THE IMPROBABLES

BY THE SAME AUTHOR

Ortog (translated by Brian Stableford)
Blood Light (*The Books of Anguish 1*) (translated by Sheryl Curtis)

THE IMPROBABLES
and
THE 32nd OF JULY

by
Kurt Steiner

translated by
Michael Shreve

A Black Coat Press Book

Visit our website at www.blackcoatpress.com

ISBN 978-1-64932-182-4. First Printing. February 2023. Published by Black Coat Press, an imprint of Hollywood Comics.com, LLC, P.O. Box 17270, Encino, CA 91416. All rights reserved. Except for review purposes, no part of this book may be reproduced or transmitted in any form or by any means, electronic or mechanical, including photocopying, recording, or by any information storage and retrieval system, without permission in writing from the publisher. The stories and characters depicted in this novel are entirely fictional. Printed in the United States of America.

TABLE OF CONTENTS

Foreword 7
THE IMPROBABLES................................... 17
THE 32nd OF JULY 131
RESEARCH DEPARTMENT 233

André RUELLAN

*A biography, bibliography and filmography of André Ruellan,
a.k.a. Kurt Steiner, is included in* The Books of Anguish No.1.

Foreword

A Conversation Between
André Ruellan and Philippe Curval

Philippe CURVAL: Let's start the beginning?

André RUELLAN: I don't remember much before 1922, which is when I was born. My first recollection is of me in a bedroom, lying down, the sheets hanging around the bed moved by a breeze blowing in from the window. From what I was able to learn later, this took place at the Berck Hospital, where I was because I had cracked a tibia.

PC: So you started your life by cracking a bone?

AR: No, I was two and a half by then.

PC: And after?

AR: A big black hole. Then I remember the visit of my cousin, who was born in the United States, was also called Andrée Ruellan, and wore her dark hair in macaroons over the ears. She had pinned above my little cot a reproduction of the Douanier Rousseau's painting of a cart. I was six years-old.

PC: Why was she born in the United States?

AR: My family had emigrated around 1910.

PC: Are you expecting to inherit a fortune from some rich uncle?

AR: Alas, no. The last known relative died at ninety-seven, without leaving anything to me.

PC: And where does this large family come from?

AR: Ruellan is a Breton name, from the Côtes-du-Nord. My grandfather, who was a shoemaker, had eight children. That's probably why he moved so often. As a result, my father married my mother in the Auge region. She was from Normandy.

PC: Then they moved to Paris?

AR: Yes. I am a Parisian of the first generation and the last of my family to bear the name.

PC: Any other memories of that time?

AR: Only fragments—mostly the picture of my father returning loaded with books he had bought on the quays. He was a welder at Delage. Five of us lived crammed into a very small apartment in Bécon-les-Bruyères. The walls were covered with piles of books; a room was full of them; there were even some in the cellar. My brother had a collection of pulp novels put out by Ferenczi and Tallandier, which I devoured as soon as I knew how to read. There was also a series of magnificent volumes bound in green leather called *The Universe and Mankind*, whose inserts and illustrations dazzled me.

PC: So your father liked books about science, esotericism, political works and philosophy?

AR: Not philosophy; he was above all thirsty for knowledge. This is why he also possessed a magnificent microscope which he had acquired after saving much money. I took full advantage of it. I was a real sponge for knowledge, which delighted my father. He was an anarcho-syndicalist; materialistic towards God, but rather mystical with respect to life in general. Like many socialists at the end of the last century, he had been influenced by a spiritualist current from India. Around the age of twelve, for example, he made me read *The Haunted Houses* by Camille Flammarion and I firmly believed in the existence of ghosts.

PC: In short, a happy family?

AR: But one with enormous financial difficulties. In 1934, everything went bust. My father became unemployed. The family exploded. I stayed with my mother and my sister.

PC: You were the youngest?

AR: Yes—the least of my worries.

PC: Did you stay in Bécon-les-Bruyères?

AR: No, since we never paid the rent, we had to move all the time.

PC: What did you live on?

AR: My mother, who had been a cleaning lady, started reading fortunes. It was then that she tried to build, with the help of a few friends, a house made of plaster tiles on the slopes of Argenteuil, in a land that didn't belong to them. After the owner had us kicked out, we took refuge in a shack at the bottom of the hill. I stayed there until the war.

PC: What about your studies?

AR: They happened normally; first, primary school; then complementary courses until age of sixteen. At that time, I applied simultaneously at the École Normale d'Instituteurs in Versailles, and to take advanced classes at the Lycée Condorcet in Paris. I was accepted by both, but naturally I chose to go to Versailles to become a teacher, since schools had always taken care of me.

PC: Did you stay there long?

AR: Until the German invasion when I left to go to Bordeaux on foot. When I returned, I continued my studies. I was paid and I had signed a contract with the Government to do ten years of teaching.

PC: What were you thinking at that time?

AR: I wanted to write! At fourteen, I had already started a novel about an invasion of giant insects.

PC: The influence of your brother's books.

AR. Undoubtedly, but with more ambition. I had read Wells' *War of the Worlds*, *Time Machine*, *The Invisible Man*, and my father's popular science works. All these ideas were running through my head.

PC: Did you plan to become a teacher or a writer?

AR: Maybe a writing teacher… In 1942, I embarked on another novel, one that I did not finish. I wrote a lot of pages, all lost today.

PC: You were about twenty at the time; weren't you impacted by the obligation to work for the Germans?

AR: Indeed. I was drafted to build a tennis court in Arcachon for their submarine crews from a nearby base.

PC: A tennis court for submariners?

AR: You're more right than you know. If I had not enjoyed the protection of a lieutenant who knew I was a student, I would have been sent with the others in a diving bell to build concrete hangars at the bottom of the ocean, carrying fifty kilo sacks of cement all day. After a week, we were told to report to the courtyard at six in the morning. I understood that we were going to be sent to Germany. But thanks to the intervention of the same lieutenant, I was given an *ausweiss* (internal passport), and took the train to return to Paris.

PC: Any more problems during the German occupation?

AR: My brother was a resistant, registered with the Communist Party; my sister was a Trotskyist; my father was an anarchist. The entire spectrum of the political left was represented in my family. My brother gave me false id papers which I was supposed to use to go and fight in the maquis of the Vercors. Luckily my family started crying about my leaving, so I stayed, otherwise I wouldn't be here to tell you my life story right now.

PC: What happened next ?

AT: I hid, first on a farm at Château-Thierry, then in Mayenne, with my sister, who by then was married.

PC: Almost a quiet vacation until the end of the war.

AR: Not quite, since I almost got shot a fortnight after the Allies' landing.

PC: By the Americans?

AR: No, by the Germans. One of their men had been shot in the village, so they gathered all the men under forty and stuck us against a wall. We waited there under the threat of machine guns. Three quarters of an hour is a very long time under such circumstances. Finally the orders came not to shoot us. We spent the night locked in a room at the town hall. The next day, we were interrogated. I no longer remembered if the date on my fake papers matched my real birthdate or not. The German officer, who saw my doubts, looked at me with clear blue eyes behind by steel-rimmed glasses, then let me go. The executions were over, but he belonged to the Wehrmacht, not the S.S.

PC: What did you do before the country got back to work?

AR: I did some business, mostly exchanging bottles of Calvados for products imported by a nearby G.I.s camp, especially gasoline. Today, I would do the opposite. My price was a liter of Calvados for five liters of gasoline. From the growers, on the other hand, I asked for two liters of Calvados for the same quantity of gasoline. I used that little profit to buy coffee, cigarettes, and K rations.

PC: Did this idyllic period last long?

AR: About two weeks, after which, I was asked to return and teach English teacher at a school even though I barely knew the language, but because I had registered for a certificate in English lit at the Sorbonne.

PC: So you were fulfilling the terms of your contract with the Government?

AR: I did—for two years.

PC: But afterward, left teaching?

AR: Yes, but I paid my debt in full; in fact, not so long ago—the sum of ninety-three francs. A ridiculously small amount.

PC: That's when you went to medical school?

AR: Yes, around 1947. I pictured myself as a doctor writing poems, an activity that I had engaged in for almost five years. I was even part of a literary society.

PC: How did you pay for your studies?

AR: I got a scholarship. I've always had scholarships. The financial situation of my parents being worse than that of even migrant workers today, it wasn't difficult.

PC: So you're a ward of the Republic.

AR: You could say that.

PC: Did you enjoy medical studies?

AR: Well enough to not start writing anymore novels until my sixth year.

PC: Did the return of science fiction in France prompt you to write again?

AR: Well, since my early childhood, I had been reading fantasy and sf, but it's true that the French publication of the first American sci-fi novel, Jack Williamson's *The Humanoids*, in 1950, made me jump out of my chair. At that time, I wrote a genre short story for *Le Hérisson*, but what really got me back was the birth of the *Angoisse* imprint of publisher Fleuve Noir in 1954. I immediately began writing a horror novel, *The Sound of Silence*, which was immediately accepted.

PC: Under the name of Kurt Wargar?

AR: No, Kurt Steiner. But as Kurt Wargar, I had published another novel, *Monster Alert*, the year before at Flamme d'or publishing.

PC: Why Kurt Steiner?

AR: I was tired of seeing French authors take English-sounding pseudonyms, so I chose a German-sounding one instead.

PC: How was your life then?

AR: I lived in Enghien with my sister, but I also rented a small apartment in Paris with some friends. We sometimes played chess there from noon to midnight. Or we invented silly recipes, like bread à la bread: "Fry slices of bread in a pan, then eat them with croutons." All of this ended at the same time as my medical studies, the year I got married.

PC: And then you practiced medicine?

AR: I had a ready-made practice, but eventually, I packed up my diploma and ran away.

PC: Why?

AR: As much as I had enjoyed studying medicine, the practice of it did not appeal to me. Through my other brother-in-law, the artist Jean-Claude Forest, who later went on to create *Barbarella*, I met Georges H. Gallet, who edited not only the *Rayon fantastique* genre imprint for publisher Hachette, but also *V-Magazine*; I had written some short stories for him which had whetted my appetite. Moreover, I had discovered a way to become even more free: the editor at Fleuve Noir had told me that a novel was fine, but he preferred to publish series by the same author; in short, he was offering

12

me a sort of contract. I said yes but I was terrified because I thought I had said everything I had to say in my first book, and that I would be incapable of writing another one.

PC: History has proven you wrong.

AR: Indeed! During the next five years, I wrote twenty-two horror novels, plus a few science fiction ones.

PC: That's when you met the small community of French authors.

AR: Yes, one day, Georges Gallet dragged me to a cocktail party at publisher Denoël where I met Alain Dorémieux and Gérard Klein. After some libations, I took them back to my place where we continued drinking. The following Monday, they invited me to lunch with Valérie Schmidt, Jacques Sternberg, Jacques Bergier, Michel Pilotin and you.

PC: Why did this fabulous collaboration with Fleuve Noir come to an end?

AR: Because of a simple economic principle: the novels in the *Angoisse* imprint barely made up half of the monthly advances they were paying me. This allowed me to live nicely, however. For example, in 1957, as I always loved big cars, I bought myself a superb used Buick convertible. But, mathematically, each time I delivered a new novel, my debt to them grew by half that amount.

PC: So it was a failure of popular literature since a writer like you could not live by his pen while producing as much as you did.

AR: Rather a failure of popular horror literature. If I had been writing novels for their *Anticipation* imprint, whose sales were double thar of *Angoisse*, it would have been a different story.

PC: But you were passionate about horror.

AR: Yes. My problem was that I only wanted to write the lowest-selling type of books. Yet, there are several of my *Angoisse* novels which contain sci-fi elements.

PC: How did this end?

AR: At some point, Fleuve Noir stopped sending me money because I owed them too much.

PC: Why didn't you turn to writing police or espionage thrillers, which sold phenomenally well?

AR: I had no inclination to write a policeman after some unfortunate experiences with the police in the past; as for espionage, I tried, but my manuscript was rejected. It must be said that editors in charge of these imprints, which sold well over a hundred thousand copies each, were not looking kindly at newcomers.

PC: You hadn't been rejected until then.

AR: No, my novels went straight from my typewriter to the printer, bypassing any kind of editorial review, probably because of their relative lack of importance to the publisher.

PC: So how did you repay your debt?

AR: In the same way as I did with National Education. As it was not indexed, inflation reduced its value over the years, which enabled me to write only one or two *Anticipation* novels instead of four to clear it.

PC: During that time, you had a medicine cabinet in Les Halles?

AR: Yes—for twelve years. The people were very nice, the customers few, but loyal.

PC: Which gave you time to write.

AR: Yes. I wrote *The Improbables, The Oceans of Heaven, Ortog and the Darkness. The Children of History, The Scratched Record* there—five books in all.

PC: These are more elaborate novels than the ones you produced when you wrote six horror books a year.

AR: Horror is based on atmosphere, so mainly on style, and the work in which I was previously immersed facilitated this. The next period allowed me more time for reflection, which is essential for the creation of good sci-fi novels which require strong structures.

PC: How did you start writing for the cinema?

AR: In 1969, comedian Pierre Richard, who was only doing stand up, contacted me. I had written song lyrics and some satirical short stories for *Hara-Kiri*. Jacques Sternberg had told him that I was the man for the job. As he was thinking of going into films, I pitched him *Les Caractères* by La Bruyère. He read the book that night and the next day, he called me and we got to work. After *Le Distrait*, we collaborated on a second film; then, he became a star, and I became a screenwriter. I haven't stopped since. It was a form of expression that suited me and turned out to be very profitable. I have worked with directors Jean-Pierre Mocky, Michel Berny, Jean-François Davy, who adapted my novel *The Threshold of the Void*, Jérôme Laperrousaz, and Alain Jessua.

PC: Any science fiction films?

AR: With these last three directors, yes. *Hu-man, The Dogs*, and, above all, *Paradise for all*.

PC: You also wrote for television?

AR: I got into it rather easily. Michel Berny, with whom I had written three screenplays, had just directed a successful series entitled *Breakfast included*. He asked me if I had an idea., so we did *Billet Doux* together. After a string of unlikely acceptances and rejections, it was finally broadcast in September 1984.

PC: Do you feel that your work reflects your life?

AR: For my horror novels, it is indisputable. For my SF novels, some clearly reflect my interest in medicine, but in both cases, the connection is on a cultural level, not on an affective level.

PC: Have you been tempted by general literature?

AR: In 1942, my unfinished manuscript of which I spoke earlier was vaguely inspired by my life.

LES IMPROBABLES

KURT STEINER

★

ANTICIPATION

Editions
"Fleuve Noir"

THE IMPROBABLES

What is true is what is experienced.

CHAPTER I

The reception room of the first rector was empty and silent when the visitor entered. He was a small man, very narrow-shouldered, but his ease and unusual agility gave pause for thought.

Varold stepped in without showing the least impatience. His attitude did not reflect that nervous shyness of common people pent up in a majestic place awaiting the appointed time for a meeting. Watching him, you could think he was dallying in an old, familiar house.

He walked over to the permanent 3D projection of the first rector in a corner of the room, a statue that made only a few, slow, repeated movements. It was obviously a loop from a film. Varold smiled at the effigy and thumbed his nose at it.

"A secret ritual, a forbidden gesture," a humorless voice said behind him.

Varold turned around. The first rector was standing on the other side of the room, a mirror image across from the central column. The look he gave Varold was ambiguous, a little patronizing but strict and with something more elusive.

The visitor bowed slightly without losing his smile, "I apologize. The gesture you refer to belongs to no ritual. In truth, it belongs to a distant past when it meant something a little irreverent but was readily forgiven. It was childish."

The first rector walked slowly, his face was blank, closed like a door, showing no hint of emotion. "Would you please explain to me why you are here," he spoke politely, with a gentle voice.

Varold took his time. He glanced amusedly at his host's black robe and went over to a dish-shaped chair where he sat down without being invited. Shortly he announced, "I have some information that your special service has no knowledge of and I'm prepared to give it to you… in exchange for a nomination to the executive committee of said service."

The first rector sat down as well. "If your information deserves such a reward, we shall see that you are satisfied. What's it about?"

Varold admired the man's control: the most important magistrate of Kaltarborog was probably not used to encountering informality and insolence.

"See how I trust you. I'll give it to you solely on your word."

He paused, watched for the first rector's reaction. But the challenge slid past like water off stone.

"From my personal observations," he went on, "I know that the archons of Babelia are preparing an expedition to the past. Oh, I'm aware that you, too, have had many such expeditions, but the one I'm talking about is different from yours because of the probability of success. This time Babelia is seeking out a particular person and it looks like he's hit on something big. If you don't act now, our enemies might soon have use of a totally new weapon. I don't have to remind you that Kaltarborog and Babelia have long been equal in power and that all our weapons are useless against the range of the other. These expeditions to the past, to some old scientist or another whose genius will guide us in one direction or another—these expeditions didn't start yesterday and Babelia, too, is constantly sending emissaries. But as I just explained, this new one has a good chance of success."

The first rector stared coldly at Varold, "By what means," he asked softly, "have you arrived at such conclusions?"

Varold smiled, "Let's just say that I'm a kind of maverick working for Kaltarborog." He leaned forward. "The person on whom the Babelians are focusing is studying genes. I suspect the archons are considering site-specific mutation that will get them what neither of us have managed to perfect: a species capable of travelling in time like in space without the need for any device—the 'chronanthrope.' Then they'd get through all the barriers that we've put up against any temporal intrusion. That's the ultimate weapon that will destroy us. If we let Babelia act alone, we'll be bringing about our own demise."

The first rector straightened up, "And what if you were a Babelian infiltrating this city?"

"Put me through the tests," Varold offered simply.

The magistrate nodded, "We shall submit you to them. In the meantime, you'll wait in the penitent's cell where you'll have time to repent the imprudence you've shown since the start of this conversation. Now, give me the details…"

Either Varold had help from the outside or else he had perfected some special means, either way there was no trace of him when they came to give him the tests. And yet, it was no mean feat to get out of the penitent's cell…

His disappearance seemed to be an admission of guilt, of treason. So, the rectors took the news into consideration—they would have to protect themselves against all traps, but Kaltarborog was vulnerable. Nevertheless, following this line of thought, they could wonder why a Babelian spy would sabotage his mission by tacitly revealing his identity by escaping. There were too many uncertainties here for the rectors to take it lightly.

They summoned an agent named Anton Borg whom they would send back, just in case, to the time coordinates given by that strange Varold and his goal was the same man whom, according to Varold, Babelia was targeting.

As for Varold, no Kaltarian ever had contact with him again, except for Anton Borg.

For their time travel the Kaltarians used a highly perfected derivative of an old device invented in New Vancouver in the 21st century: the time transfer, whose principle was based on the negative duration of certain particles which were themselves discovered a century earlier. But time transfer could only move inanimate objects, excluding all biological organisms, and only for a very short time. Contrary to this, the Kaltarian mechanism allowed virtually all kinds of possible voyages. All, except for the famous 30th century barrier that had always been impassable. But, travelling from the 24th to the 30th century was of little interest since the whole period in between was in a state of latent war that marked the relations between Kaltarborog and Babelia.

They had, therefore, focused their research on the past and each side was striving to use the work of an ancient scientist, trying to get the most out of what had not been published. There were enough men of science over the past centuries that the field of research would never run dry. Both sides were sure that this method was the only one that would decide the winner because nothing of what they discovered remained secret for long. In fact, Kaltarian commandoes, by dematerializing, could pass through the Babelian energy shields and vice versa. Each camp was teeming with spies from the other side and anything considered ultra-secret was immediately targeted by the unstoppable agents.

The two giant cities represented the final elements ferociously devoted and attached to the mother planet. For two centuries they had evolved side by side, fighting for supremacy while the rest of humanity had emigrated to other worlds in the solar system like Alpha Centauri. These colonies maintained no relations with the metropolis that they considered populated by a bunch of madmen—which was not exactly true. The cities on the Moon, being so close, were keeping a suspicious eye on the people who lived only for war but they never sent a ship to Babelia or Kaltarborog.

For their part, the two rival cities were completely uninterested in extra-terrestrial affairs. Both considered the emigrants as despicable foreigners because of their desertion. But they did not have a space fleet at their disposal and were limited in the field of robot ships, all of which were considered diabolically clever but simply ineffective.

It was this ineffectiveness of the most cleverly designed weapons—and the deadliest—that enraged the two opponents so violently and fed their mutual fury. With the perfection of a new destructive machine in the shadows of the past being impossible since they could not transport the necessary technology out of it, their last hope of victory was spying on the ancient geniuses followed up with work that was so different from the current trends that the enemy would not understand the impact. However, as this mindset was held on both sides, it was inevitable that their emissaries would meet and the war, far from ending, was simply carried into the past.

Jorik was floating in non-time. At the bottom of an air sac in the main palace of Babelia lay his inert body, but the microwaves emitted by his mind were all passing through the delicate receptors of the bluish sphere that the archons had cast outside of duration. The thing was keeping vigil, beaten by the waves of eternity, those swells that are invisible to the human eye, whatever their country or epoch. The chronons struck it in their constant eddying, but it had been programmed not to react except to a specific frequency. Thus, through the intermediary of the searching sphere, Jorik was floating in non-time.

No thoughts, no dreams, no feelings could produce an array of images as rich as what Jorik was experiencing on his motionless and instant voyage. In the hazy fog of hundreds of mixed-up epochs he grazed stars being created and worlds being destroyed, multi-colored suns whose planets had been stolen away, dark universes where races perished, the dust of humanities and billions of births. All of a sudden, he changed scales and saw himself surrounded by the weirdest microorganisms, pass like subtle steam through all kinds of sharp-edged crystals, witness the exchange of electrons that was the life of giant seaweed. Then he entered the core of a human thought, followed the frozen twists and turns, tried to figure out under what reign it would vanish. Another showed up, trained on incomprehensible problems. The sphere moved away from it and returned to the void.

Jorik paid scant attention to these visions. He had a mission to accomplish and was waiting, in his personal time span, until the thing floating where his mind was focused gave him the signal of arrival. The goal of his mission was fitting for his dry, somber soul, his cold, joyless heart. He belonged to the classified brigade of the time emissaries and nothing except death would stop his hand when the instant came.

Something happened inside the sphere, a click that echoed in the hibernating man's brain: the cortical emission that Jorik also used as a channel, guiding the waves of the thing on the lookout. The signal-carriers travelled against the current. Through this mechanism the emissary had already received a bunch of useless information. Now something new was coming.

On his bed in the 20th century, in the old city of Paris, a man sat up. He had just been startled awake by a noise, the noise of a metal object falling on the wood floor. Automatically, his sleepy eyes drifted to the luminous hands of the alarm clock on the bedside table. They showed three o'clock. Sitting on his bed, Manuel did not move for a second. It was not easy to tell the difference between sounds coming from outside and what might have banged inside the bedroom because a hard rain was hammering the windows and the wind was raging around the roofs. Somewhere in the night an impatient horn was honked. A long silence, then the three strikes of a clock came through the storm. Manuel searched the shadows. No noise could have come from the room. There was no real doubt about it. And then he heard it again, the same sound—

he remembered the exact, faintly metallic tone. A sound that seemed to come out of a dream.

"I wasn't dreaming," he said in a low voice.

He reached out toward the lamp. A yellow light flooded the room. Manuel Esteban blinked, briefly blinded. When his eyes adjusted to the light he examined the floor, but to see it all he had to get up, which he did reluctantly.

And he jumped back. At the foot of the bed there was an object that should not have been there. Gripped by fear Manuel began a slow retreat toward the door. At any moment he was expecting an attack of some kind from the bluish sphere whose presence was unexplainable.

Then he stopped with his hand on the doorknob. If anything happened, he would have time to escape... but the ball was just lying there, once in a while throwing out some wild lights against the bluish glow. A kind of weak vibration, barely noticeable, also seemed to be emanating from it. Esteban felt possessed. He watched it with a kind of terror, a detached terror that he faced with uncommon courage by staying in the room. He would have been long gone if this weird paralysis was not nailing him to the spot.

By reflex he threw open the door. No, he was not at all paralyzed... and maybe that was something to worry about even more. Where did this thing come from and how did it get through the closed windows? Manuel dodged these questions.

Okay, a sphere at least 20 inches in diameter, made of some material that reminded him of nothing he had ever seen before except maybe soapy film with fewer colors. Little inclined to mysticism he sensed superior technology—was one of the superpowers that rule the world working on some new experiment? If so, Manuel was going to find himself on the front-page news very soon... unless they wanted to keep it a secret, which would put the primary witness of this success in great danger.

The attack was lightning fast. Esteban staggered under the blow of the psychic battering ram like being hit in the face by a shockwave. He tripped and held onto the doorframe to keep from falling. His mind started reeling under the wave of strange thoughts, all brutal and insistent, a tumultuous current that unfurled before him the scattered fragments of the personality attacking him.

However, Manuel soon pulled himself together and used the full force of his will against the unseen enemy. He managed to take three steps back, three slow, heavy steps like he was walking in an old diving suit.

Slowly, silently, the sphere rose up and floated in midair. Once again in possession of his consciousness and reason, Esteban felt chilled to the bone. The fright he had not yet fully felt was now rising up in him like a tide. He knew that a formless, terrifying danger was threatening him, that the object out of nowhere was something deeply evil, nothing to do with the petty quarrels in the news or with the level of science he knew about. He took another step and fell backward onto the floor with a thud.

Like being carried on soft waves the sphere floated towards the man lying still. It stopped in front of him and started vibrating while the weird lights got brighter inside. Outside the rain beat down even harder.

Manuel had not passed out. Stripped of all energy and initiative, reduced to an object, his dilated eyes watched the movements of the assailant. The first mental attack had, in the end, targeted his body, not his mind. A second attack was in the works, which scared him even more. On the surface of his brain, countless hypotheses, each one crazier than the last, were running wild, trying to explain the situation he was in. For a split second he even considered what truly reflected reality. But he did not stop there, judging it less acceptable than the others…

The sphere drifted slowly down to his chest. The wind and the rain in the city raged on more fiercely than ever, as if the elements were partner to the aggression that Manuel was suffering. Surrendering, defenseless, conscious of little, he ended up confounding the fury of the skies with his present danger.

The second attack came. The ball was spinning faster and faster while new colors appeared inside—unusual, constantly changing, flashing and glowing colors that Manuel stared at in awe. Like this he went through a period of apathy about himself, feeling like a spectator at his own demise.

The real defeat came next. A strange mind, cold and determined, hastily insinuated itself in his brain, taking control of his innermost circuits, settling into the language zones, invading the strongholds of voluntary movement, blocking the reflex arcs, poisoning the peripheral conditioning. It captured the cerebellum, rushed down into the lower centers, polluted the emotions and dammed up the instincts.

The victim's personality grew smaller and weaker. Manuel was still aware of his body, a huge thing around a shrunken mind. He felt like his limbs stretched to the ends of the world, that his feet lay over the horizon. And at the same time, his ideas were gradually reduced to childish notions, his will to fight turned into a temper tantrum. What clarity remained in him knew that he had to cut his losses to save his individuality. He took refuge in the most primitive core of his being, the most elementary part of his self. He felt like he was rolling into a ball, another sphere mirroring the attacker. Back to this intact center he dragged the wreckage of who he had been, the aching debris of his thoughts and sentiments, the remains of his exhausted will.

Jorik launched a devastating flux of maximum power against this mental ball and the sphere turned pitch black as it spun dizzily. The waves bounced back and put in danger the internal mechanisms of the transmitter, causing Jorik's mind to burn with pain.

"Doesn't matter," the emissary judged, "we'll use it like it is…"

In the final moments of consciousness, what remained of Manuel started repeating frantically, "This being is called Jorik and he comes from another time… This being is called Jorik and he comes from another time…"

Manuel Esteban scrambled to his feet. Behind his drooping eyelids a flame was shining that did not belong to him. A thin smile, another's smile, was on his lips. He sprang toward the bathroom. No hesitation—the memory and habits of Esteban were at Jorik's service. Being commanded from another place and another time, Manuel's organism obeyed like a remote-controlled device, better certainly because of the involuntary help given to the attacker by the amount of his knowledge and by the traces of his past. Of course, there was still this resistant kernel stuck like a tumor in the middle of the conquered terrain… but what could it do now against the occupant?

The blue sphere shrank. Soon it was the size of a rugby ball, then an orange. When it reached the diameter of a marble, Jorik picked it up with two fingers and dropped it into the pocket of a coat that Manuel had left on the back of a chair the night before. A moment later the sound of the shower could be heard and in it Jorik's hearty whistle.

CHAPTER II

This morning, someone was pacing up and down the glass corridor that led to Manuel Esteban's office on the second floor of the building occupied by the laboratories of applied biochemistry. Coming out of the elevator, the young and distinguished professor of biological chemistry froze for a second.

"They're already here!" Jorik thought, baffled and bothered.

The person had his back turned. But there was something in the shape, in the general appearance, something that could not fool the emissary's expert mind. Jorik consulted Esteban's stock of memories while starting down the corridor with utmost calm. According to the memories imprinted in the chemist's cells, the man had showed up more than a year ago under the name Anton Borg of the University of Prague. Since then, he had come back many times to annoy Esteban under the pretext of being deeply interested in the Frenchman's work on gene metabolism.

Jorik considered the situation coldly. "What's so surprising about that?" he thought. "Why would the Kaltarians be behind us since we're equal in strength?"

This "Dr. Borg" turned around and came to meet him, his face lit up with a warm smile. Jorik knew that Esteban had to stay cold toward him so as not to sound an alarm.

"Ah, my dear professor…" Borg almost shouted.

Esteban gave him a distracted smile and held out his hand reluctantly. The other took it and shook it enthusiastically. Jorik wondered how a Kaltarian could be so tactless. Was he really one? However, doubt was not allowed. A quick reference to chemist's memory: At every meeting they had, Anton was trying to push the Frenchman's efforts in a direction that he himself saw as a dead end. The most surprising thing of all was Borg's diabolical perseverance despite suffering continual rebuffs. Surprising for Manuel but not for Jorik who recognized the dominating trait of Kaltarborog.

"Well, come into my office," Jorik said with a weariness that sounded utterly sincere. "But you know you're wasting your time. I've already told you that your suggestions don't hold any interest for me. Again, why not follow up on it yourself since you're also a specialist in the matter?"

The other shook his head hard, "But no, they're your ideas and I have no right to draw the least conclusions from them. You need to recognize their value!"

The door of the office closed behind them.

Looking bored and annoyed, Jorik sat in an armchair and motioned to his visitor to take the uncomfortable, straight-back chair. Dr. Borg frowned a little but smiled again as he took his seat.

"It's my turn to do something stupid…"

Jorik noted the surprise on Borg's face. It was clear that Esteban would never behave so rudely. He thought fast while the other spoke. The attitude to adopt lay between two extremes, both of which must be avoided. The slightest mistake would put the Kaltarian on alert and to be honest he was not feeling up to playing this game so abruptly when it was hard enough with reasonable preparation. Anton Borg had gotten used to the chemist's reactions over the past few months whereas Jorik had only controlled him for a few hours.

"My dear Anton," he replied to the speech that he heard with only half an ear, "I'm no more an expert on the enzyme reactions of the genes than any other biochemist in the world. You claim that I slipped into this area of personal hypotheses…"

"Slipped into?!" Anton cried out. "You're putting words into my mouth that I never said."

The pseudo-Czech had once again caught something unusual. Jorik, whose mind should have been paying attention to what the other was saying while at the same time constantly examining Esteban's brain circuits and also searching for the proper behavior to remain unsuspicious, knew that he had overestimated his strength. There was only one solution: give a little free rein to Esteban despite all the possible risks. He lowered the intensity of his inhibitor emissions that the sphere was sending to the chemist's nerve centers.

Since the moment his personality had been violated, Manuel had been living as if at the bottom of a well full of cotton. Echoes from outside and the movements of his own body reached his consciousness through miles of veils and insulation. All of sudden there was a kind of gash in the atmosphere and he felt as if a strong wind blowing in from all parts of this body was lifting up his mind. He surfaced into his own face, which Jorik had been careful to keep lowered. Slowly, cautiously, the Occupant was letting his guard down and Manuel was taking control of his sensory organs. His will was still feeble and his muscles sluggish, but the nightmare of the last few hours was becoming bearable. On the other hand, his partially restored clarity showed him that he was in an atrocious, impossible situation. Nobody could help him because his reprieve did not give him enough freedom to ask anyone for help. And who could help him in such a state? Deep down inside, however, he had an inkling that if he had to count on someone it would be the very man who had been bothering him for so long. But he kept this idea out of the reach of Jorik who was also tracking his thoughts.

More directly in contact with the usual reactions of his victim, the Babelian modeled his behavior more adequately, all the while keeping a close watch on the deeper reactions of his host. Apparently, Anton calmed down and banished the doubts that had crept up. Likewise, Manuel instinctively used the regions of his brain that were free again to devise an action plan with personal symbols that Jorik had not had enough time to decode.

In short, Esteban was on the battleground of two enemies whose origins and real natures were totally unknown to him. The little he knew of them came from Jorik's callous mind: the names Babelia and Kaltarborog, barbaric names that meant nothing to Manuel… and also the muddled, abstract notion of a huge fight going on somewhere at some vague time. This Jorik and this Anton were obviously acting like enemies and Manuel felt like he had some key part to play in the combat. But he had no idea why.

Anton had shown up a while ago trying to influence him in an absurd way and Jorik came after using different methods for his undoubtedly similar objectives. Manuel was fed up with being the playground and pawn of these two beings. He decided to turn the tables and use the first to free himself from the second.

The meeting was coming to an end. Seeing no reaction from his host, Jorik had eased off a little. Manuel knew he had to act fast—he might not have another chance anytime soon. Mobilizing every ounce of willpower available to him, he launched a rebellious impulse into his right arm and before Jorik had time to block the movement his hand reached into his coat pocket. His fingers closed over the small sphere that Manuel knew was there. But Jorik was balking the movements now. Caught off guard by the swift initiative, he was back in control of the situation and Manuel's fist remained closed, stuck inside the pocket.

However, Anton was always on guard and Esteban's sudden movement put him on alert. He jumped up. And his own hand was pointing a tiny object at Manuel. A menacing object that was shimmering red.

"Slowly take your hand out of your pocket, Esteban," he said coldly, enunciating each word clearly.

Manuel clearly felt Jorik's dismay. A tempest of rage and spite but not the least fear. In an instant he lost the pleasure of witnessing the outcome of the showdown. Jorik had shot a high frequency wave through his brain, which turned into a burning but silent scream during which Manuel passed out.

When he came to, Anton was still standing before him and watching him curiously. On the desk between them a bluish marble was rolling around.

"How do you feel?" Anton asked.

The interest he was showing seemed genuinely directed at Manuel himself and not what the chemist represented in the context of his strange preoccupations. But Esteban, who was suddenly feeling wonderfully free, had now paid the price for not trusting anyone, particularly the person who had been hanging around for so long and who belonged to a world as weird as Jorik's universe...

"Pretty well," he answered feebly. But he decided to keep up the ruse. He hardened his voice and said, "I don't know what got hold of me. Kind of fainted, I guess. I've been overworked these last few weeks."

A smile crossed Anton's lips. "No need to pretend."

With a sweep of his hand he grabbed the marble just before it fell off the desk. His attitude and tone of voice had changed. Esteban was seeing and hearing a total stranger he had never met before.

He demanded weakly, "What do you mean?"

"Just that. What miracle do you think made your nasty guest disappear? Don't you think I had something to do with it?"

Anton tossed the marble up and caught it.

"Don't tell me you didn't know about this little object..."

Manuel dropped the charade. He had won despite the uneven balance of power. If Anton was also going to act like an enemy, at least they could talk in person and face each other like humans.

He took a deep breath and waited for his heart to stop pounding before he asked, "Where do you come from?"

"Wrong question," Anton replied. "You should ask *when* do you come from."

Esteban shrugged, "I'm a chemist but I have some knowledge of physics. Enough to know that time travel is a mathematical impossibility."

Anton rolled the marble into his left hand. "I'm sorry. I didn't mean to upset mathematics with my presence here. Especially not the poor little math you know." He leaned forward. "Seriously, don't you think your present situation is full of, how can I put it, unusual aspects?"

He put the marble in his pocket and his hand came out gripping the red thing he had pointed at Manuel-Jorik before.

"Look," he said.

He aimed at the wall. The electric clock vanished silently. A wisp of smoke was floating in the room, smelling strongly of ozone. He had not looked away from Esteban, who gulped hard.

"I'll tell you what happened just now," he concluded paternally. "I used this weapon against you but turned it down to minimum power. When your guest also passed out, I searched you and found the transmitter I suspected was in your pocket. I just had to break into the emission linking your mind to Jorik's without destroying the device, which I can do. So, I learned the identity of your occupant before liberating you."

His eyes twinkled as he looked at the marble.

"Destroying this old thing would've been a big mistake. I'm holding one for the first time and want to make good use of it… with your consent."

"What'd you do with Jorik?" Manuel asked.

"I threw him back to where he came from."

Manuel was overwhelmed with fatigue. He closed his eyes for a moment. He thought: "Anton might be as dangerous as Jorik in the long run, but right now I certainly have less to fear from him." He opened his eyes again just when a dark form took shape behind the glass door of the office. Someone knocked three times softly. Anton swung around with extraordinary swiftness.

"Yes?" Manuel called out.

The door opened and a man entered.

"Oh, sorry," he immediately stepped back. "I didn't know you were with Dr. Borg."

"It's nothing," Manuel let out a sigh of relief. "Can you come back in a few minutes?"

"Naturally, professor…"

The door closed. It was the most common incident imaginable but exactly because of this Esteban realized how crazy his situation really was.

"You sent Jorik back," he said after a long silence. "So, right now he's in… in Babelia?"

Anton nodded, "You see, you know more than you think."

"And you," Manuel shot back, "why don't you go back to…"

"To Kaltarborog?" Anton finished for him cheerfully. "But of course my place is here with you, my dear Esteban. For a year you've refused to help us by pursuing your hypotheses. If you weren't so stubborn, you would've been left alone a long time ago. Now I have the feeling that you won't be getting any more than us out of your intuitions. I believe we have to accept this and I'll write my report accordingly. However, the unfortunate efforts of Babelia are giving me the idea of using you differently. When I've explained things to you, I think you won't mind helping me… We have nothing in common with the people of Babelia, you know."

All of a sudden Manuel felt cold. What outrageous powers lay hidden behind this person speaking so obscurely? The name of Babelia brought to mind a universe copied out of a demented bible and Kaltarborog a civilization of the steppes, dripping with gold and ancient jewels. None of this fit with what Anton was claiming.

"Your own mathematics," he said sarcastically but revealing his uneasiness, "is it part of the future… or the past?"

"Of your future," Anton answered politely. "When I said we won't be getting much from your intuition, that meant that in your publications before today we found the seed of ideas we were hoping would blossom. As for what you'll publish in the future, it's of no interest to us. All this is given up now, let's not talk about it anymore."

He straightened up. His eyes were twinkling again.

"The methods of Babelia—more aggressive than ours, I have to admit—did give us a new idea about you, however. Do you want to do the same to our friend Jorik?"

Without waiting for an answer from Esteban he held up the marble.

"A Babelian transmitter," he explained. "A somewhat old-fashioned instrument, no, really old-fashioned, which I suspect was used as a trick. They were hoping, justifiably, that we wouldn't put up barriers against this old thing. They have a lot better but they know that we know and we can defend against them. Apparently, they're interested in you for the same reasons as we are and not sure whether they're first to arrive."

Manuel sneered, "I thought you all knew everything about my private life in the past, present and future. Jorik should've expected to meet you, right?"

"Listen up. The spies from each camp know in general what's afoot in the other, but neither side necessarily knows which project's been discovered by a spy. In my case, Kaltarborog learned that Babelia sent an emissary to you at a certain time in your life. My leaders, therefore, got me to contact you a year before him."

He put the marble on the table.

"But it's been seen to that if you refuse my offer now, you'll never have another chance to accept a similar one."

He raised his hand to silence any argument.

"Yes, someone *over there* knows if you'll accept or not, but not you or me, and your freedom is intact, especially since, as you know, my methods are not coercive."

Manuel tried to buy some time, "Why didn't they check beforehand by sending another agent? Why not give him some backup?"

"They don't have enough people at hand to be using more than one for a minor operation. Don't kid yourself into thinking you're the pivot of our battles…"

Manuel nodded. They were calling him conceited now. "I have no false pretensions," he said coldly. "So, you're going to ask me to take the place of Jorik."

He realized that he was slowly, in spite of himself, accepting Anton's crazy conceptions. They were crazy, no doubt, but how else could he explain the mental invasion he had suffered and how did this so-called time traveler destroy the clock?

"Let me add," Anton replied, "that you have here an opportunity that no other man of your time could even dream of. Oh, I understand your hesitation. You're almost 40 and you naturally lost your sense of adventure a long time ago..."

"Please, your tricks are a little too obvious."

Manuel thought about it. No, of course, he hadn't lost his sense of adventure... but what kind of adventure were they talking about? He feared, once again, some plot being hatched by a very contemporary foreign power. But in the end, what was the risk? He did not see how his work could be used by the military. As for the nonsense...

"And if I accept your offer, how will we proceed?"

"I'll put you in hibernation and link your encephalic emission to the Babelian transmitter. You'll become our agent in Babelia immediately. When the mission's over, you'll be well paid, of course."

"Like how?"

"Well, we're prepared to deposit in your account what you will consider quite a hefty sum. In usable currency, naturally. Or, if you prefer, we'll give you some little inventions or discoveries that won't upset the natural course of progress but will assure you fame and a healthy income."

Manuel stared at the other. "A pact with Satan," he said seriously. "What kind of parchment do I have to sign?"

Anton smiled, "I'm not who you think I am and the mission will turn out to be more exciting than dangerous."

Esteban considered it for a minute. "Accepting that this isn't all a web of outrageous deceit," he finally said, "I have no desire to get a reputation as a clever inventor. I won't refuse, however, a small fortune if it's not in Spanish doubloons or galactic credits. Anyway, I have to admit that a truly new voyage is more tempting than anything else. Too bad if I make a fool of myself by playing this ridiculous game. But allow me to take a few basic precautions, like bringing in a doctor if I have to really go into hibernation."

"That's only natural," Anton protested. "When will you be ready?"

"I'm at your service," Manuel said curtly.

CHAPTER III

In the 11th vault of the Black City Jorik was deep in frozen sleep. His confused dream was full of slow and sluggish images, fraught with the distant jangling of indestructible chains. He knew that the past had cast him out into the deepest depths of his body and the archons would punish him cruelly for his failure.

But to get punished he would have to wake up. He felt that the transmitter had come back, that it was very close. Why was he stuck in this semi-coma? He accepted the delay with mineral patience. At least he was now sure that the chemist in the past was useless to both Babelia and its enemies.

The 11th vault suddenly started to glow with a yellowish light in which there were glints of steel. The sphere was materializing over the inert body, slowly vibrating, gradually getting bigger. It had just crossed six centuries in "no time's land", in the non-time where the mind travels inside the time ball. There was a synchronization reaching out from the vibrating emissions whereby Jorik learned the truth.

He could already recognize the mentality he had invaded, the current of tattered thoughts and contradictory feelings that he was steeped in during his intrusion. But the situation was reversed now. He felt as weak as a baby against the man he had defeated and who was defeating him in turn. He remembered the Kaltarian. Of course, he had helped Esteban. Here lay the weakness of the archons' plan. Although an outdated device like the transmitter could pass undetected, it could also pass into the wrong hands and be used against them… and if there were anyone to punish, it would have to be, logically speaking, the executor of the plan.

When he evaluated the amount of information in the hands of the one settling into his brain, Jorik realized, with fear and trembling, that he would not even be punished.

The Kaltarian had obviously given Esteban detailed information about Babelia. The triumvirs of Kaltarborog were ignorant of almost nothing concerning the Black City. As a result, it would be practically impossible to foil their plan: a false Jorik could freely go and destroy, commit crimes and sabotage the inner workings of Babelia's resistance. Ach! The agent of this plan would be uncommonly successful in the damage he could do.

These furious thoughts were the last that Jorik had. He put up a mental barrier against the invader to protect his personality and guard the precious secrets that the other would need. But the pseudo-Anton must have paired the device to a Kaltarian instrument because Jorik felt all consciousness escaping him like water through a sieve. Soon he was just a shell, an empty void, an absence of being. The transmitter started spinning faster and faster. Manuel Esteban slowly opened Jorik's eyes.

Manuel had been forewarned. He was expecting the ambiance and the things around him. But expecting the unfamiliar is not the same as being in it. Moreover, he had just gone to sleep in a very skeptical state of mind and had to admit that he never dreamed of opening his eyes on this unimaginable scenery. In short, there was a weird depersonalization, the sensation of being another person, weirder even than being invaded by another.

He regretted having surrendered to this crazy experience. "Surrender" is the right word... But there was no turning back now. He had no control over the preposterous sphere spinning above him, creating a light breeze, and the transmitter was the only link he had to his native universe. He was at the mercy of Anton Borg's pleasure and Lord only knew what he really was or wanted or was thinking. So far, surprisingly, he did not seem to be a liar.

Esteban was lying in a kind of deep sarcophagus and he was terribly cold. Deathly cold. His angle of vision allowed him to see only the vaguely luminescent ceiling above the ball that was shrinking and losing its colors. From the angles of the ceiling hung bundles of transparent coils, ugly to look at and impossible, of course, to imagine their use—if there was one. The size of the vault was pretty small and the walls reflected a little of the ceiling's light creating a dull, kind of gooey atmosphere.

The smells came after the sights and Esteban regretted it. There was the awful odor of rotting vegetables, which did not fit with the unbearable temperature of the place. At times he got whiffs of something burning, which terrified him for reasons he could not really figure out.

Then came the sounds. Or rather the deep silence was penetrated by distant rumblings and short, metallic bangs. Listening carefully, Manuel tried to learn as much as he could about his environment, starting from these fragmentary echoes. It was not an easy task. He really was *elsewhere*. But his strength was coming back and he could raise himself on one elbow. His head peeked over the edge of the coffin so that his field of vision widened. He saw in front of him, a few feet away, an oval screen mounted on the wall. It appeared to look out upon a dreadfully dark night, compared to which the obscurity of the vault, softened by the ceiling light, felt more like dawn.

Absorbed by these surprising observations, Esteban had forgotten about the sphere over his chest, continuing to shrink. When he thought about it again, his heart wrenched: the device was the size of a pea and still going. All he could see now was a fading shimmer. Manuel remembered Jorik's reaction on a similar occasion. He mustered all his reviving energy and managed to raise a hand toward what was now a shiny dust particle. But his panting pushed the dust out of reach. A second later it vanished. The bridge linking him to his original time had just collapsed.

The traveler fell back down. He was so utterly desperate that he could not face the situation, could not make a single decision. He stayed like this for several minutes, cursing the absurd pact he had made with Anton who had not said much about what was awaiting him. However, the unbearable cold in the vault forced him to do something—his despair was not so complete that he would let himself die of cold.

When he sat up the second time, he saw a figure in the dark screen that slowly took shape. It became clearer, bigger and looked like a small human silhouette. Shivering, Manuel eagerly watched the growing image, which took on proportions that were incompatible with the screen. He saw it materialize in the middle of the room: a tall person bathed in a bright light. The man was thin and bald and his narrow face was oozing hostility. His uncommonly pale eyes stared at Esteban.

"So," a bitter voice came out, "are you coming to report on your miserable failure?"

Manuel took a few seconds to realize that the newcomer was speaking an unfamiliar language but he could still understand him. Very quickly he remembered how Jorik had used his own memory and mental conditioning and he knew that he had the same ability even though Jorik's personality was, for the moment, nowhere to be found. He stared the man down, making a quick inventory of the gray suit and soft boots and the belt from which hung a case in the shape of a comma. Then he shot back with the same apathy that Jorik would display.

"Don't you think you should speak more coldly in a place kept at this temperature?"

"Very spiritual," his face remained wooden. "I suppose you'll keep clowning around even in the presence of the counsel of archons…"

Manuel searched for a response. The man must be used to handling people like Jorik. Maybe he would be rattled by the behavior of a 20th century chemist? But it would be very unwise to put on a show. On the other hand, the give and take was happening so fast that Manuel's reaction was delayed. And here he noticed something else that stopped him: the vault had no door. The oval screen was apparently the only way in or out and from he could tell, you had to turn into smoke to use it.

"All right," he said, "let's get out of here."

"Stop blabbering," the other's voice was impatient. "You can see I'm waiting for you!"

Manuel saw only one thing: he had better probe Jorik's cortical zones and fast. But he found no clue to guide his actions. How in the hell was he supposed to get out of this cell by passing through a screen that was 15 inches wide at most? If he kept hesitating, the man was going to get suspicious.

"Oh," his own voice became shaky, "those ba... they got me!"

And he dropped back down so heavily that the other might think he had passed out. He felt ashamed for resorting to behavior that was only fit for a teenager, but what else could he do? The results, however, exceeded his expectations. The man swiftly backed up to the screen and made a sweeping, drastic movement. Two other Babelians popped up next to him and went up to Esteban who was watching them through half-closed eyes. Seeing them approach, he could not stop thinking about the words he had spoken in a language as different from French as French is from Latin... and apparently with a perfect accent.

The two men leaned over him, lifted him by the shoulders and legs and carried him towards the screen. On the way, Manuel tried to be as heavy as possible. Then he had the strangest, most unpleasant feeling of his life. It was like a compression of himself in every dimension of space and, paradoxically, feeling lighter. He was becoming steam, a cloud, just fumes at the same time as his porters whose shape he could no longer see. It did not last long. Soon his usual sensations were back in a place flooded with a different light, in the middle of a silent gathering.

Someone put a cold disk on his forehead and in an instant all his thoughts became sharp and strong like he had rarely felt before. His eyes opened by themselves and his muscles forced him to sit up. Surrounded by all those green, almost white eyes, he felt like he was in a nightmare.

Another man came forward. He was totally bald, like the others, but flabby and obese, unlike most of them. "Report", he said curtly. His voice sounded like a shard of glass.

Manuel opted for the truth. Thus, he would not reveal himself by hesitating even if his words all had double meanings.

"They were there. They intercepted the transmitter beam and sent me back before I had time to get anything out of the chemist. Besides, you gave me an almost empty head to invade. I doubt they'll get any weapon out of it, even a primitive one."

The archon grimaced with disgust and turned to a man of medium height with shifty eyes. "Make sure the head of this ill-prepared mission be assigned to the light units."

He turned back to the fake Jorik. "As for you, go back to the on-call station. If the State hadn't invested so much energy on you in the traveler training, you'd be going with your chief."

Once again, everything became blurry around Esteban. The assembly vanished into thin air like ghosts and Manuel remained alone with the men who had fetched him from the vault. He understood that all these people were really somewhere else and he had seen just a 3-D projection that was vividly real. He was about to say something but his companions were already gone. An exit suddenly appearing in the wall had swallowed them up and closed behind them as unfathomably as they had appeared.

Manuel thought fast. He had gotten his strength and energy back and nobody seemed to have caught on to Anton's trick. More importantly, the events unfolding were not part of a dream and he had to keep up with them because the bridges were now cut off from the normal, comforting existence that had once been Esteban's. He tried to forget his loneliness and prepare for the dangers to come by telling himself that he had started off well, better than he could ever have imagined under such conditions.

Now he had to get to the "on-call station". Something in Jorik's brain gave him directions to get there, instructions to get past the obstacles and the right attitude to see him through. He got up and stood for a minute examining the layer of elastic metal he had been lying on, then the domed ceiling, the walls joined to the ceiling by those weird, non-Euclidean surfaces… One of the walls, perfectly smooth, reflected the image of a thin man dressed in gray with short, black boots, whose aquatic eyes glistened in a finely chiseled face. He swung around but understood in an instant—he was face-to-face with himself, with the new man he had become, with Jorik.

He had to get used to this body, to the different height, the length of arms and legs, its unfamiliar lung capacity. His voice was cold and dry. He kept his back to the image and marched to the wall through which the others had disappeared.

There was no photoelectric cell controlling the panel like he had first naïvely believed. The technology was much more sophisticated. Apparently, the matter itself disintegrated at his approach. People could do as they wished with matter—thus the transportation of human organisms through obstacles as well as the shrinking and enlarging of bodies. This control over the physical universe was witness to the extent of their power. A power that brought shivers to Manuel just thinking about it.

He went through a short tunnel and was suddenly outside under the pure sky of a summer night. A warm breeze caressed his face and he breathed in the odors… and right away screwed up his face in disgust. The wind stank of grease and burnt rubber or something like that at least. Looking up at the sky Manuel almost yelped: a beautiful green covered the surface of the moon where there were no dark spots of craters.

There must have been lush vegetation growing there. It was certainly inhabited.

At his feet stretched the city. Here, too, Manuel was stupefied. He was expecting a magnificent, harmonious city, sparkling with lights, scattered with glistening buildings, but what he saw was a disordered mass of motley buildings, shapeless and mostly ugly, all of them glowing green like gigantic fish corpses. This was Babelia, as far as the eye could see, a city that inspired nothing but fear and loathing.

Esteban looked back at where he had just left. A little less ugly, but still menacing, the buildings rose up in the shape of a trapezoid against the sky. Manuel figured that he was looking at the central palace. While he was watching the top of the walls he spied a red dot in the distant west. It grew rapidly bigger. The light it gave off was soon bright enough to pale the city's phosphorescence, drowning everything in its frightening, bloody glow. Manuel got goosebumps as he looked around in vain for a hiding place. He was about to run back into the tunnel he had just come out of when the red globe exploded into streaks and sparks, then a stream of fire that drowned the stars. The fiery stream was strange because it seemed to flow over an invisible dome whose curve extended over the city.

The stream of celestial lava poured into the distance and eventually disappeared over the horizon. The sky became as clear and pure as before. Everything remained perfectly silent.

"Kaltarborog!" Esteban thought. "That firework was meant for Babelia but the archons protect their city with a forefield that covers it with an indestructible dome."

He remembered Anton's explanations now and their meaning became clear with Jorik's memories, which Manuel was starting to use more easily. Knowing that the Kaltarians' worst weapons could do nothing against Babelia, he started walking to the quarters below the palace. He, Manuel, was perhaps the only Kaltarian weapon against which the Babelians were helpless. Would he play this senseless game now that he was exiled forever? Thinking about it, Manuel realized that this was the only way to forget about the exile or rather to make it bearable. He also had to keep in mind that if there was some way to get back to the 20th century, it would have to be through the enemy city. Thinking of his body lying in the abyss of the past, Manuel decided to get the most use out of these people who meant nothing to him…

There were no streets, strictly speaking. The buildings butted up against each other without any order, without any overall plan, less even than the most primitive conclave of huts. It was an unpleasant contrast with the high level of scientific development whose effects were seen elsewhere. On a small esplanade where only three or four houses stood, a rough square of some kind, Manuel passed a column of marching men. Dressed in black, they were all carrying a triangular object hanging over their chest.

"The night watchmen," Manuel thought. "They're the ones who'll eliminate, if need be, any Kaltarian who dared to materialize in here."

He knew, almost instinctively, that the triangular weapons had an effect like Anton's little weapon in the lab when Jorik was defeated.

The forms of the watchmen faded into the maze of Babelia without Manuel getting worried. As he went on his way he wondered how Jorik could get through such a labyrinth without getting lost. It was his city, of course, but as it stretched beyond the horizon and since the layout looked to be ruled only by the laws of chance, he had difficulty seeing what could serve as markers.

Nevertheless, Manuel reached the area for people ready for duty. He had not seen a single vehicle on the way. Did they exist? Were they rarely used, maybe only for defense or economy? On this subject Jorik's memory circuits were silent.

The area was a much better organized zone than the rest of the city, at least from what Manuel could see. In the pile of buildings this area was like a patch of healthy tissue on a body riddled with cancer. However, the clearly military appearance of the lodgings here was no more welcoming than the crazy jumble around it.

Esteban met no sentinel, no guard. No alarms went off. He got to his allotted cell without incident. In his mind, however, he could see a danger: so far he had relied on Jorik's memories, but what if they failed him? In such a case he would be caught completely off guard, unless he could fall back on what he had from Anton.

The cell was round. It did not look comfortable enough to feel relaxed. The archons were obviously keen on keeping their emissaries ready for action. A bed, round like the walls around it, stood in the middle like an altar, creating a weird contrast with the rest of the room despite its smooth curves. Whether it was meant for sleep or something else, it was the only thing in the place that might put your mind at ease. Someday, Esteban had to figure out the nature of the ambivalence in Babelian society it symbolized.

He noticed a low piece of furniture stuck in the wall. His hands, conditioned by the same gesture performed over and over again, open it and without ever having seen them before he recognized the photoacoustic crystallizations that the emissaries used for documentation. He grabbed one at random, put it in the piezoelectric transcriber and waited for the machine to start working. Meanwhile, he opened another piece of furniture that held packs of nutritive jelly. Then he sat down on the round bed to eat. The jelly tasted rather odd but also rather delicious.

The ambient light gradually faded and was replaced by a purple light that was suddenly swept away by the glare of the sun. At the same time, the walls seemed to fall back and vanish into the distance. Manuel found himself alone in the middle of a burning desert where the dry wind seared his lungs. A caravan of camels appeared on the horizon.

Squinting, Manuel could make out the columns of horsemen riding alongside it. They were carrying spears, bows and arrows. Soon the horizon was covered with armed men and although they were far in the distance, he could hear their noise. There was something barbarous about them and the rhythm of the war chants reminded him so little of what he knew about primitive songs that he almost forgot about where they were coming from.

When he shook himself out of his reverie, he felt terribly uneasy. He saw the conical helmets and the braided beards of the horsemen approaching and he feared being surrounded by their winding ranks. Jorik's memory abruptly failed him. Was he watching a temporal projection or had he really tripped a mechanism that had thrown him into this age of fury?

He jumped up. The round bed had turned into a pile of sand. With shaky steps he headed for the place where, logically, but unseen to him, should have been the analyzer. He found nothing. 100 yards away the Mesopotamian horsemen were galloping and hollering straight for him.

Bathed in sweat, Manuel turned every which way like a frightened animal. He felt hunted and a quick glance only heightened his fear. Out of the depths of time, the warriors of Teglat were rushing at him.

Something hit his face hard. At first he thought it was an arrow... but the space was protected by an invisible wall. Desperately, he felt along this wall, ran into the jutting furniture and turned off the analyzer. The huge caravan with its ranks of guards melted into a purple haze. The walls came back, the sand turned back into the round bed and Esteban, exhausted, dropped onto it.

"Are you alright, Jorik?" a woman's voice said, as soft as morning dew.

CHAPTER IV

With his head pounding, Manuel turned around. She, too, was sitting on the round bed, directly opposite him, and was watching him calmly. She had very light hair and long eyes whose green was almost white. Her brown skin, on the other hand, made her look like a strange animal and the tight-fitting, iron gray bodysuit showed off her curves that were so graceful and harmonious that Manuel had never before seen the like.

He cursed his emotional reaction. If this woman had been watching the ridiculous dance he had just stumbled through in his panic, she would certainly think something was wrong. But what could he do about it? He had just landed from a distant time and was still not ready to admit to anyone this reality—the reality of his voyage, of his incarnation in another body. The girl had come in more quietly than the wind, using the time projections to sneak into his cell. What gave her the right?

"I…" Esteban started.

"Yes?" she was all ears.

Manuel quickly found the name of the intruder in Jorik's brain: she was Gelia and she was also a time emissary.

"Listen, Gelia," he felt better having remembered her name, "I think my last expedition has kind of traumatized me. I failed and I just ran through the historical documents… I think I lost my head a little with those Assyrians…"

He smiled tensely. Gelia remained cold and kept looking at him curiously. "You're not usually so childish," is all she said.

Manuel felt himself turn pale. Since the Babelians could trespass psychically, why wouldn't they suspect that Esteban, with Anton's help, had invaded Jorik's personality?

"I'm coming back," he stated, "from a childish time and I tried my best to fit in there. But maybe I was too successful and it changed my behavior."

All of a sudden, he knew what he had to do to assuage Gelia's suspicions. He got up, walked slowly around the bed, stood in front of the girl and slapped her hard. She jumped up and covered her face with her left forearm in a gesture that belonged to every age. But Manuel could see her eyes gleaming with satisfaction.

"In any case," the steely voice of Jorik went on, "I still won't put up with insults."

He sat next to her and held her in his arms where he felt her melt. He thought, with a smile, of how amazed his colleagues back at the university would be if they could see him acting like this... but in that case they would have other reasons to be astonished.

"I was afraid for an instant, true," she finally said, "that the enemy had put you through some kind of transformation. They could develop a new weapon any day and we might not know about it for days."

"You're absolutely right," he agreed while hiding the humor in the response. "And you're still as patriotic as ever, which just deepens the feelings I have for you."

He felt like he was in a stage show. But Gelia's supple shape was an outcry against the unreal nature of their words. And the girl disturbed Manuel much more than he wanted to admit.

"I feel better," she said in a breath. "I have to go now. We'll see each other at the saturnalia?"

Manuel had no idea what this meant.

What saturnalia? He queried Jorik's neurons in vain. There was no trace of the thing.

"Of course," he whispered tenderly.

Gelia disappeared suddenly without making any more noise than when she had come in. Alone, Esteban thought for a moment about their meeting, about her being an amusing distraction amidst the dangers but also about the very danger she had and still did put him in. Gelia was like a two-edged weapon: she could help Manuel a lot, but she was just as capable of ruining him completely. He would have to think hard this new factor so abruptly thrown into the turmoil that was sweeping him along. She was a bomb to be handled with the greatest care.

And what about this romantic rendezvous at the so-called saturnalia? "I couldn't care less about this girl," he reflected. And the fact that he dwelled on the idea proved to him that he was already feeling a little jealous at the unlikely tryst that Gelia could make with just anyone. But no! These people were more like Spartans than decadent Romans.

Stirred by a conditioned reflex, obviously deeply rooted in Jorik's being, Manuel went to a section of the wall that vanished at his approach. He found there a walk-in closet where he took off his clothes. As soon as he had put them on a ledge jutting out at eye level, a sound, at first low then higher and higher, surrounded him. It quickly became unbearable, then completely inaudible.

"The frequency has risen into the ultrasounds," he thought.

He had done these meaningless things without thinking. Now he was starting to understand that the device was cleaning his skin with an ultrasonic shower.

"In my time we couldn't get this method to work on surfaces. We barely even used it for medical purposes, except for destroying living cells of course."

The shower was over. Grabbing his traveler suit Esteban noticed that he not only felt cleaner than ever, but his muscles were limber and strong despite not moving during the long hibernation. Obviously, it was a compound radiation which also contained "starter-waves" that worked on his fibril metabolism. His clothes were also squeaky clean. He gladly put them on and left the "bathroom".

Outside, he heard a constant racket in which no single, individual voice was intelligible. One thing he knew sure: it was the sound of a moving crowd.

A very recent and very unpleasant memory came to mind: was he once again getting just illusionary messages from some mechanical projection like when he turned on the audiovisual documentation? And yet, the sound was not coming from inside the room and no image came with it. Manuel left.

The zone was teeming with men and women walking and talking in tight-knit groups. Laughter broke out here and there and Manuel remembered, surprisingly, the cold and dreary personality of Jorik, which he had observed when the emissary was controlling his mind. Despite the dim light spread sparingly in the night, you could still see many faces with the trace of a smile. So there, not all Babelians were cast in the same mold...

Manuel mingled with the crowd, secretly observing the appearance and behavior of those around him. Their faces were lit up and their speech sped up with excitement. They stayed in groups where loud discussions arose about performances. Several times Manuel heard the word that Gelia had spoken and that did not seem to have any other translation except "saturnalia". Connected to the "performances", it was food for thought.

"Let's go," a tall man said, "someone's going to get past two hours! Why not you?"

Manuel felt concerned: in the semi-darkness the eyes of the Babelian were riveted on him. Always those almost colorless pupils, strangely swimming in the white of the eye.

"Why not," Manuel said curtly.

He felt like he had just answered an unreal person met in a dream. But all this was real. The people were actually walking on the hard ground. Shouts echoed through the air that really filled up the lungs.

And yet, they had imprisoned Manuel in another's skin, centuries away from his home. A physical dream, crazier for being so material, so obviously present.

They left the zone and entered the chaotic maze of the city. Not far from Manuel, the man kept talking to a girl who looked very young and who cackled loudly. Esteban was not annoyed by this diversion but he gradually faded away from the couple and took a different street without changing the general direction. Sometimes he passed a squad of night watchmen and the fluorescent green glow of the buildings spotlighted their expressionless faces.

Scattered through the jumble of streets, the crowd could only be heard now. Esteban placed more trust on the sounds than in Jorik's memory, which was useless for the moment. Why had he gone along with the crowd? Curiosity? Deep-seated habit in the emissary's being?

The buildings lit up. Manuel stopped on the edge of a lake that was vaguely brightened by wild lights from the depths. A kind of shiny, metal pier stood nearby. The emissaries were huddled together there and Manuel noted that there could not have been more than a hundred of them. Along with a few straggling couples he joined the group. Everyone seemed to be champing at the bit. Some eyes stared at the hazy glimmer of the water, others at a rectangular building on the pier topped by a three-pronged pole slowly swaying.

A man jumped onto the edge of the flat roof of the building. He raised his arms and his voice, with the help of an invisible mechanism, reached Manuel:

"Now it's time for the saturnalia. Let's all get ready."

Surprised, Manuel started thinking of two things at the same time: the immediacy of the saturnalia that Gelia had talked about as if it were a future ceremony and the weird effect of the hidden speakers that amplified the voice in distance but not in volume. It was like the man on the roof was talking to each of them individually, standing right next to them and whispering.

But his attention was soon focused on the emissaries and he searched desperately in Jorik's brain for something that might give him a hint of what to expect. With some anxiety he realized that the brain was giving him less and less information. If he were left all alone, he would undoubtedly be found out soon and executed shortly thereafter. He felt like he was hiding behind a shield that was getting smaller by the minute.

The door of the building opened and the emissaries were lined up to pass by it. Manuel got in line and shuffled forward with the others. When he got to the door, some figure in the shadows handed him an object, which he took. The others kept nudging him on. A few feet on he noticed that the object fit his hand comfortably. A weapon probably. He handled it cautiously. Nevertheless, without knowing how it happened, a bright flash sprang out in front of him, hollowing out a three-foot hole in the ground and causing those around him to panic for a brief moment.

"What happened?" a wary emissary asked.

Esteban bluffed in Jorik's cold, calculated voice, "I was trying it out, making sure it hasn't been sabotaged by a Kaltarian who might've infiltrated our defenses. In my humble opinion, you're all getting a little sloppy, every one of you…"

The Babelian looked uncertain, wavering between disbelief and distrust.

"I wasn't being clumsy," Manuel tried to double down on his bluff. "No one got hurt, right? I was careful…"

"Anyway," the man said gravely, "no one got hurt but just one death and you know very well…"

He walked away without finishing the sentence. Manuel could tell his excuse was not convincing. Jorik's brain was really starting to break down. But for every bad there is some good because Esteban now knew the nature of the object he was holding. He would have really liked to know what he had touched to trigger it, but this was not the time to examine it.

A hand fell on his shoulder and he spun around. "Oh, it's you, Gelia."

Her worried eyes were staring at him. "I saw the explosion. Any damages?"

"Of course not," Manuel said softly. "I'm not as careless as you think! But I have to admit that the trigger is extra sensitive. Look at it."

He held the weapon out to Gelia. At that moment he would have given his eye teeth for a little more light. Still, he could see where Gelia was taping with her finger before handing it back to him.

"I don't think so," she said.

"So, my brawn is too much for my brain," he joked a little, feeling proud of his trick.

Now that he knew how to work the weapon, he felt less nervous. First of all, if they gave it to him, it was for a reason. And then, more generally, he felt more confident about the future since he would not have to rely solely on brute force...

All these reflections were soon swept away by the image of the girl standing motionless and so close. Manuel breathed in her subtle perfume, which he had hardly noticed when he was holding her in his arms. With the still water in the background, the Babelian girl looked like the eternal youth of the world and the centuries he had to cross to reach her only made her that much younger.

The master of ceremony's voice came out of nowhere and everywhere. "The games will begin on the third radiance."

Manuel put his arm around Gelia's shoulder and hugged her.

"We might not ever see each other again," she said dreamily. "The Kaltarian prisoners fight with desperate energy."

Esteban did not reply. So, was this the saturnalia? In a flash he understood his mistake. The Babelian word he had translated like this really did have its root in the name of an ancient god, but it was not Saturn. The god who lent his name to this particular ceremony was Neptune. Now Manuel understood the choice of a lake or sea for the site of the games. Games that, from what Gelia said, sounded like a return to the barbarity of ancient days. In spite of everything, he had a little laugh at himself because of the mistake, probably explained by subconscious reasons that he dared not admit.

"Come on," Gelia said, "I have to join the women. Goodbye, Jorik." She skipped away without giving Manuel time to respond. She was definitely not very expressive.

But new events were about to divert his thoughts. A bright flash had just lit up the landscape with snowy light, revealing the entire, unbroken surface of the lake and casting sidelong shadows of the misshapen buildings of Babelia, like a photo negative against the star-studded sky. The travelers separated into two groups, women on one side and men on the other. Manuel mingled with the latter, still blinded by the first radiance.

At the bottom of the lake, ghostly movements and shifting lights seemed to be organizing themselves, forming a kind checkered dance on squares linked by the swift trails of the pale light.

A second flash as bright as the first glinted off the light clothes of the emissaries, freezing the crowd like in a photo. The chessboard blanketing the bottom of the water suddenly went dark. So suddenly that Manuel thought it was due to his blindness, but he could still see everything around him.

The shores of the lake fell completely silent. Conversations and mutterings that could be heard only an instant before were immediately hushed. The sky and water awaited the third flash.

Coldly, soundlessly, it blazed as brightly as the other two. Then everyone started moving toward the water, Manuel with them. A dozen men dove in first.

Esteban watched the surface. No one was coming back up, but this did not seem to bother anyone on shore. So much time passed that Manuel was sure the commando team had perished in an ambush by the Kaltarians at the bottom of the lake. Such an outcome was, however, highly unlikely: the Babelians could not be so crazy as to give all advantages to the prisoners and none to their own fighters.

Another group dove in. Instinctively, Manuel had stepped back in order not to be one of them. He congratulated himself after a few minutes when this group, too, did not re-surface. But his thoughts took another turn when he saw the first line of women walk to the edge of the water. He could make out Gelia's face and figure among them. By reflex he moved closer to them, but he realized that the slightest inter-vention on his part would give him away.

It was then that he saw several men rising up from the water on those fantastic beasts. Dripping with water that the moonlight turned into sparks, they leapt 30 feet high, legs squeezing the flanks of those long creatures that were some-thing between a swordfish and a cuttlefish. After a short ride in the air, the men and beasts disappeared again into the lake with huge splashes, sometimes kicking up big bubbles that popped and let loose thick green vapor. Thus the semi-aquatic, semi-aerian joust went on. But how did these men lacking any kind of breathing apparatus stay so long underwater without drowning? Here was a mystery that Manuel did not feel able to solve.

Nevertheless, it was his turn. The group he was joined to was getting ready to dive. Esteban stepped back to get a better jump, to say the least. After all, he only had to do as the others did... he took the leap.

First of all, Manuel swan hard, straight ahead, opening his eyes cautiously. His first surprise was that the water did not sting his eyes any more than a dry, warm breeze. His sec-ond surprise was what he witnessed: through the unnaturally clear liquid he saw the beasts lying along the dock, 15 or 20 feet down. They were lined up like horses along a drinking trough and the Babelians were already clambering onto their backs. In the distance, in the blue-green world streaked with red lights, things were quickly taking shape.

But his greatest surprise was when he saw a Babelian near him open his mouth and eagerly fill his lungs with the cold water...

Naturally, Manuel had kept his mouth hermetically sealed. But he felt like he could not hold out for half a minute longer. He heard his blood beating in his ears and a terrible weight was crushing his chest. He let out a little air, still swimming slowly toward the beasts.

A bright light suddenly flashed in his mind—the forbidden regions of Jorik's brain had just unveiled a new cache of hidden information. In short, the emissaries were amphibian. Whether it was congenital after a mutation brought on by guarding the acquired hereditary traits or rather that each emissary, as a child, had undergone a ghastly surgery to graft gills onto his body— either way the fact was there.

A prey to his own, personal reactions again, which were always interfering with the Babelian body at the wrong time, Manuel still hesitated to imitate the others. The painful image of suffocation kept popping up in his mind, but it was not as dreadful as it would have been in Manuel's own body. He opened his mouth and breathed in a little water, very gently.

The feeling was extraordinary, almost miraculous. Esteban remembered a legend he had read as a child that was about Ys, a drowned city, and the people living there, among whom was a young girl who lured a fisherman's son one day into her palace. The boy followed her and was able to breathe in the new element thanks to a charm… for a moment Manuel believed he was the hero of this legend. Wouldn't Gelia be the heroine?

But he had to hurry. The fighters were snatching up all the available beasts and their squadron was moving off quickly into the sea. Manuel filled his lungs—or gills—with water that seemed to satisfy every fiber of his being and swam to the dock. At this moment came the thought of sirens whose hair waved softly like white algae. Having any kind of commerce with them was obviously a serious breach of custom.

The exile from another century perched on the back of one of the sea monsters, which immediately reacted with unhoped for docility. As they swam off together, he glanced back. Other beasts were slowly coming out of trapdoors, rising up and forming a barrier to block the way. They were ridden by Kaltarians wearing masks.

The water suddenly felt colder, less fit for maintaining life. From the moment the torrent of extraordinary causes and effects had seized him, he had not really fought against it—physically, of course. The only act of violence he had committed was to slap a woman. Now he would have to go up against determined enemies who, although they were already conquered theoretically, were still warriors, clever and full of hatred, whereas he, Manuel, had never been anything but a peaceful professor.

Luckily, they had provided a kind of saddle, firmly attached on the back of the fantastic fish. With his feet in the loops, Manuel could stay pretty well balanced even if a fall in this element was nothing to fear, still the changes of direction were really abrupt. He wanted to scream out, to call some Babelians over to help him, but how could he make a sound, how could water vibrate his vocal chords? He managed only a pathetic gurgling noise with the last air bubbles in his lungs—the rattle of a drowning man.

The others were already shooting at him. His right shoulder felt a sharp pain where a puff of green vapor rose slowly through the water. Manuel held his weapon in his left hand and fanned shots out in front of him.

He had nothing against these people. Plus, they were prisoners who belonged to the same camp that he had chosen to support. But they thought he was a Babelian, an enemy to kill if they could. The energy beam had hit a Kaltarian who slid slowly off his beast and floated to the surface along with the weird green bubble. The strength of the weapon must have been diminished by the density of the water, so the Kaltarian was certainly not killed by the shot, for which Manuel was thankful. But what an odd impression to see a wounded man soar up like a bird instead of falling to the ground…

Carried away by his enthusiasm, Manuel crossed the broken line of enemies. His shoulder was just sore, like after getting a moderate electric shock. A twitching in his back muscles told him he was hit again. The barrier had closed up behind him and the weapons had him in their sights. He had to get rid of this painful cramp that was tensing his body like a strung bow. Desperately, he steered the best toward the surface. He came out of the water into the dim phosphorescent night, dripping with sparkling water, got his bearings and looked for his adversaries. But they, too, had fled, pursued by a party of Babelians in which he could see a few women. So, they were allowed to mix together? Esteban thought of joining Gelia, wherever she might be.

When he swung his beast around, he saw her. The girl was a few feet away, breaking the surface and dragging behind her, at the end of a rope, the lifeless body of a Kaltarian prisoner.

Even though the weapons used by the Kaltarians were weak, the Babelian emissaries suffered three casualties and a number of seriously wounded. Of course, the Kaltarian prisoners, on the other hand, were massacred.

A grand nocturnal feast was going to bring the Babelian fighters back together, during which it was the custom to celebrate the funeral rites for those who had perished in the battle and to give out the rewards that the winners deserved.

Manuel climbed onto the dock with the others and his wound was patched up right away—it was far from fatal. A strange wound, however, and it would have troubled any of Manuel's contemporaries. It was neither a bloody lesion nor a big bruise nor a closed fracture, but rather a swelling with punctuated bleeding that partially paralyzed his arm. Something apparently got through to hit the blood vessels as well as the nerves and the edema was surrounding the lot with a hard, painful mass. The bandage was special, too: they taped a green metal plate onto his shoulder and that was all. From that moment on, Manuel felt like his shoulder was shrinking while he slowly recovered the use of his arm. Esteban suspected that the weapon used electromagnetic waves that affected the molecular arrangement of cells, but reversible enough for a treatment of the same kind could heal it. The metal plate was obviously doing just that.

During the match, they had set up banquet tables on the dock. Like the buildings they had an unhealthy glow about them, which did nothing for Manuel's appetite. Between this sight and the memory of the Babelian girl dragging behind her the dead body of a Kaltarian, Manuel was seeing a common thread that disturbed him. He could not tell exactly why, but he felt like everything in Babelia belonged to the bad side of man. How could Gelia be an exception? Jorik was the first example he had encountered and he seemed typical.

The on-call emissaries sat with their friends. Manuel looked around the esplanade bordering the docks, searching in vain for the girl. Finally, he saw her sitting at a table nearby. In the sickly glow she looked like a wicked flower. And yet, he could not stop himself from sliding in next to her.

"Hey," she said, "are you hurt?"

Her voice did not sound terribly worried, but she looked a little concerned and this was enough to make Manuel feel better than he would have imagined.

"It's not serious," he said casually.

Childishly he swung his wounded arm in a circle, which made him cry out in pain.

"What's wrong with you?" Gelia looked surprised. "Can't you wait a few minutes before moving it?"

He had tried to act tough and he looked like an out-of-control idiot...

"So," he pouted, "what's on the menu?"

Gelia's surprise turned into bewilderment. Then she broke out laughing, "Don't you know how many Kaltarians died? There's enough for all of us."

Manuel took a few seconds, maybe a full minute, to stop his shuddering. Learning that you have gills when you hit the water is one thing, but this revelation, not yet fully digested, that you are participating in a cannibal feast would make anyone lose their marbles. Manuel lost enough of them that Gelia's smile vanished.

"What's wrong?" she asked coldly.

Manuel slumped on the polished metal bench and forced himself to breathe deeply.

"My injury must be worse than it looks," he stammered. "I feel dizzy and cold. I think I might not be able to stay here for this."

Gelia's suspicious air turned into a sneer, "As you want. But I don't have to tell you that I won't be hanging out anytime soon with such a crybaby."

She turned her back to him. Manuel was furious… against himself, against her, against this whole savage city and against Anton the Kaltarian who had sent him to this hellhole. He started hoping that it was all just a nightmare, that he would wake up far away, long ago, in his own bedroom. For a few minutes he took refuge in this idea to escape from the complex, frenzied conflicts surrounding him. But he had to come out of it…

A noise rumbled out of the nearby buildings and the stretchers appeared. They came forward, automatically, remote-controlled apparently, from the tower of radiances. There were a dozen and each of them carried a corpse. From all directions came infrared spotlights. Hanging off the edges of all the tables were saws and knives.

Manuel stood up. "I've never seen the use of all these ceremonies that just make us regress to the earliest ages of mankind."

Gelia turned to him. And she was not the only one. Other emissaries were looking at Manuel as if they could not believe their ears. The traveler started to regret his comment. All those colorless eyes riveted on him, the silence surrounding him, and in the background that dismal rumbling of the corpse-laden stretchers along with the tinkling of the flesh-cutting utensils… they were all competing to make Manuel lose the little clarity he was still hanging onto.

However, the great risk he was running suddenly gave him more energy. He buckled down, looked around and said, "It will never be said that Jorik supports these outdated traditions. I'm going to tell this to the archons themselves."

"Tell what?" a barrel-chested man with wide shoulders asked slowly without taking his eyes off him.

Manuel looked him up and down in silence. He just remembered that he, too, had the same colorless eyes and this equality gave him comfort as if it were a real weapon.

"Everyone should be able to dispose of his victim or prisoner alone. Sharing should only be done if the owner wants to," he spoke forcefully. "The archons ought to let us decide for ourselves."

Untroubled, the man asked, "What do you mean by this reference to the earliest ages of mankind?"

Manuel felt like he was tripping over his shoelaces while making a long jump. But he did not get flustered, "In the earliest ages of mankind, apparently, which you know as well as I, these festivities were sacrificial."

He paused a moment. Why was he going off on these reckless, contradictory detours? He could almost feel the hostility around him. Then suddenly he knew why he had spoken like this, how he would settle the issue. He was getting a clear picture of Jorik's memory.

He took another deep breath and went on, "It's no longer the case. Our time travel missions have a biological drawback that no one in Babelia has been able to fix: our metabolism is changed slightly so that our food must contain nucleic acids of human origin. We're unable to assimilate any other kind of nucleotide. There's nothing sacrificial about this and we went straight to the corpses when all other methods of storage from biochemical extraction failed."

"Yeah, so," the man said, "that's nothing new."

"I'm saying that these meals taken together under the pretense of false equality are relics of long-dead religious festivals. I'm afraid their need will start taking on the stench of religion. I'm afraid it'll weaken our power against Kaltarborog where nobody's disguising reality."

He made a brief pause before continuing.

"Giving to each what he himself earned by his valor will clear things up for good and will get rid of this crippling tendency to deify everything, which we're not immune to, I'm afraid. Plus, this new method will first of all motivate us more in the battles, putting real strength back in fighting, as is fitting for a genuine Babelian. Come on! Have the courage to give up this security that guarantees sharing the spoils after the battle and let's get back to more vital and virile actions."

A spark of interest flashed in the colorless eyes. Manuel knew that he had won the round. He kept silent for a few seconds, then struck the final blow.

"I'll set the example myself because it's easy to just talk and not do the work. It so happens that tonight I didn't get a victim or prisoner. So, I'll publicly refuse any share."

He stood up and left with dignity. In the midst of the flattering whispers that rose up behind him, he heard Gelia's voice call out:

"Jorik! Come back! I was wrong about you!"

He noted that for the first time she was using the "informal" you. He did not go back to the green shades where the radiation cookers were starting to heat up. Nobody followed him since they were all so tightly disciplined by the archons. In the formless maze of the Black City he felt weak right when the retrospective fear hit him with the danger he had just scraped through. At the same time, he felt less sickened by the cannibalistic practices of the time travelers. However, he still could not imagine eating with them and was proud of his cleverness.

CHAPTER V

Back in his circular cell, Manuel started eating. The nutrition pill quickly quenched his hunger and restored his strength. How lucky he was to have found like this, *at the end of his rope*, some of the most important information in Jorik's memory.

He was startled. Since he had incarnated in the body of the Babelian emissary, he was dependent on its metabolism. How long could he live on the store of nucleic acids in this body? How long could he resist the mandatory cannibalism? Now that he was prisoner of this century he had to consider his limitations. If, instead of changing times, he had just changed bodies and if he had landed in the skin of a man-eating tiger, he would have to obey the killer instincts of his new body. There was not much difference here.

He suddenly felt exhausted. Gelia made his skin crawl, but he still felt attracted to her. Wouldn't it be easier to simply adapt to his new metabolism—the same as Gelia's—and go down to her level in order to live and break down the wall separating them?

But he could not bring himself to do it. There was another solution. Now that Gelia was part of his life, he saw no way of getting her out of it. Therefore, he had to keep on the track set out for him by Anton: sabotage as much as possible this messed up society even at the risk of killing Gelia and himself in the process, which would resolve, once and for all, these complicated problems.

Manuel delved into Jorik's memory. At all costs he had to find the necessary means to carefully prepare an effective and rapid attack. Rapid so as not to question the difficult decision he had just made. Effective so that the results would be as damaging as possible. He managed to clear his mind of all other considerations and started probing blindly.

He remembered. He remembered a place where he had never been. He knew what was done there, what it would take to stop it, and how to accomplish it. He still had the weapon they had given him for the games, lying there snugly on the round bed. He grabbed it and left the room.

The images that had just surfaced in Manuel-Jorik's mind were superimposed pretty well, certainly clearer and more precise, on the directions given by Anton. He thought, "Getting a good look, I see these directions would never have been enough for a real raid." But they were, in fact, inseparable from the situation of clairvoyance where his incarnation had put him in this century. They were just a preface and a guideline. A spider's web along which beads of a foreign memory were forming like dewdrops in the morning... or in the twilight...

Manuel realized that he had not yet made the most out of Anton's instructions. They were, in the end, like a link between his own mind and Jorik's brain. He would not forget them again.

He was walking along the darkened streets between two dimly lit facades. For the first time he was aware of what this darkness meant in Babelia and he appreciated the real merit of the nickname "The Black City." Babelia had not been built underground and nobody had managed to stop the rotation of the planet so far. No, Babelia stayed in the shadows because of its protective forcefield. Through a saturation effect, the light rays passed through the shield only if their flux was under a certain limit, beyond which the photons were simply reflected. Thus, from under this invisible dome that could blow up enemy missiles, you could see the bright stars and even the moon's disk, but never the sun or its light diffused by the atmosphere.

Manuel looked up and saw that the day was just dawning, which he could tell by the total darkening of the sky, a paradox that was really not so surprising if you think about the intensity of the solar rays in the saturation effect that for an observer under the energy dome would eliminate the weak luminescence of the moon and stars and so their image on the retina. In Babelia, nothing was as nocturnal as the day.

"This city is like the flipside of a coin," Manuel thought. "Its defensive weapons have cut off the light while its offensive commandoes have turned into cannibals because their time-traveling prevents them from synthesizing nucleic acids."

He walked on, so wrapped up in his thoughts that he did not see the patrol come up on him. He was thinking, "I should be well placed to notice the link between the swapping of chromosomes and their movements in the continuum…"

"Where are you going," a voice barked, "and why are you carrying that weapon?"

Manuel snapped out of his reverie as the watchmen surrounded him. He barked back, "You can see I'm an emissary. I've just come from the games where I was hurt…"

He showed them the bandage on his shoulder.

"I was taking a rest in my room where I'd brought the weapon because I didn't want anyone taking it and causing any problems for me. Since I couldn't return it before, I'm taking it back now."

The watchmen eyed him suspiciously, then one of them waved him on, "All right, you can do what you have to."

Without a word, like a good, proud, surly emissary, Manuel marched through their line and vanished into the night. The fulfillment of his mission had just been seriously threatened. He hurried through the maze of jumbled buildings.

The power plant was a huge, hemispherical building flanked by a kind of minaret with a bright purple, pointy tip. Everything around it was barren, so Manuel slipped into a little alcove at the foot of an almost vertical building. During the few minutes of surveillance, he started questioning the decision he had made. However, the efforts he was making to spot a human figure in the darkness kept him from thinking too much. Then he felt his whole body go on alert automatically when the silhouette of a guard stepped out of the monumental entrance of the building. A Kaltarian commando could materialize at any moment in this strategic location so this guard was not supposed to be alone. Violence was no good. Manuel would have to get clever again.

He came out of his hiding place as if he had just turned the corner and headed for the guard as casually as could be.

"Halt!" the man raised his weapon. "Stay where you are."

Manuel did not move. His ray gun was hanging from his belt. He slowly raised his empty hands.

"Don't you recognize my emissary uniform?" he spoke with the dull cheerfulness that time travelers use in their best moods—except during the games.

"Sure," the other replied, "but I don't trust it."

Manuel smiled. They could talk.

"So, you're going to make me look foolish in front of my friends?"

"What friends?" the guard looked around worriedly.

"The ones hiding behind that wall…"

The guard took two steps back and grumbled, "Is this some kind of joke?"

Manuel tried hard to make his voice sound patient and tolerant like he was talking to a child, "No joke. I was just betting my commando buddies that you city guards didn't know how to play hopscotch."

The man shook his head and repeatedly stupidly, "Hopscotch? What do you win?"

"Not money," Manuel was struggling now to stay serious. "There are six of them hiding behind both those corners across from us and six others over there to the right. I promised them not to say anything but I want to be honest with you even if you don't know how to play."

The guard shook himself like a rain-drenched horse and brayed, "Hey, come out of there!"

Manuel stood still and silent. The man looked at him with growing suspicion.

"That's enough. I don't know this game and I don't want to learn it. Put your hands behind your head. I'm taking you to the guardhouse in the plant."

Manuel obeyed and shrugged, "If you guards are jerks to me, you're going to have every emissary in Babelia coming after you. They'll clean up the mess later."

The guard did not answer. He knew that this, at least, was true. The emissaries had a bad reputation.

"We're just going to do a little check," he mumbled.

As Manuel was expecting, there were ten men in the guardhouse. The one who had brought him in addressed the others.

"He says he's got a dozen of his buddies hidden nearby waiting on some kind of bet. I think you should go check it out while I watch him."

"Hold on," one of them said. "I'll stay and watch with you. Who knows?"

Manuel started laughing, "You're all chicken. Not a single one of you has the courage to go through emissary training!"

He stopped laughing and looked daggers at all of them.

"Watch me?" he pointed at the one who had just spoken. "He sends you all off to get beat up by my friends and you stay here, pretending to watch me."

"Don't listen to him," the accused guard yelped. "Can't you see he's trying to separate us?"

A giant of a man measured him up and growled, "You're coming with us. No one has anything to fear from the emissaries here. I'd be honored to be one of them. We're going to do a little recon as a matter of principle." He nodded his chin at Manuel. "And if this guy's telling the truth, I'll be glad to invite his friends in here and offer them a drink. Then we can talk about whatever this bet is. Me, I'm in."

The brute dragged the others outside, leaving Manuel alone with his guard. He lost no time.

"I see how this is going to end. You'd better go get the bottle while there's still time."

The other looked suspicious again, then started smiling, satisfied with himself. "You won't have a chance to play any tricks on me. The bottle of Gzerb is right here."

Keeping his eyes on Manuel the man stepped back and felt around behind him with his left hand. His right hand kept hold of the ray gun. About three feet of wall dematerialized, revealing a hole in which the guard grabbed a flask made of soft, transparent material. He brought it out and like a gourd squirted it down his throat.

This was taking too long to Manuel's liking. "Hey, I gave you the idea! You could think of me!"

The man laughed, "Here, catch!"

He tossed the flask at Manuel who caught it in mid-air and pointed it at the guard's eyes. And he squeezed hard. Blinded by the spray, the other stumbled and called out for his comrades. Manuel was on him in a flash and knocked him out with a karate chop to the neck.

Now he knew what he had to do: first, find the control of plastimetal shield that surrounds the whole plant in case of an emergency. Anton had given him detailed information for this. The breaker was in the middle of the control panel in the guardhouse.

Sounding like the soft rustling of silk the shield sealed off the entrance to the power plant. Then Manuel left the guardhouse and entered the huge building itself.

In the center stood the great fusion generator where a plasma that could reach a billion degrees was vibrating. This plasma created the energy needed for the force field that held it captive, just like it provided the energy required for the protective dome of the city.

Manuel remembered that it was daytime outside the dome. Soon the Black City would not deserve its name, he mused. It would become the White City when the shield disappeared. And it would be a very short time before a Kaltarian missile turned it into the Flaming Red City… brighter than 1,000 suns, as someone said in his time.

He took out his ray gun and walked over to the generator's little controller booth. Gelia's face popped up in his mind.

How could he condemn her like this? Was everything forever lost for him who was doomed along with her? And these Babelians? He had been sullied by all their possible faults, but did he, Manuel, take himself for a god to murder a city like this?

Everything reset back to zero while the guards calls echoed behind the plastimetal screen. There was certainly some way to get to the intruder without going through the opening. A few more minutes and the mission would fail.

Manuel thought he should shoot without thinking. You never kill if you think about it first, unless you're a monster. With his forehead soaked in sweat Esteban wondered what twists and turns of destiny had yanked him out of his epoch to come and mess things up here. And what a mess! But this very question was just a way to escape the problem rather than face it.

A human form materialized out of nowhere, exactly in the line of fire of his ray gun and a voice boomed out:

"I don't like this! You're going to create mayhem everywhere!"

Stunned, Manuel could not take his eyes off the little man. He noticed, unconsciously, the iridescent bodysuit he wore, which was blinking in the trembling light of the plasma.

"This isn't Anton," he thought, "but it must be a Kaltarian. So, they can materialize inside the strategically important Babelian buildings? In that case, what am I doing here and why did Anton…?"

The man interrupted his thoughts, "My name will tell you nothing. I am Varold. But I think I've got a pretty bad reputation in Kaltarborog." He chuckled. "And I'm afraid I have something to do with your being here. It so happens that by a chain of events…" He waved his hand before Manuel who was staring at him with furrowed brow. "In short, I beg you to remember what's most precious to you in the world… Put your weapon down and let's talk."

"Don't you see?" Esteban shouted like he had just sobered up. "They'll get in here any second now. I have no time!"

But he had already put the gun in his belt, only too glad that this weird guy stopped his trigger finger at the last minute and spared him from making a decision that was too hard.

"I said 'let's talk' because I know for sure that it'll take them some time to get in here."

Manuel looked at Varold, then at the plasma column. An absurd idea crossed his mind: Was Varold the spirit of the plasma, the goblin of the generator conjured up by a Dickens of the future? Such a thought was ridiculous and demeaning for a scientist, especially in this age dominated by highly developed technology. Whether Varold was an agent from Babelia or Kaltarborog mattered little, really, because Manuel belonged to neither city.

Nevertheless, the 20th century man asked, "Who are you working for?"

Varold smiled with a hint of bitterness, "You wouldn't understand fast enough. We'll talk about that someday, maybe, if we see each other again. For now, I'm asking you to trust me but I have no way to prove to you my goodwill. I can only tell you that I know where you came from—you are not from the here and now. So, believe me, don't get too involved in politics that are beyond you."

A look of surprise crossed Manuel's face, then he resumed his composure, "*They* got me involved."

"No," Varold said softly. "You know perfectly well that even though the Babelian agent attacked you by surprise, you still signed up to join the Kaltarian ranks of your own free will."

Manuel kept silent. Varold was speaking the truth.

"Well," Varold continued, "here's what I advise: drop these homicidal projects of yours and go back to a certain person who is right now participating in a feast that you can't stand but is necessary for her body—just like for yours, by the way. If you let her live, as well as everyone else in this city, I guess it's not to give up on her? I think she'll fall pretty easily into open arms ready to embrace her. And yours are not the only ones…"

In spite of everything, Manuel felt a wave of jealousy surge up, searing him like a brand. This was obviously some cheap trick of Varold's, but it was working, even though Manuel was fully aware of the ploy. Whoever he was, he was very well informed, as if he had been alongside Manuel the whole time, everywhere he had gone. You could even believe that he was reading his thoughts…

The more Esteban watched Varold, the more he believed he was dealing with a Kaltarian. But what did this present attitude mean? Was he playing the double agent by protecting Babelia or had Kaltarian politics taken a different turn after Anton had sent Manuel on this mission? And what did Varold mean when he said he had something to do with Manuel being here?

Gelia's image came back to mind and filled it up completely, wiping out all of Manuel's other temporary problems.

"What should I do?" he asked curiously.

"I told you. Go back to the emissaries and bear the sight of their feast so you can watch over the girl who matters to you. For the rest, events beyond your control will decide your behavior. You've already chosen sides, so you'll see how you can affect the results of these events."

"And how do you think I'm going to get out of here?"

"Like me. Let me take you."

Varold came close and took his hand. The contact felt so weird that Manuel stepped back. It was almost like the guy was not really real, materially. Was this because of his way of traveling, a way that seemed common practice in this epoch? The sensation did not last long. Manuel saw the things around him turning blurry, melting into each other, swirling around, then gradually vanishing before his eyes. This was a different transformation from what Manuel had experienced in the vault when he first came here. The dematerialization mechanism must be based on a different principle. He admired these people who had various methods for such fantastic operations.

Another scene materialized around him before he had entirely escaped the last. Or rather, his body came back to a reality that allowed him to receive new information from outside. The endless night of Babelia was fading away before the fluorescent façades. Nearby, the surface of the lake shimmered. Strange smells wafted through the air along with the noise from the banquet.

Varold had disappeared.

Manuel was half expecting this disappearance. He compared it to film editing, a cross-fading in which the director had cut out his accomplice with some fancy special effects. But who was the director if not Varold himself? Manuel felt like he was no longer in control but being controlled.

Looking down the long line of tables, he found Gelia. Varold had not lied: the girl was leaning against the shoulder of the guy next to her, both of them laughing and chewing those foul tidbits with gusto, which Manuel was trying to ignore. The wave of jealousy that had crept in before was flooding him now.

He walked over to them, still unnoticed, and called out to Gelia. She looked surprised at him. His voice almost caught in this throat, "*Bon appetit!*"

"Oh, it's you, Jorik! Why'd you come back and what do you want?"

Self-preservation got the upper hand. Manuel managed to repress his rage, figuring that he had already made the emissaries suspicious enough. But the other guy jumped into the fray so rudely.

"Something bothering you?" he put down his piece of human meat.

Jealousy, anger and disgust came rushing back and he felt his blood boiling. A red veil spread out before his eyes.

"I wasn't talking to you," he sounded barely understandable. "Eat your rotting carcass and be quiet."

The other stood up slowly. The noisy conversations had given way to a heavy silence. Though cool and composed, the voice of Manuel's rival rang through the silence like an alarm bell.

"How do you want me to kill you?"

Manuel swiftly drew his ray gun and aimed it at the emissary's gut. "I won't give you a choice," he said, drunk with fury.

At the same time, he was grabbed from behind and someone snatched away his weapon. A voice said, "He's crazy! When has this kind of fight ever been settled except with bare hands, with the freedom to use lethal grips?"

"I repeat," the traveler spoke as if nothing had happened, "what kind of fight do you feel most comfortable in?"

"Whatever you've got!" Manuel's voice was turned flat and monotone by hate.

They formed a circle around them. The emissary who had taken Manuel's weapon let him go without giving it back. In a flash Esteban saw the insanity of the situation: plucked out of his peaceful biochemistry lab in the 20th century, he was on the verge of fighting to the death with a merciless brute who would be born four centuries after him and only because of the pretty eyes of a cannibal. And hadn't he turned into a man with gills who could travel instantly from one point to another? He started to think again that he was living through a nightmare and he wanted to wake up right away to escape this absurd duel.

But he did not wake up. The man was approaching him, his two hands opened like vise grips. Manuel dove desperately into Jorik's memory to find the conditioning for hand-to-hand combat. He did not have to use it. What happened next was completely unexpected.

Exactly as Varold had popped up in the power plant, so a bunch of men materialized in the shadows near the circle around the fighters. These men appeared so suddenly that they looked like condensations of the air. They all wore long, black robes, belted at the waist, and their heads were protected by round helmets. All of them held short but thick weapons, like flattened tubes. A few of the Babelians had already shouted in alarm. And the battle began.

The emissaries had been taken by surprise and many of them fell before they could even touch their ray guns. Manuel knew instantly that he was looking at a Kaltarian commando team armed with weapons that could freeze their molecules. Anything caught in the beam hit a temperature near absolute zero.

Manuel saw a few Kaltarians taking prisoners and dragging them down by the lake. Along the way, the plunderers and captives disappeared abruptly. Gelia was one of them while Manuel's adversary dropped to the ground, stiff as a board. These were the last images engraved on Esteban's retina—an instant later he was hit by an unbearable cold spell. He knew they had killed him. His final thought was for Gelia.

CHAPTER VI

Two men in white lab coats—one was young and clean-shaven, the other had a gray, square-cut beard, but the eyes of both were full of surprise and worry: the man gesticulating before them with reckless abandon had been introduced as the right-hand man of a VIP in his country.

The bearded professor shrugged his shoulders and spoke out harshly in outrage, "I can claim to be up-to-date on the most recent work all over the world concerning controlled hypothermia," his voice got louder, "and I'm amazed at how flippantly you're treating your patient. How can you hope to avoid myocardial anoxia if you bring down the temperature below 40 degrees? Go on, then, but I won't be responsible for monitoring his hibernation."

Dr. Anton Borg glanced at him, "This is between Esteban and myself. I'd appreciate it if you'd keep that in mind."

He took off his coat and left without saying goodbye. In the hospital corridor he took a few steps, then stopped to make sure he was alone. He opened his jacket to reveal a weird vest made of metallic fabric. Instead of a pocket there was a small, thin disk that bore unimaginably complex markings. He played with it for a second, then the corridor was empty.

Anton Borg had decided to take a few precautions. Not ones expected by the two clinical experts, but ones that he judged necessary. Before continuing, he needed to make sure, in some way, that he held the threads of Manuel's future, those threads that the ancient Greeks believed were held by the Fates.

This was not his first experiment of this kind and the vest he wore was made for this. An accessory had been built in that allowed him to hide in a hollow of the continuum where he had a special angle of vision. Here, outside of space and time like the Babelian transmitter, he could watch, unseen, a specific destiny—Manuel's for instance.

The sight of what would happen was never perfectly clear because the future of anyone was always subject to unknown factors. But there was a mathematical relation between the precision of received images and the probability of existence.

What Anton saw made him scared stiff. In an inhospitable gloom, a series of doubles were running around, each going off on different paths that were impossible for Anton to watch simultaneously. But the clearest image showed the motionless form of the chemist along with a Babelian who was unknown to Anton.

He had to start with this vision to guarantee Manuel's safety, despite the life-threatening dangers that seemed to be looming in the near or far future. Now, such visions did not give any clues on how to fix anything because only the factor of the initial danger existed in the hibernation. So, he would have to transport himself to the time in which Manuel was acting by proxy—as a Babelian whose form was superimposed on Manuel's, most likely Jorik's whom Anton should have expelled from Manuel's brain.

Anton decided on the spot to go back to the 24th century. However, he could not risk infiltrating the Babelian defenses. Therefore, he would go to Kaltarborog where he could get in touch with the head of the commandos and with the agents of the triumvirs. Surely it was possible to call Manuel back to life right now, but such a move would be admitting defeat, which Anton hated. He thought it more elegant to avert the danger at the last second than to simply keep Manuel from experiencing it.

Anton acted accordingly.

In the Borg apartment in Kaltarborog the main room was used as monastic cell, laboratory and office for the technician of political-economic problems. In fact, though the walls were white and bare, half the space was taken up by all kinds of instruments and machines. The home of a Kaltarian emissary was very different from a Babelian's who showed no sign of this freedom of action, this decentralization, at least in appearance.

Oscillographic diagrams fluttered on the screens, understandable only to an expert who could summarize the economic level and political tendencies of the last six centuries. By examining them you could spot certain fluctuations that came out of the actions of emissaries in the concerned epoch. It had always been voluntarily limited and so remained undetected in the past. But the purpose of these "nudges" were part of Kaltarian tactics as they tried to help along the development of thoughts that were more original among the old geniuses whom they intended to steal from. A double-edged sword because it could also be used by the Babelians... but they were doing the same thing.

Anton changed out of his 20th century clothes into the black robe that everyone wore in Kaltarborog. He got in touch with the first rector and reported the results of his mission.

"Why were you away for so long?" the magistrate asked in a paternal tone. His meek and mild face on the screen did not fool Anton who know him well.

"I had to go through non-time," he said, "in order to observe the future of Manuel Esteban. You know how much that slows down the trip."

"You took it upon yourself," the first rector reminded him without smiling, "to actively use the man whom you were only supposed to watch and maybe guide. If the consequences of this initiative turn out to be disastrous, you alone will bear the responsibility."

"And if the results I get are spectacular?"

"The honor will fall upon the triumvirs, who were wise enough to choose you."

Anton was used to this cynicism and made no comment. He simply asked for news of the agents and commandoes.

"Nothing interesting about the agents, most of whom are still out there. A commando team, on the other hand, came back yesterday after taking a few prisoners. You can go down to the cells and question anyone who will talk. They all belong to the emissary brigade of Babelia."

Anton saluted politely and thanked him. The screen went dark. He thought, "Now that's just fine." And he did go down to the cells.

At the entrance to the underground, he stuck his head in the sensor beam that sent to a computer a reading of his electroencephalogram. The forcefield blocking the corridor vanished for a very short time as he passed through.

The first cells were occupied by the hostile Babelians who remained stubbornly mute to all questions. Some of them were injured, obviously by the abuse they had suffered in captivity. The wounds were being treated only superficially. Anton wasted no time on them.

The last cell drew his attention: there was a young woman in tears who got hold of herself surprisingly fast as soon as Anton entered her prison. Like the other prisoners she had undergone psychic probing and the file outside her door mentioned her name as well as the most pressing concerns detected on the surface of her consciousness.

She was called Gelia and what seemed to matter most to her was the fate of a certain Jorik. Anton began interrogating her with utmost caution—he did not want to start off antagonizing the one person who had information about the man whose personality Manuel had usurped.

Even though she showed astonishing self-control, this prisoner did not seem prone to the same resources as the others. First of all, she did not give him the silent treatment. She started by insulting him, which in Borg's mind was potential common ground for the future. He was right because he was there only a short time before she went back to crying. Feeling now that he had the upper hand, he pressed his advantage.

"Tell me about Jorik," he said.

She insulted him again, calling him a murderer and executioner.

"It's true," he admitted, "that the Kaltarians act like murderers in Babelia. But when the Babelian units get into Kaltarborog, how do they act? That's called war and nothing has changed in thousands of years. For me, I'm not a time traveler like you and I don't believe I've participated in the acts of violence you insult me for. I won't go so far as to say that I'm trying to help you, you wouldn't believe me, but it's true. Imagine if I wanted to help Jorik?"

"No one can help him," she said with a lump in her throat.

"What do you mean?"

"He's dead!" she shouted full of spite and sorrow.

Anton was quiet for a moment. Then, "Was it our commandoes who killed him?"

"You know very well!"

Anton thought some more. If Manuel had done something inside of Kaltarborog or even if he had been in danger during a temporal mission, it would have been possible to intervene at the last second. But this case was different.

"You loved him, didn't you?" he asked.

It was Gelia's turn to remain silent. Finally, she spoke as if to herself, "It's weird. I never really found him attractive, not his body or his face. And I didn't like his personality much. Of course, I'd never rejected his advances like the stupid girls of Kaltarborog usually do, but there was nothing between us that really turned me on."

"And then?" Anton gently encouraged her confession.

"And… I suddenly found another Jorik. A Jorik I didn't know. It was only for a few hours and then you killed him!" her voice grew louder at the end so that the last word was shouted. Sobs came back and she could not go on.

"What's your explanation for Jorik's change in behavior?" Anton wanted to distract her but also found out how much the Babelians knew about this kind of substitution.

"I have no idea," she muttered. "At first, I thought his last mission had exposed him to some kind of trick of yours. And then he acted like a real Babelian while still showing... how can I put it?... heightened sensitivity."

"Towards you?"

"Towards me, sure, but more than just that."

She got lost in thought, staring at the ground, and Anton did not interrupt her bleak reflections.

A deep silence loomed over the underground cells. The dim light never varied and the air was recycled. Everything was designed to create a feeling of constant stagnation, the impersonal breath of eternity. And yet, many of the prisoners were promised a quick death. They were the lucky ones. The others would soon be begging for the final blow with all their heart.

Anton Borg popped up in the clinic he had just left, not exactly in the same place but close. He had been gone less time than it would have taken him to run down the corridor. He went back, opened the door he had just closed and rushed into the room

"Oh," he sounded remorseful, "I think you're right to tell me to be careful. I believe it'd be better to gradually warm him up now. We'll try this again later with a better chance of success. For the moment, gentlemen, I have no more need of you."

The professor and his assistant took off the lab coats with grand and haughty gestures, put their own coats back on and left without saying goodbye. Alone with his guinea pig, Anton smiled faintly. He took out a small flask, poured something into his hand and rubbed Manuel's forehead with it. The liquid seemed to evaporate on the spot. In truth it was absorbed by his skin. It was a substance that mobilized all the pre-anesthetic medication, the nerve agents he had to inject into Manuel before starting the hibernation per se and that would quickly be eliminated by his kidneys.

After that, Anton started warming up his patient with a current of air and increasing the dose of cardiotonics in the IV drip. Then he gave him pure oxygen to breathe.

After ten minutes or so, Esteban opened his eyes. A few seconds later he opened his mouth, "The Kaltarian weapon… it's so cold!" He struggled to lift his head and let out a feeble cry, "Gelia! They took Gelia!"

Anton patted him, "Stay calm. I've seen Gelia."

Manuel closed his eyes again, exhausted by his outburst. Anton kept adjusting the reanimation. Soon Esteban was strong enough to sit up.

"What did you just say me?" he asked. "First of all, how is it that I'm not dead? That was certainly the last thing I felt. How awful!"

"Wait a minute," Anton replied. "I can't tell you everything at the same time. And first of all, you don't look so surprised at getting back your strength so quickly. Did you know that it usually takes two days to get back on your feet?"

"Doesn't matter," Manuel declared. "Since I landed in Babelia, I've learned not to be surprised at anything."

Anton brought him his clothes, which he put on slowly.

"Still, it feels good to be back in my own body. It's like going back to the house you grew up in. I didn't like Jorik's at all."

Anton smiled and tossed out, "It wasn't too pleasing to Gelia either before your excursion."

Manuel jumped and stammered, "Tell me now. You said you saw her…"

Anton did not keep him in the dark any longer.

After Borg's explanation, Manuel stayed silent. Soon, however, he looked up and said, "So, Gelia is a prisoner in Kaltarborog right now…"

Anton winced, "Right now… is not exactly the correct term."

"Yes, of course," Manuel shrugged. "I meant that our knowledge of the future stops at Gelia's imprisonment. Was she in danger when you left her?"

He realized that he was talking about the future in the past tense after confusing it with the present, but these bizarre situations could not be translated into suitable language. Besides, all that counted was Gelia's fate.

"Not any immediate danger, but…"

Manuel pursed his lips and then spoke bluntly, "I have the feeling that Kaltarborog is fully equal to Babelia in terms of viciousness. But what does 'immediate' mean? Can't we target a precise time like we can a specific place? Then we'd be able to…"

"We?" Anton interrupted him. "So, you're willing to go back?"

"Naturally," Manuel furrowed his brow.

"Well, what did you do with the Babelian transmitter?"

The blood drained from Manuel's face as he sat there speechless. Afraid that the emotional reaction might cause another fainting spell in the weak patient, Anton raised his hand to keep everything calm and showed Manuel the strange piece of clothing he was wearing under his coat.

"No worries," he said, "that device is not absolutely necessary. I have better. As for the transmitter, I guess when you got there you let it shrink down to nothing until it just vanished?"

Manuel nodded. "My mind didn't clear up fast enough for me to grab the sphere in time."

"Sphere in time… that's the right term," Borg nodded in turn. "But it doesn't matter. You were wondering just now how it is that you're still alive after that Kaltarian weapon hit you? It's simple: you weren't there in person since your body was here. If they could kill you, it would have to be by hitting your body through time. You were just controlling another body remotely and it's that body that felt the effects of the entropic weapon."

"The entropic weapon?"

"Yes. Stopping the movement of molecules comes down to accelerating the deterioration of energy that we call entropy to an infinite degree. Jorik died in the same way the universe will die billions of years from now. Your brain waves were cast off, cutting off your control of the now lifeless body."

Manuel thought about it and mumbled, "So that's how the weapon works..." He looked up at Anton and said, "But that requires the use of infinite energy!"

Borg shook his head, "A great deal but not infinite. It's only for a momentary stoppage of molecular movement that's limited to a restricted volume. But this stoppage is enough to cause the death of any biological structure."

Manuel thought about it. "That doesn't do it for me. We know about a procedure called freeze-drying that also uses a very fast lowering of temperature but it preserves the physio-chemical potential by preventing the decomposition of organic substances, even living cells."

Anton glanced at him with an ironic smile, "Do you think we don't know about your miraculous inventions? It's not the same phenomenon." Then his expression changed. "Even though it's theoretically possible to save victims of the entropic weapon, by heating them back up gradually, I don't know if the Babelians ever tried it and there's no guarantee of a crowning success."

Manuel smiled back at him with a hint or irony as well, "Another thing. Since you can change the architecture of matter as you want and thumb your nose at any obstacle, why are the Babelians guarding their power plant so closely?"

"Their generator prevents any human materialization in the area of the plant."

Manuel did not tell him that he had seen with his own eyes the materialization of a certain Varold. That Esteban was a Kaltarian ally did not stop him from keeping a few aces up his sleeve.

"I managed to get in through the door," he said cautiously. "But the weapon I was using ended up being useless against the forcefield generator."

Anton glared at him briefly but did not press him. Manuel was sure he had sensed the lie but for some reason he did not want to show it.

All he said was, "I'll warn you that you'll be a lot more exposed if you go with me now because you'll be fully part of the trip, not just emitting brain waves across time."

"I see," Manuel replied. "I have my own reasons for going with you—I want to see that Babelian girl again… without any chance of betraying you since she's your prisoner. But why would you want to bring me along with you? I'm not so naïve as to believe that it's just because you like me."

Borg smiled, "You're right. You're not much use as a specialist in the field of science you've been exploring for so long and all your efforts to rise above yourself have failed, it's clear. But you naturally see the problems in a different light than us and what might be even more important you see them differently than the Babelians. I keep thinking that it might be better for us to use the whole man instead of just some random products of his intuition, even though your first mission was not very reassuring."

"Well now," Manuel admitted, "I don't see exactly how I can be of use this time but anyway you've got me since it's the only way I'll be able to see Gelia again."

An idea came to mind that made him frown.

"One detail worries me," he added. "What effects does time travel have on the assimilation of nucleic acids?"

"I see where you're going," Anton observed. "You're afraid of being forced, if need be, to do things that disgust you, right? Well, don't worry, the Kaltarian methods don't force travelers into the foul feasts you witnessed in Babelia. Still, there are other inconveniences to deal with."

Manuel waited uneasily for the explanation.

"Time travel doesn't matter, but the length of stay in a foreign time does. It counts for double what normally passes in your original epoch. We also undergo a metabolic change, but it ends up as shortening the traveler's life."

Manuel shrugged, "Does this only happen during the travel and not during all their life?"

"Yes."

"So, are the needs of the Babelians also limited to their travels?"

"Exactly."

"Then I can hope that Gelia will give up this heinous stumbling block someday."

"Why not?"

Manuel straightened up, "If you promise to help me save her, I will convince her to stop time-traveling."

Borg nodded, "If you have enough influence over her to manage that, I see nothing wrong... but have you considered the fact that when she sees you, she won't recognize you since she's never seen you in person before?"

Manuel spread out his hands, "I've thought about it, but you told me she wasn't really interested in Jorik until I started controlling him. I'm ready to win over Gelia's heart a second time."

"What passion! Will you go so far as to bring her into our ranks?"

"Without a doubt. I made no commitment to Babelia, so I'll be willing to stand by you if you help me."

"Perfect. From this moment on you can consider that you are not only enrolled in the Kaltarborog forces but also that you are my personal ally. I will always be the one to tell you what you are expected to do. Plus, I will do my best to help you with the Babelian girl. Deal?"

"Deal," Manuel agreed. His heart skipped a beat.

CHAPTER VII

The second metallic vest brought by Anton Borg was unbelievably light. In one of those moments of downtime during the preparations for the new trip, the biochemist had examined the clothing under a microscope, but there was nothing unusual about its structure. Just some micromachining that was far beyond anything he had seen before—the architecture of the mesh was at the molecular level. Manuel wanted to look at it under the electron microscope but he was afraid the beam would destroy the material or alter its operation. He therefore learned to use it without knowing anything about how it worked.

The departure was very simple. Anton had said, "You don't have to do anything. You'll be transported to Kaltar-borog without even realizing it and you'll materialize next to me. Then I'll introduce you to the head of our expeditions."

However, though the departure was just as he said, the voyage itself was another matter.

Manuel had just turned the dial built into the metal vest as Anton had told him. Had he misunderstood the instructions? Had his fingers fumbled it? He felt like he was pulled out of himself, ripped out like a membrane yanked by an opposing force, swollen to bursting like a soap bubble about to be popped by a playful child. The familiar scene around him vanished in a kaleidoscopic whirlwind at the same time as a shrill noise pierced his eardrums.

Soon, the sound lowered in intensity and stabilized on bearable frequencies. All around Manuel was empty space where dim lights drifted around, constantly changing colors. He had lost his weight and was floating in a position that he could not define. He no longer felt his heart beating, could not even tell if he was breathing. This weird place seemed to have as little air as it did physical objects, but apparently the human physiological functions did not suffer. The scene was more intangible than a dead man's dream.

The lights blinked off. Strangely, Esteban did not care about what awaited him and even though he suspected that none of this was going to plan, he had no fear. He was floating in blissful serenity, especially since he had survived the violent start, and waited eagerly for the end of the journey. Wasn't this the non-time that he knew about through Jorik's memory? Just like with space, he had to follow whatever path he fell upon to get from one point in time to another…

However, something stirred Manuel's interest. The lights were back but this time they were even weirder. Still flickering and perpetually shifting, they actually looked like they were taking on a human form. Arms and legs akimbo, Manuel watched them suspiciously, like a drowned man eyeing swimmers. They were made with a dark core surrounded by a brighter and brighter aura—exactly the same image as the spiritualists described for "astral bodies". Without knowing why, Esteban had the clear impression that their mutations were organized for a specific purpose. As if they had performed a dance around him to prepare a pre-arranged path. And all this melted into the grayness of a nebulous tunnel.

Then darkness. His mind was confused, distraught. He believed he was dead and was surprised to still be aware of his being. This weird spatial impression, too—the impression of being in a bizarre position like gravity was pulling in all directions at the same time and there was no plane of reference.

Slowly, the veil scattered. All around him shapes gradually emerged, at first vague, gossamer shreds torn out of a dream, delicate rudiments of a nascent universe. Little by little it took shape, combining its pieces by some strange magnetism, making the unbelievable more credible by the minute. Motionless between existence and nothingness, Manuel felt his body taking on more tangible reality as the images, sounds and strong smells took possession of his senses. Before anything else he saw the trunk of a huge tree standing a few feet away and he remembered a distant time when they put him in corner facing the wall. But an odd sound made him turn his head: in the green light drifting through the branches, there was the impossible shape of a kind of tapir with a short snout but with huge tusks pointing straight down and it must have been ten feet tall, digging furiously in the ground. Mounds of dirt piled up behind it while it quickly sank.

Manuel understood right away: this Deinotherium proved that he had landed in the end of the tertiary.

Despite the moist and sticky air in the humid heat, the traveler was quivering with mortal shivers. Thrown weaponless into the heart of a carnivorous epoch, he could do nothing but wait for his demise, which would not take long. There was only one way out, but what a way! He had to fiddle with the control on the time vest and risk making another jump that might put him in an even more dangerous position. He missed Babelia and its inhuman civilization.

It was no good dwelling on the reasons (random or premeditated) for the error. He had to survive now or start blindly on a series of jumps through time that could take him to a period before the birth of the planet or after its destruction, to the peak of an ice age or into some society of the umpteenth century where they would lock him in a zoo before opening his skull to weigh his brain in front of a snickering audience. Thinking of the luminous shadows he had seen in the non-time, Manuel feared, moreover, that they could interfere again if he tried the perilous experiment of trusting in the time vest…

He realized that he was standing up, stiff as a stake planted in the soft ground. He stepped forward and turned his back against a tree trunk. Like this if danger came, he would not be taken completely by surprise. An ironic grin crossed his lips when he pictured what dangers surrounded him in the form of unspoiled nature and fearsome creatures. A trail of hot wind blew past, carrying with it the heady scent of the rainforest. In the distance he heard a monstrous roar that sounded like it came out of the depths of the biggest living organ, then the thick silence crept back. Nearby the giant tapir had disappeared into the ground without paying any attention to the stranger and nothing was left of its presence except the mounds of dirt around the hole.

Manuel kept a wary eye on his surroundings. As he panned around slowly he stopped suddenly. He had just seen, between a leafy bush and the foot of a giant tree, a shape that hid itself rapidly. All his attention was focused on the suspect spot. But nothing else moved. Even sharper than what he had just felt, a fear penetrated him that was impossible to control. It was useless for him to recall the inextricable situations he had already been through since the start of his voyages. Here he was more helpless, more vulnerable than ever and this feeling weighed uncomfortably on his shoulders.

He convinced himself that he should avoid, at all costs, focusing on a single point when every part of the forest presented threats. A quick glance proved that the *things* of the tertiary knew how to move stealthily. The semi-human face that was watching him from between two giant leaves made his hair stand on end. Despite his fear he could not help remembering certain engravings that pretended to reconstruct the Neanderthals. At first sight you could admire their insight and accurate imagination gleaned from a few pieces of a jaw and skullcap.

Except that what Manuel was seeing was alive and well. He thought fast but in vain to find what attitude he should adopt in the presence of such a distant ancestor. The other did not give him time to choose his behavior when he came out into the clearing and the rustling of leaves could be heard all around. Nearby arose the rhythmic rumble of a tom-tom.

The jutting-jawed, hairy face with constantly moving eyes in deep-set sockets belonged to a body whose appearance made Manuel gasp, even so far as to forget his terror. The Neanderthal was dressed in an elegant, shimmering tunic and carrying a kind of walkie-talkie on a shoulder strap.

Now they were coming out of everywhere. They all looked the same except that few of them were wearing the same clothes as the first one and none of them were sporting such an eerily anachronistic device. However, they were all armed with heavy clubs or long spears and Manuel felt terror jostling again with the bewilderment inside of him.

The circle closed in. The traveler suspected now that he had been preceded by emissaries from Babelia or Kaltarborog who had given gifts from the 24th century to the tribe. But the attitude, both respectful and aggressive, of the subhumans did not fit with this hypothesis. That kind of exchange or gift-giving usually comes from a relatively long visit, which would, in theory, pave the way for easier contact. And why would commandoes from either side make allies so far in the past? This did not accord with their missions.

All these thoughts flew through Manuel's mind like a storm in the brief time it took the Neanderthals to encroach on him. They kept their relative positions and Manuel figured it wise not to move or speak. Odds were that if he tried to escape, he would be taken down immediately. Despite their caution these people were surely fast and expert marksmen. It was crucial that he show no fear.

The first one stood in front of Manuel and fumbled with the object he was carrying. He put it in the grass at Manuel's feet and took three steps back. The number was certainly part of a ritual because all the others did the same. "Common origins of mathematics and religion", Manuel mused. Along with his fear, the amazement started fading away. They were replaced by a faint desire to smile. Setting aside any hesitation, he walked straight to the rectangular box, picked it up and slung it over his shoulder. A flood of howls crashed through the forest. The disruption of history was repeating history— the explorer was playing god.

Everything remained at a standstill for the moment. Manuel wondered how the primitive being could have guessed that the walkie-talkie was carried comfortably by the shoulder strap. When he looked down at the object, he was stunned to see that the metal strap had changed place without him realizing. He had thrown it over his shoulder but now it was lying diagonally across his chest.

Like this the device was kept over the heart, while the fastener was placed over his brainstem. This was nothing like any kind of radio. This was nothing like anything he knew. He wanted to examine those shimmering tunics more closely, but he could not display any curiosity. Where things were headed, he was sure he would have plenty of time to satisfy his curiosity shortly.

Somewhere deep in the brush the drum kept beating and Manuel had never heard anything so wild. He turned to the one remaining closest to him and slowly raised both arms. The other did the same and grunted, followed by a few brief shouts. Everyone came forward, bent double, grunting in rhythm. The chief turned his back to Manuel and took another three steps, after which he turned around. Manuel followed him.

The whole tribe was now showing signs of the deepest worship. It surrounded the traveler in the chanted march in which everyone repeated two rough syllables formed out of two tones. Two of them were dispatched in advance to check the route and give warning, probably, if a wild animal appeared. With his mind calmer, Manuel felt protected by the wall of broad chests and the clubs that must have been terribly heavy. He found inside himself a kind of sympathy towards them as he realized how totally alone he would have been and really helpless despite his advanced state of evolution, if the tribe had not met him. He was turning into a social insect, an ant or bee. His free mind—completely relative—began to examine the device he was carrying. It taught him nothing at all. Someone else must be as high on the evolutionary ladder compared to him as he was compared to these hominids. The more time passed, the more he was convinced that the emissaries from the rival cities had nothing to do with the presence of this object.

Then they came across another clearing. Manuel found the key to the enigma when he saw, partly hidden by the huge branches of the trees, a spherical ship around 15 feet in diameter whose surface shimmered just like the tunics worn by his guards. So, the earth had been visited in the tertiary by intelligent life from another planet. The box and the clothes came from this. And they were apparently humanoid, judging by the shape of the tunics. Gnawed at by curiosity, Manuel scrutinized all around the ship, but he saw no trace of non-human activity. He just saw a rock wall at the edge of the clearing with deep holes in its side. He was approaching the village of the troglodytes. Manuel got ready to act as divine as possible.

As he got closer to the ship he saw a circular opening in the bottom part of it, where the lowest edge of the opening was around twenty inches off the ground. When he passed by he snuck a peek inside. There was a cabin lined with rosettes that glimmered faintly. When he was about to walk away, he thought he should look acquainted with this sphere that was probably taboo. He went over to it calmly, mustered all the courage he had left and climbed alone into the open cabin.

This action was answered with shouts of joy that became frenzied when a bunch of objects sprang out of the side of the spaceship and landed in the high grass. It was obvious that everything that happened from now on with the ship would be credited to him and his prestige would only grow stronger.

But Manuel was himself a primitive here and he knew it. He was anxious to leave the creepy ball before one of its owners came back. He was about to do just that when that monstrous cry he had heard before deep in the forest rang out again nearby. The troglodytes swiftly and orderly rushed back to the ship. Just then the bushes parted and a giant beast came screaming through, bellowing like a foghorn. Its appearance confused Manuel: it was, apparently, a descendant of the big lizards of the former era but covered in fur. The beast whose head bobbled over 30 feet high was heading straight for the spaceship.

What happened next, Manuel barely had time to see. First a low rumble came from the depths of the ship, then a bright bream, blood red, sprang out of the side near the opening. The mammal-reptile started shrinking fast, so fast that in an instant it was the size of a housecat and buried itself in the ground. Manuel jumped down and ran to the spot where the beast had disappeared.

The hole was very deep and he heard, like from the bottom of a well, a kind of pitiful whining. The Neanderthals around him were overjoyed, dancing hysterically. Stupefied, Esteban pondered the effects of this diabolical weapon that shrank the size without changing the mass. The troglodytes had obviously seen it before because their religious fear did not stop them from celebrating.

Manuel went back to the sphere. No one came out, no presence showed itself. Whatever it was, it had made a choice of which target to hit. Manuel felt a great relief. He imagined being shrunk to the size of a fingernail but still weighing 155 pounds.

Surrounded by gratitude, he headed for the grottoes. As they started off, he wondered if the ship might not be a robot. Just then he tripped over one of the objects thrown off by the sphere. It was another rectangular box but different from the one he was carrying. He had an idea. He went back, climbed into the spaceship and compared the faint light of the rosettes on the wall with the surface of the walkie-talkie. They were the same. It made him think of some kind of recorder transmitted by an amplification system destined for a home port. Maybe they were recording right now his pumping heart and fried nerves to stick them in some archive on Arcturus…

He left the sphere, suddenly afraid that it was some kind of specimen collector and it would take off without warning.

In Manuel's opinion, the number of savages had grown. Others had obviously been waiting in the caves or hunting in the forest, so the ones around him, leading him to one of the most accessible cavities, must have been a clan and not an entire tribe.

In the grotto it stank horribly of rotting meat and excrement. Females, more like apes than women, were nursing simian babies that they hugged harder as they stepped back into the shadows when the stranger entered their lair. The survivors of a Homeric battle that would probably be sung about for centuries were carefully cleaning the remains of an animal 15 feet long with a gigantic jaw—a huge plantigrade. Manuel realized the power of the group and his own weakness faced with extraterrestrials—or even Babelians—and it inspired more respect in him for these prehistoric wild men.

In a language that was mostly barks and whistles the chief of the clan was talking to him now. Maybe he was begging him to bless the hunters or to chase away the big predators. Manuel just answered with some nonsense syllables while he raised his arms again. It seemed to work because they all dropped to the ground and bowed before him. The bouncing-breasted women howled. Some were bold enough to even touch his clothes and they were obviously comparing them to the shimmering fabric. The traveler used the opportunity to feel those strange tunics: they were feathery light and softer than goose down. The little transtemporal vest Manuel was wearing under his coat also attracted their attention, more than anything else.

"Look in awe," Manuel chuckled, "you've got a long way to go before you reach the age of metals." Once this age was reached, that of electronics would not be far behind. Esteban suddenly had a clear revelation about how fast history moves.

Many of them were still prostrate. The chief got them up gently, glancing sideways at Manuel as if asking his permission. The traveler helped him raise the worshippers and this caused a new explosion of joy, which ended by offering a hollowed out stone full of clotted blood. Manuel pinched his nose and tried to lap up the clumps. He did not succeed, but the gesture was enough. The clan lived on symbols.

Struggling to control a surge of nausea, Esteban left the cave wiping his lips with his sleeve. The disgusting dish had squelched his growing hunger, but he knew it would come back soon. He would have to ask the clan for edible fruits or roots then. These thoughts pushed into the background his despair of being abandoned in this terrible time without any familiar landmarks. He walked over to the weird sphere.

A trap? Evidently the machine could take off as soon as he got inside. Unless this was no vehicle at all? Was it a station, dropped here by a departing spaceship? Manuel really wanted to enter it again, so he decided on the latter hypothesis to steady his mind. And he went in.

The cabin he entered was too small to take up the whole interior of the sphere. There was more, a place more difficult to access. Manuel tapped the walls cautiously, but he found nothing. Dropping the sensor that was still slung over his chest, he put it at the foot of the wall. The strap was immediately sucked into the device.

"What if this was one of the passengers?" This fleeting idea made him scared again of being kidnapped. But as soon as he stepped through the opening a small, alert, jolly fellow stood before him. He recognized Varold.

Since his meeting with this odd character in the nuclear plant in Babelia, Manuel had not had much time to think of Varold. The only thing occupying his less conscious mind was Gelia and the dilemma he was in now was especially painful because it meant a definitive separation from her.

Standing unexpectedly in front of Varold, his reflex was to step back. Then he remembered that the man had already helped him once before. Maybe he was bringing him the only salvation to escape this epoch buried in the mists of time.

"Tell me everything," Varold said cheerfully. "I know you left the 20th century again but I don't understand how you ended up here."

"And you," Manuel replied, "how did you find me?"

Varold waved that off, "Oh, I travel a lot... and you obviously don't know that your time vest emits chronomagnetic waves for which I have the right receiver. But let's drop that. Who dragged you out here?"

Feeling more at ease Manuel told him how Borg had said they would meet in Kaltarborog and he described the "luminous shadows" he had seen in the non-time. He thought he saw Varold shudder at that moment. But only for a split second.

Their conversation was interrupted by a group of hunters bringing back a deer, a big deer, stabbed all over by spears. It had certainly been caught in a trap, a hole dug in the ground—so far Manuel had seen no throwing weapons. While the hunters were gathering at a respectful distance, the clan that had greeted Manuel came scrambling down the steep slope at the foot of the cliff, yelling and waving their arms. The two groups met and got into a heated argument. In the eyes of the primitives, it was obvious that two divinities were better than one.

Manuel turned his attention to the group that had just dropped the animal corpse in the grass. This offering was no more appetizing than the last one considering there was no fire. But Varold's arrival was changing the situation so favorably that Manuel did not care about the food. He was remembering the mission he had agreed to accomplish for Borg on behalf of Kaltarborog.

"Look at this," he picked up a cube that shimmered faintly in the grass. This thing came from the sphere that I believe was built by intelligent aliens. Do you think the Kaltarian specialists could figure out its purpose and how it works and maybe use it to fight against those awful Babelians? Theoretically the commandoes are supposed to contact old geniuses, but that doesn't necessarily mean human geniuses."

Varold shook his head, "I'll just remind you that the shadows of non-time helped or rather forced you to be here, precisely so that you'd bring this box back to Kaltarborog. Now, you have to trust me—those shadows are, for me, dangerous enemies and so they are for you too. Leave those things here and you won't be playing into their hands."

Manuel shot him a suspicious glance, "How did the shadows figure I would get out of here?"

This was the second time that Varold got in the way of his plans, for one reason or another. The first time he did not get upset but such behavior cast a questionable light on Varold's intentions. He was really acting as if he were working for Babelia... and yet, no, in that case he would bring the box back himself. Manuel dropped this idea.

Varold answered Manuel's question, "They knew that your vest emits waves that Kaltarborog can pick up like I did. Anyway, you won't be abandoned here. That's kind of the reason I'm offering you to leave right now so you don't see anyone. I'm surprised we haven't met your friend Borg yet..." He forced a smile that Manuel tried in vain to interpret.

What should he do? Leave right away with Varold or wait for Anton's arrival, which Manuel believed would be very soon, and see what he thinks?

"Where will you take me?" Manuel asked.

"To Kaltarborog, of course, and just when Borg himself gets there."

"Listen," Manuel improvised, "I'm burning with curiosity about this sphere. Let's go take one last look and then I'll go with you without bringing anything along."

In fact, Varold was not acting like an enemy and since the destination was exactly where Manuel wanted to be, he could confide in him. Gelia was at the end of the road.

"Let's go," Varold smiled again.

They entered the sphere and Manuel pointed to the box he had put on the floor. "You see, the strap there..."

He stopped. Like a camera lens the opening of the ship had just sealed itself shut while the giant hand of incredible acceleration plastered both of them to the metal floor. The sphere had taken off and was blasting into the cosmos like a bubble shooting off the surface of boiling liquid.

CHAPTER VIII

Varold had quickly managed to overcome the terrifying acceleration and with some difficulty get upright again. Crushed against the hull, Manuel felt his head pounding and was desperately trying to keep breathing. Was an oxygen refill supplied on the spaceship? Through a red mist the chemist barely saw Varold and his brain, feeling squeezed by a vise, could only register wonder at his behavior. What was the guy made of to be able to resist the force of acceleration? A vague memory recalled the weird texture of the hand he had touched back in Babelia. Some words struggled past the pulsing beat of blood in his ears:

"Quickly," Varold was saying, "we have to get out of here before it gets too fast. After that, there's nothing I can do and we'll have to stay for the whole trip and that's too risky—it could last for centuries."

He leaned over Manuel and took his hand. Once again that feeling of grabbing a thick cloud. Manuel's entire body hurt and he felt like he was falling down a bottomless well. The intolerable feeling lasted only a second or maybe ten years. Then they were standing side by side in a cold, dark tunnel.

Manuel was wobbling as he rubbed his face. He felt like he was coming out of the grave. Varold looked fit as a fiddle and his eyes sparkled.

Manuel stammered, "I thought I was in hell. That feeling of being torn apart hasn't gone away. I think it never will."

He jumped to another idea.

"How did you fight against the acceleration? Are you really here or am I standing next to a space-time projection of you? Your body doesn't feel normal…"

Since Varold did not answer, he continued more steadily.

"You've brought me to a real place. There's something I can't quite grasp: when we travel through time, in whatever process is used—yours, the Babelian or the Kaltarian—we must end up in the same place we started from. But the Earth and the solar system have to move in the meantime, which means we're materializing in space far from our habitable planet…"

Varold deigned to respond this time, "Time is inseparable from space. You knew that in your age when they talked about gravitons without ever having seen one. Since then, the chronons and spations have been found. We needed those discoveries to build a transtemporal machine that could use these quanta of space and time that are completely bound together. We never travel through time without travelling through space and this is because of the existence of gravitons, which bind them together by a common energy field. This means that with an elevated acceleration, we risk being thrown far from the point of departure defined by the three coordinates I mentioned—even farther than we're going from our original gravitic sphere. If it's easier for you, think of time travel as happening in five dimensions, the three dimensions of space plus time and gravity."

He started walking down the tunnel as if his explanation was clear and final. Esteban had no choice but to follow him.

The walls emitted a weird glow like is produced by a lot of phosphorescent animals, and a light breeze, very cold, blew down the tunnel. Presently they reached a fork where Varold stopped.

"You go left," he said. "It'll take you directly to the laboratories of Anton Borg. I have things to do down the other way. Goodbye."

He went to the right, which was much darker than the left, and seemed to dissolve into the darkness before Manuel could move an inch. The 20th century man stood undecided for a moment, then he shrugged his shoulders and followed Varold's advice.

While walking he was surprised to be brought back in Kaltarborog in a manner stranger than the time sphere or the vest with molecular threads. This Varold had something more than human about him and Manuel was like a puppet in his hands. And yet there was one important point: Varold was helping him, even if he behaved like a spy from the enemy city.

The corridor rose slightly. Manuel had still not met another living soul and he did not like that. After 10 minutes or so of walking he found himself at a dead-end. A kind of intangible curtain stretched across the corridor, glowing green, beyond which was a wall maybe seven feet away.

Manuel put his hand out toward the curtain, then drew back. Was he going to be electrocuted or disintegrated? He thought, "Varold told me it led to Borg's labs. Would he send me into a trap? It wouldn't make any sense considering his attitude…"

He reached out again and touched the area with his index finger. Immediately he felt sucked in and in a flash was on the other side just when an irresistible force rose up from the ground. He rose slowly through a wide chimney that he had not noticed before crossing the glowing curtain.

"Antigravitational shafts."

The sensation reminded him of a dream in which you fly and it was not unpleasant. A little alarming nonetheless—if the energy suddenly turned off, he would drop like a stone and crash at the end of the corridor whose light he could barely make out. An elevator without a floor, that's what was unnerving. Before him stretched a huge room flooded with sunlight where crystals of all shapes and sizes and colors were mounted in black metal settings. In the middle stood Anton Borg, staring at him with obvious surprise.

"Where did you come from?" he asked suspiciously.

Manuel thought about it. He had not yet told him about Varold and saw no reason to do so.

"Something threw me off course," he suggested. "It sent me underground, where I've just come from."

Borg looked away and asked casually, "Something?"

Manuel thought that if he did not want to talk about Varold, who apparently knew all about those luminous shadows, he was better off not mentioning the shadows at all to Borg.

"I don't know, maybe I misunderstood your directions about using the time vest. Whatever the case, I arrived later than you and farther away."

Borg shrugged and looked at him again, "The important thing is that you didn't have any mishaps in the non-time…"

Manuel saw the ambiguity in this remark. He even sensed a kind of ridicule. Borg was not fooled but for some reason he decided to drop it. Manuel swore to pay closer attention to the Kaltarian's words and deeds in order to clear up the matter. Maybe, after all, he would have to mention his stopover in the tertiary? In such a case, how could he act wisely?

"All right," Borg straightened himself up, "let's talk about the schedule and make good use of our time."

Manuel smiled unwittingly at the expression that took on such strange significance at this moment: for some time now, you could say that time had been well used and that being at the wrong time was gaining time… He mentioned this to Borg who had to smile, too, before continuing.

"You're going to be introduced to the magistrates who run the city. Since you're coming from the distant past," he lingered on the word "distant" a little, "you'll be the guest of honor at a meal."

Manuel twitched involuntarily.

"No," Borg assured him, "you know our methods are different from the Babelians and they don't ask of you the same sacrifices. And that works on many levels. As you've no doubt noticed, the forcefield around our city doesn't block out the sun's rays—it's thicker but less dense."

Manuel walked over to a huge window that let in the full sunlight. From this vantage point he could see the extraordinary panorama of buildings that looked both splendid and severe, built according to a very harmonious organization. Exactly the opposite of the indescribable jumble of the Black City. A sea of greenery stretched along the horizon.

Borg had just put on a black robe over his clothes, cinched with a soft metal belt. He was holding out the same robe and belt for Manuel wear.

"Let's go," Anton said. "We can't keep the wardens waiting, especially not the rectors."

He led the way.

The banquet room had a high, high ceiling where colorful arabesques were woven into such complex designs that the eye could not gaze upon them without blinking. In the middle of the room they had set up a round table surrounded by a shallow ditch. The table was around 50 feet in diameter, even though the center plate was maybe three feet lower.

Manuel was introduced by Borg as one of the geniuses of his generation and the reception of the newcomer was as warm as it was natural. Contrary to what had happened in Babelia, Manuel did not understand a single word of what was said, but the more than friendly smiles on their faces translated their words. And yet, there was something forced about this welcome and Manuel felt surrounded by a general atmosphere of hypocrisy. He was glad he had stayed next to Anton, with whom he could talk and whom he thought was mostly acting for his benefit. Of course, Borg was Kaltarian and if the Kaltarians were hiding something…

"Time will tell," Manuel thought. And deep down in his consciousness a voice was murmuring, "And if it tells too much, maybe it'll be fatal."

Borg said to him, "You see, they're sending in the Teratos."

From an invisible door in the middle of the center plate rose up creatures dressed entirely in black, their heads hidden under hoods.

"Teratos?" Esteban repeated without understanding.

"The teratological products grown in test tubes," Borg kindly explained.

And he explained further: the high dignitaries of Kaltarborog maintained very costly laboratories specialized in human embryology where Babelian fetuses gave them an endless supply of monsters with multiple arms, razor-sharp claws or standing on two or three pairs of legs that makes them fiendishly fast. The main attraction at their feasts was to pit them against each other until the weaker was torn to shreds.

"And you call the Babelian barbarians?" Manuel was indignant.

"Shh," Anton said. "Not so loud. Some here might understand you. But what do you expect? The constant war against Babelia affects our customs and we end up imitating our enemies unintentionally but in different ways…"

"Pious hypocrisy," Manuel thought.

But they were bringing in the dishes and their conversation had to end. Before starting in on the slices of blue and orange vegetables they served as hors d'oeuvres, the first rector stood up and spoke softly.

"Let this frugal meal," Anton translated for Manuel, "be dedicated to the friendship that our illustrious guest has shown us today. Professor Esteban, a kind-hearted researcher of his age whose work is partly responsible for our present civilization, has in fact already accomplished a dangerous mission for Kaltarborog, but alas without appreciable results according to the prober Anton Borg. We all hope, don't we (and here his voice became vaguely threatening), that this new ally will be crowned by fate and that he will be an extra factor for the political unity in a city where I too often lament the antipatriotic intrigues of some of our brothers blinded by ambition…"

Manuel was disgusted by the deceitful meekness of this character, "The speeches haven't changed much in style or content."

Some wardens forced their grins to look warmer and kinder. They started the meal in an atmosphere of hatred, jealousy and suspicion. Manuel already saw that the Babelian savagery had some good in it compared to this stifling ambiance. All the way down to the physical appearance of the

Babelians, conditioned by centuries of artificial ultra-violet light, even though cold and icy, they finally offered more security.

In the center of the table, the Teratos had thrown off their robes and hoods. Manuel sat hypnotized, neglecting his creepy hors d'oeuvres to watch the monsters who were pounding each other while growling deeply. So, this was the point of embryology for the Kaltarians? Two or three skinny ones with multiple legs were fighting a deformed thing with sharp claws, spinning around so fast it was hard to follow.

"These monsters would've become normal Babelians if the Kaltarians hadn't manipulated their gestation," he thought with disgust. But in this world that was more twisted than the one had come from, his moral code was obsolete and it was impossible to interfere in any way whatsoever.

The feast, which the rector had called frugal, went on, course after course, as the massacre continued. Two of the speedy freaks had been ripped apart but the solitary brute was losing so much blood that it almost gushed onto the dining table. The last Terato standing against it seemed to have waited for this final combat because it showed no sign of fatigue and the awkward swings of its adversary hit only empty air. Defeated by the agility and constant barrage of its lighter enemy, the stronger, heavier monster slowly sank, practically bloodless. A stale smell floated among the diners whose appetite was not at all disturbed by the spectacle.

Then the second rector stood up and announced cheerfully, "As is customary, the victor will receive his reward."

From the back of the room some servants came pushing forward a terrorized Babelian woman. Manuel recognized Gelia.

His first reaction was to jump out of the throne they had sat him on and run to her aide. Three reasons stopped him: First, Borg's hand was grabbing his arm with surprising strength; then he remembered what had happened when he interfered with the Babelian banquet; and finally a familiar voice echoed strangely in his mind, the voice of Varold saying: "Be patient. For now, they're just showing her to the crowd. She'll be given up later. I'll deal with the matter myself before it's done."

Manuel's knuckles were white as he gripped the table. But he was convinced that the inner voice was not a hallucination because after some applause and cheering Gelia was dragged away by the servants, thus verifying the truth of the psychic information.

"You're right," he grumbled to Borg, "all is not lost."

"That's what I was going to tell you," Borg whispered back.

They slowly finished their black salads with spots of red while Manuel took his time calming down. Had she seen him sitting amongst her persecutors? He feared their next meeting and even hoped it would never happen. But how stupid was he? Gelia only knew him as Jorik!

Although his mind and heart were elsewhere, Manuel had noticed that they were feasting on only vegetables— vegetables with the consistency of meat but whose taste was unmistakable. He blurted this out to Anton who answered ironically.

"We eat nothing else, unlike in your barbarous century. We don't raise animals just to devour them…"

Manuel did not get upset. He did not even hear the end of the sentence because he feared for Gelia's life. And if they met again, how would she react to him? Most likely with no emotion whatsoever because she had never seen his real face.

The dessert consisted of oblong fruits that were slimy and too sweet but the others seemed to delight in them. Manuel could not finish them. And he was relieved to see that the meal was ending. As he stood up from the table, the inner voice drowned out the warden praising the committee as the first magistrates looked on skeptically.

"Stay calm," Varold said. "I took Gelia into the city where she's safe for now. I'll see you again."

The telepathic communication cut off. A few minutes later a servant came to whisper something to the warden who turned timidly to a rector. The latter could not control his anger. Manuel overheard him saying, "Find her right away or heads will roll!"

CHAPTER IX

The new mission of the Kaltarian probers Borg and Esteban looked like it was going to be sensitive and dangerous. The dark forest around them occasionally rang out with the calls of wild beasts, mostly the howling of wolves. The long, leafless branches sparkled with snow whenever the clouds unveiled the risen moon.

Manuel shivered under his frayed brocaded coat. He missed the luxury and refined comfort of the room they had given him in Kaltarborog and he remembered the gentle warmth in the air when he left. Unconsciously he rubbed the grip of the zero weapon hidden inside his coat—the weapon that could stop moving molecules. It was agreed that he would only use it in case of dire emergency.

Before leaving, the triumvirs had granted the probers a private hearing. For Manuel it was a more unpleasant memory than of the Babelian archon. Compared to the triumvirs the rectors appeared open and sincere... Manuel shook his head with disgust: Kaltarborog was no better place to live than Babelia.

The howling wolves sounded closer. This place and time did not seem such a good place to live either. But they cut the probers some slack when it came to choosing their goal and Borg had chosen this—against the wishes of Manuel who doubted it would be of any interest.

Esteban quieted his thoughts because they were passing through a group of windowless shacks whose mud walls swelled in the gusty wind. Soon a crenellated wall appeared in the gloom. They walked along the foot it, which was sunk in half-frozen water. The land rose. They passed a round tower after which the moat went on for a distance that was impossible to guess. An ogival door appeared in the wall.

"Let me do it," Anton whispered. He walked up to the thickly barred portcullis and shouted, "Ho, is anyone there?"

Jangling metal came out of the dark behind the gate and a hoarse voice barked from the top of the wall, "Who goes there?"

Manuel thought, "You couldn't dream up more conventional dialogue." He smiled a little, despite the cold and the danger they were facing. But his smile vanished when he looked up at the patch of moonlit sky and saw a man pointing a crossbow at them. Manuel knew that these primitive weapons fired with lethal force and he would be pierced through if the guy shot. He could not use his zero weapon, so he fell on his belly and tried to camouflage himself.

The watchman on high was confused and lowered his weapon. In the meantime, Borg had finished talking. The red light of a torch lit up the arch behind the portcullis, which was slowly rising.

"I guess you didn't understand," Anton whispered. "I told him we were tower builders coming hastily from Nemours, bearers of a message from the duke for the manuscript seller of the University. We've come more than eight leagues today on foot because highwaymen stole our horses."

Manuel had followed the conversation distractedly. Above all, he realized from this translation the great difference between the French of this time and that of the 20th century. Since he had turned to chemistry and physics at a young age, he had never taken much interest in Old French. Among the wild, dancing torch lights he followed his companion through the arch. It was January 14, 1398, five in the morning, and the gate they had just passed through was where, more or less, five or six centuries later, the Jardin des Plantes would stand. The man they were going to meet was called Nicolas Flamel.

Leprous houses were crushed against the ramparts. While walking up the narrow road leading to Sainte Genevieve Church, Anton showed Manuel the rolled parchment that he had waved at the watchman.

"Even if he had unrolled it," Borg said, "he would probably not have been able to read it, which is a good thing. This parchment is one of many from the trial of Joan of Arc, which won't take place for another thirty years. I grabbed one at random before leaving. But it'd be better if we didn't show it to anyone who can read because it dates from Charles VII and the reigning king right now is Charles VI."

Manuel pondered the dangers looming over them. Even the reassuring presence of the zero weapon in his belt could not outweigh all of them. As if answering his thought, Anton went on:

"Watch out for the cutthroats who haunt the Latin Quarter. Clerks and crooks alike carry daggers and know how to use them. In a real pinch, use the photophore."

Manuel remembered he also had a tiny electric light with a nuclear battery, the size of a pencil but able to cast a blinding light over three hundred yards.

"The freeze gun would draw less attention.'"

"Indeed," Borg replied, "but just one murder can have repercussions down the centuries and wreak havoc with history."

Manuel bit his lip. For a short while they walked side by side in silence. Then Manuel turned around. He thought he had heard muffled footsteps behind them. Since the alley was lit only by intermittent moonlight, he saw nothing.

"Don't be so nervous," Borg scolded. "We'll probably run into some city watchmen before any thieves."

Noises were coming out a tavern around fifty yards ahead of them. "There," Anton said, "we'll get the address of the man we came for."

Manuel kept his anxiety hidden. What kind of people were they going to meet in there? Students in the 14th century were not little saints, far from it... and there was a good chance they would be mixed up with real thugs. Esteban glanced at Anton and had to admit that he did not look like much in his ratty doublet that fell all the way to his oversized shoes. The gray, wool coat wrapped clumsily around his body was no help. And Manuel was afraid the wig was going to fall apart. He thought, "I can't imagine."

They had to go down half a dozen steps after pushing open the heavy door to reach the common room. The place was rife with a thick stench and a deafening racket. The stink came from the many candles or maybe from the rats in the cellar—Manuel could not tell—a foul mix of sweat and squalor and the heady fumes of spilled wine.

As for the noise, it came from the hoarse voices, the shrill laughter of the four or five half-dressed women and the banging of metal mugs on the thick wooden tables. Three quarters of those present wore monk's robes with hoods barely covering their tonsured, brightly colored heads.

Since all eyes converged on the newcomers Borg raised his arms to call for silence and spoke some horrible mumbo jumbo in a French that was incomprehensible to Manuel mixed up as it was with mangled Latin. His speech must have been crystal clear, however, because a huge guy answered with a guffaw that kicked off a wave of laughter in the room.

"He's making fun of me and insulting me," Anton whispered to Manuel.

Without getting flustered, the Kaltarian addressed his speech to someone else but a fairly drunken girl cut him off with a shrieking voice.

"Charming reception," Manuel thought. "I'll be damned if he gets anything out of these people." He regretted his thought right away. Wasn't damning people to death pretty common in an age when the courts didn't mess around?

He could feel the hostility grow palpable in the room. The name of Nicolas Flamel was passing from mouth to mouth, along with other names among which Manuel heard Lucifer, Satan, Belial, Astaroth and many he did not recognize. It was the time when the reputation of the gold-making alchemist was going to force him to pretend to bury his wife, Pernelle, along with himself in order to flee to Switzerland. Manuel thought it might have been better to aim for a less critical period in Flamel's life.

"Why don't we go back one or two more years?" he quickly asked Anton.

The other shook his head without answering and took a step back toward the stairs. But a scruffy guy with wine-soaked hair jumped behind him and barred the way with his arms outstretched. He yelled, "Christus! Christus!"

Manuel took the photophore out of his belt but Borg ordered, "Get your back against the wall."

In an instant they were protected behind a table in a corner. Anton said, "Since they already think we're sent by the devil, let's show them."

Manuel pressed the button on the photophore. A blinding light flashed silently, throwing bluish glares on their faces, making them look like corpses. The same scream of fear was wrenched from all the chests even as they rushed into the opposite corner, shielding their eyes with their forearms. Anton shouted at them rudely while Manuel kept them rounded up with the ray of light. No one was listening. They dropped to their knees and mumbled stammering litanies, repeatedly crossing themselves. Suddenly one girl ran screaming away from the group, stumbled up the stairs but tripped on her long dress and fell on the doorstep. She scrambled to her feet, sobbing with fright and vanished in the night. They heard the sound of her hastening footsteps fade away down the alley. The door gaped open onto the darkness. A gust of icy air rushed into the tavern and blew out all the candles. Manuel turned off the photophore. The darkness flowed around them like a greasy river. Anton and Manuel felt their way toward the door, the rectangle a little less black in the night, trying to blink away the dazzling flashes as they went.

When they climbed the final steps, they had the impression that an avalanche of iron was poured into the street. The sound of a mob, a chaotic clamor, weapons pounding against shields. They went back down. The alley was full of armed men whose helmets and armor gleamed in the light of the torches.

"We've got to get out of here," Manuel said. "Let's go two or three days away."

"No," Borg said curtly.

"But why? Are you crazy? We're going to have to freeze everyone!"

"Not a chance. Wait for them to come in. We'll start by blinding them."

"And if they riddle us with arrows?"

"Think about it! They won't do anything but back off and cover their eyes like the oafs over there in the corner."

The oafs in question were starting to stir. Even though they did not put much trust in their crude weapons against the evil spells from hell, they were scheming something in whispers.

"They're hoping the watchmen will hold us at bay before the arrival of the bishop specialized in exorcism," Anton said.

"If we let things go that far," Manuel remarked, "there will be traces in history. I'll remind you what you said about that."

"This isn't so serious. There are other traces, well known in your age, that come from Babelian or Kaltarian interventions. If tonight's adventure isn't mentioned by a chronicler, it's because it didn't have much of an impact."

"And if it does get so out of hand that the royal and ecclesiastical authorities decide to snuff it out completely?"

"In that case, there will be even fewer consequences. Don't worry, everything will probably work out just fine."

Manuel did not respond. "Probably" was not enough for him. He turned back to the street where orders were being shouted. The sergeant was talking to the woman who had called the patrol and treating her like a cunning wench. Obviously, he was looking for an excuse to avoid making a search of the black hole where two demon henchmen had taken refuge. At this moment something happened over by the huddled drunks. Then all of a sudden several of them ran to the steps yelling and were about to throw themselves at the feet of the guards who started whacking them with their swords. Within seconds the tavern was empty and heated arguments ensued outside.

"They won't come in," Borg stated categorically. "Let's wait for them to leave. If they stay too long, we'll go out by the stairs I saw at the back of the room, where a man disappeared at the start—no doubt the tavern owner. We'll be able to open the wall to his rooms. I've got what we need."

A torch came rolling along the ground, followed by another and another... They kept burning and the light was enough for the sergeant bending down in the entrance to see the two Kaltarian probers. He stepped back and sent in his men. Cautiously, three archers descended with arrows taut in their bows. Manuel engulfed them in the photophore ray. They dropped their weapons and covered their eyes with one hand while fumbling to cross themselves with the other.

Manuel and Anton started slowly toward the door but before they could reach it, ropes fell on their shoulders. The photophore rolled on the ground and went out. Other men had come down the stairs that Anton had planned to take, which led to a side street although Anton thought they led to the proprietor's private rooms. Swiftly bound, the travelers were dragged away amongst prayers and insults.

"They'll have the stake burning soon enough," Anton observed with stultifying calm.

In the dungeon where they were thrown, they had brought in a huge crucifix. The guards looked very surprised and more disturbed than ever on seeing that the holy presence did not cause the prisoners great pain and suffering, that they did not scream as if being branded with red hot iron and they did not spit in the face of God while writhing like lunatics. Since they had managed to catch them, they were obviously humans guilty of signing a pact with the Evil One, but even in this case they should be reacting like the demon possessing them.

When the guards left, Manuel looked at Anton with a melancholic eye, "What fate do they have in store for this poor Christ?"

In the morning light that filtered in through a tiny hole bored into the ceiling, Borg looked stranger and more anachronistic since he lost his wig. The loss had frozen the blood in Manuel's veins as he saw himself left on his own, meaning like any other helpless criminal facing judges of this time. And nothing left to chance: the scared men had taken great care in handling the objects rank with sulfur. They had picked them up with their fingertips and carried them on cushions decorated with crowns of thorns.

Thinking of this Manuel went on, "They very well might burn at the stake the objects we were carrying."

"They'll keep them," Anton declared. "They'll raze the city and a lot of the surrounding countryside."

"How can we make them understand this? Your lack of concern is mortifying on every level. You've just accepted everything's that happened, from start to finish, without lifting a finger."

"You know perfectly well why," Borg said mysteriously. "But it's true that I'd like to be a few hours older…"

Borg was right to talk about "a few hours". While events of more or less satanic appearance usually took weeks of inquiry, the distinctly horrendous nature of this one got sent before judges in record time. Three cardinals were swiftly summoned and decided on a sham trial in order to rid the world of the Antichrist on the spot. That very afternoon they led the probers into a big room where they had set up the judges, executioners, assistants and torture instruments of all kinds.

The three cardinals in red robes presided in the midst of several bishops dressed in purple and a swarm of monks from all the orders. The room was full of royal guards in black armor. Anton was smiling but Manuel felt cold sweat beading down his back. They had knocked him to his knees and one of the cardinals took the floor. Anton whispered the gist of the speech to Manuel who found it even crazier than he expected. The cardinal finished with this:

"…notwithstanding that the black night never ends in Hell, we shall condemn them to see and recognize each other, thus does Divine Justice wish to magnify their torment."

He made a sign and a man, wider than he was tall, his face hidden under a red mask, grabbed Manuel by his hair and dragged him toward the instruments of torture. Borg touched his partner on the shoulder. Manuel's head was surrounded by a spectacular orange glow and the executioner's aide fell to his knees, groaning in pain. In an instant the whole room was on its feet shouting exorcism rites. Amidst the din, celestial music suddenly filled the hall. Everyone looked up and stood silent, mouths agape. From the ceiling, slowly descending, came two beings wearing shining tunics.

"Hallelujah!" a monk yelled. "Two archangels are coming to save us from the detestable and…"

The rest was lost in the thundering music. Light as feathers Jorik and Gelia alit in the middle of the cleared space.

The music stopped abruptly. An awful silence squeezed the heads of those present like a giant hand. As stunned as the members of the tribunal, Manuel gawked alternately at Gelia and Jorik. At first he refused to recognize the Babelian—didn't they all have the same tanned skin, light hair and those pale, ice-cold eyes?

But he could not mistake him. He almost still felt in command of the body, remembering the harsh orders of that will to his own muscles. And the dangerous person as not dead! Worse: he had restored his influence over Gelia, an influence that Manuel had given him.

Jorik glanced briefly at Anton and a faint smile crossed his lips. He looked at Manuel whose eyes were filled with hate. Then he raised his voice. He spoke in Latin, a very pure Latin, as befit an angel. Manuel, who was a poor Latinist, only understood the general idea of the domineering speech—basically that the angel was giving orders to the court to withdraw from a fight that was bigger than them and let the heavenly powers combat those of darkness. He also commanded the judges to give back the weapons to the devil's henchmen as they were forged in the underworld by the damned found guilty of crimes.

The three cardinals heard and obeyed, bowing on bended knees as they gave orders in turn. The crowd stared on, trembling, but slowly moved toward the doors, not really wanting to witness the battle of Titans that was in the making. Within minutes the cardinals' orders were carried out They put the cushion with the foreign objects in front of Borg and Esteban.

Then the room was emptied. The Kaltarians were only facing the Babelians. Gelia eyed Manuel with disgust.

"Could he have a chivalrous soul?" Anton addressed Manuel in 20th century French.

Manuel could not answer. He could not stop thinking of Gelia, closer and yet farther away than ever. Then Jorik spoke to his adversaries in 14th century French. Manuel remembered enough to understand him, but he did not pay much attention since he was burning with the desire to tell Gelia the truth that she surely did not know, that he had held her in his arms through an intermediary, and that from then on she seemed to show an interest in Jorik, whom she never cared about before.

"Use the weapons when the time comes," Borg whispered. "Anyway, just now, I surrounded you with an energy field. The generator's housed in one of my arm muscles."

Manuel remembered Anton's remark a few minutes ago: Jorik the chivalrous? This could lead one to believe... Unless he did not trust the judges to get rid of his enemies? This was more likely. Manuel felt no qualms about fighting if he were being protected by an impenetrable forcefield. But who could say if Jorik, too, had a similar shield? The energy field did at least explain Anton's calm during the tavern fiasco. Part of Jorik's speech came back to Manuel, who had recorded it unconsciously in his mind. It was something about fighting for honor, avoiding useless deaths and especially about not waiting for the men gathered outside the doors to come rushing in. On this subject, Kaltarians and Babelians were in agreement.

"I refuse to fight a woman," Manuel said in mangled Babelian.

Gelia puffed out her chest, furious, and shouted, "Coward! A Babelian woman is stronger than a Kaltarian runt and you know it!"

Manuel knew not what to say. He would have to pretend to fight while trying to get her to safety against her will. Anton was holding his zero weapon, the disintegrator, and another small object they had left behind. He dropped the photophore, which was of no use anymore. Manuel and he divvied up the meager arsenal but kept a wary eye on their enemies' arms: the blaster and two other weapons that Manuel had never seen in Babelia. They separated from each other.

The crowd at the door was more curious than terrified, pushing and shoving to watch the combat they had just run away from. A droning Gregorian chant rose up. They were trying to support the envoys of God in whatever feeble way they could. For the first time, Manuel felt a little lump in his throat from this crude, for sure, but so strong and naïve belief...

Looking back to Gelia and her companion, he wondered how they could be mistaken for angels. They both looked more like the kind of demons people of this time could dream up. Was it the ambient accompaniment of music? Or Jorik's forceful declarations? In any case, they had played the role well. He turned to Anton to stop his plan of action—he had tossed over a time helmet and was fumbling with a dial. He vanished before the horrified eyes of Manuel.

Jorik laughed, ominously, like the hooting of an owl. At the doors they clapped and cheered, followed by a strident Hallelujah because one of the demons had just fled from the avenging angels. Manuel saw his final hour approaching. This sudden betrayal was handing him over to his ruthless enemies.

For, Gelia felt for him the exact opposite of what he felt for her.

"Drop your weapons," she offered coldly as if answering his thoughts. She made a sign to Jorik and added, "Let me kill him. I know all the lethal moves and can take him out in no time."

Jorik's piercing eyes looked him up and down. The result of the examination was mortifying because he just shrugged and took the weapons that Gelia was handing over. She walked over to the traveler, hands empty and eyes paler than ever.

Manuel considered the situation. Dropping his weapons would save him temporarily because despicable Borg had taken the energy field with him. But the Babelian woman's attitude and the memory of the fight he had scraped through in the Black City did not inspire much confidence in him against a woman he loved but who was set on killing him.

"You'll be able to take me easily," he said, "because I won't defend myself."

Jorik's laughter sounded more cheerful this time, but Manuel went on calmly.

"All I can do to you is give you another slap."

Gelia squinted at him, not understanding.

Manuel explained, "I mean the slap you got in my room in the on-duty zone right before the water fight against the Kaltarian prisoners."

"What are you talking about?" she grumbled. "And how do you know that Jorik slapped me in *his* room?"

It was Manuel's turn to smile as Jorik stepped forward. "So, Jorik didn't tell you that until the Kaltarian commando team attacked it was me controlling his brain and body?"

She turned to Jorik who was frozen now. Manuel pressed on.

"He didn't tell you what miracle saved him from the freeze gun, which never fails?"

Right then he had the sudden impulse to flee because he himself could not explain the miracle. But an idea popped up, which he threw out there.

"It's the same reason that I survived. His body was used to thinking like in the 20th century because of me. Even though he was there, he was affected by a web of time frequencies that shielded him from the energy blow. It's thanks to me and me alone that he's still alive."

For the first time, Manuel saw Jorik look confused. As for Gelia, she had lost three fourths of her self-confidence.

Esteban pushed harder, "Do you see now why you started looking differently at Jorik from that time on? Do you see that the feelings being stirred up in you are not meant for him? And now you want to kill me, the one who sparked all that in you?"

Gelia wiped her forehead. The songs and litanies got louder. Jorik slowly lifted his blaster, but Gelia waved him off.

"Stop!" she shouted. "What do you have to say?"

His lips became thinner, if that was possible, and he said, "It's true. I have to admit it because I can't describe the details of the battle or the banquet. He'd pushed me deep down into myself and I remember only scraps of it all. But he won't be able to do it again. If you betray Babelia, I'll deal with it—you can never trust a woman."

He raised his weapon again, but with a well-aimed blow to his forearm she knocked the blaster out of his hand. In a flash he was on her and a quick fight ensued. Was Jorik afraid of hurting her, of killing her? Or did he misjudge her strength and his reactions?

After getting caught in a death grip, Jorik fell, jerking on the ground for a short while, then nothing. His body lay still. At first Gelia looked crazed, then she slowly broke down in sobs. Still on the defensive, Manuel came over to console her cautiously. She collapsed in his arms, all her energy drained.

Outside the room a horrified silence had hushed the choir. What were the men going to do if the angels were fighting amongst themselves and teaming up with hell?

CHAPTER X

"Let's go," a reassuring voice said behind them. "Don't be sad, all is not lost."

Manuel turned around. Smiling and looking sly, Varold was standing a few feet away. He was still wearing his shiny bodysuit.

"We're all sorry for the death of poor Jorik," he went on. "But you've got to admit he had it coming. His hatred of Esteban was more important to him than his feelings for Gelia. That's what killed him when he first decided to destroy his rival. And so it goes ..."

Manuel narrowed his eyes. Had Varold showed up just to play the philosophical narrator?

Gelia, too, had turned around. Despite her distress she had strength enough to ask, "Who's this?"

"I don't know him," Manuel said softly, petting her cheek. "I've met him a few times... usually he acts like an ally."

She pushed away his hand but stayed in his arms. The doors of the room, still wipe open, were filled with a kneeling crowd muttering desperate prayers.

Varold pointed to it, "Do you understand, Manuel, why this adventure won't be found in your century? The church won't let it be spread. The death of an angel, killed by another who fell into the arms of a demon... enough to revive the Albigensian heresy. Everyone here will rot in the bishop's dungeon. As for the cardinals, they'll be made monks with a vow of silence. No evidence will remain because I'm going to give Jorik the burial he deserves."

He leaned over the sprawled body and it disappeared under his hands.

"I sent him into non-time," he stated.

Gelia gawked at the place where her companion had lain a moment before. Overwhelmed by Varold's tranquil power, her mouth stayed closed.

Then Varold said to her, "Admit it now that after the Kaltarian commando attack you saw nothing in him of that spark that attracted you during those few hours before."

He talked in Babelian with the same ease as he spoke 20th century French to Manuel. She kept silent even though she understood.

"Let's get out of here first," he went on. "I've got a lot to tell you and I need a time and place a lot calmer than here. Give me your hands, both of you."

When Gelia felt the cottony contact of Varold's hand she recoiled. But she noted that Manuel did not seem bothered, so she accepted docilely. Savage Gelia was giving way to a confused and forsaken woman.

"Pick up your knickknacks," Varold ordered them.

Manuel grabbed his time vest along with the weapons. All three of them vanished. A few minutes later the room started echoing with the booming tones of a Te Deum, which drowned out the woeful Miserere.

This voyage was very different from the others Manuel had taken with Varold. He did not feel the hard jolt that wrenched his entire body and he kept his notion of personal, biological time, enclosed in a kind of bubble in "no time's land". They were floating in a gray fog, thick and noiseless. Manuel saw Varold's face nearby, tensed up like expecting some unknowable danger. A little farther away he saw Gelia's turn to him for an instant. Her lips parted in a mute question, then closed again. Varold had noticed her because he spoke in Babelian to be understood by her and Manuel both.

"Silence is not necessary," his voice sounded like it was coming out of a long pipe. "What matters is to stay vigilant. The Conditionals are all around us."

"The Conditionals?" Manuel repeated. His own voice belonged to someone else located thousands of miles away.

"What you were calling the 'luminous shadows'. Remember? You mentioned it back in the Tertiary Age."

Gelia listened, glancing from one to the other. Maybe she was thinking that Manuel and Varold were actually old friends if they had met in the Tertiary Age, but in fact they had met before… or rather afterward.

A shadow passed by, haloed in light. Varold's suit flashed a series of various colors. The shadow went back into the fog.

"It's time," Varold murmured as if to himself and this remark made in the midst of a timeless country gave Manuel a weird feeling.

"We're going to pass the barrier," Varold said.

"The 30th century barrier?" Manuel asked.

"Yes."

With this, Gelia snapped out of her silence, "That's impossible."

Varold looked at her, "For you, yes, but not for me. I cross it all the time going both ways."

Manuel shuddered, "You are…"

"Yes, I'm from the other side. But watch out. Help me, both of you. Focus your willpower on driving back what's coming."

A group of shadows surge out of the fog. They were shining brighter and brighter as Manuel felt like he was being pushed back inside himself, his body turned inside out like glove. He saw things take shape around him—the vaporous forms of the tribunal room he had just left.

"Quickly," Varold's distant voice ordered, "help me! Help me!"

Terrified by the Conditionals' power and at the same time vaguely satisfied that Varold needed him, Manuel focused his will. The murky traces of the 14th century faded away. The shadows struggled harder to force them back. The forms took shape again. Then Varold and Manuel felt another will helping theirs. Gelia was joining the party with everything she had. After more and more painful pressure, everything vanished. The three of them were once again floating in the gray universe of non-time. The fog was empty.

"They're dangerous," Varold said. "They fight for their life."

"Us too," Manuel remarked.

"No, you're fighting not to lose it. They, like me, are fighting to get one."

"What do you mean?"

"Wait, we're there. We only have to get through the barrier set up by my own."

A shimmering surface rose up before them. Varold stretched out his hands. The surface warped, vibrated with faster and faster ripples, and it glowed brighter and brighter until it was hard to look at. Then it cracked and splintered. The pieces flew by them, dissolving in the fog. Manuel turned around and saw it reforming behind them.

"There you go," Varold said.

They were in a sunlit valley. Nearby was the slope of a hill topped by majestic trees with spear-shaped leaves. A lyrebird sailed by with a tiny chirp.

"This is the time and place I talked about. We're in Manoon and the 30th century is over."

Manuel looked at Gelia and simply said, "Thanks."

She remained distant but not unreachable, "Thanks for what?"

"You...," he spoke more intimately now, "don't you think we noticed that you helped us out back there in the non-time?"

Gelia did not answer. The lyrebird was back and keeping a jubilant eye on them.

Varold waved to Manuel to drop it and said, "Follow me. I want to give you some idea of Manoon before explaining things."

He started to climb the hill. Manuel and Gelia followed. The farther they went, the thicker the trees became and the more animals there were. For Manuel it was nice to see them but Gelia was clearly beside herself.

"These are little beasts from past centuries," she ended up saying. "How did they get here?"

"We brought them here. Hundreds of years of war between Babelia and Kaltarborog had destroyed them."

A rabbit scampered between Gelia's legs. She yelped in surprise and awe. The rabbit was friendly. It scratched its ears sitting on the feet of Manuel who crouched down to pet it. Gelia watched on, smiling.

As Varold passed under a low branch he told Manuel, "Just give it time, brave sir, and all that..."

From the summit of the hill they saw a landscape like nothing else. Mingled with the thickets and streams was a city or rather a series of elegant and colorful dwellings, all one-storied and obviously made for just one family. They spread out on all sides as far as the eye could see and certainly beyond. Nothing like the huge, architectural synthesis of Kaltarborog and even less like the dreary hideousness of Babelia.

"All of this is the work of the Defectors," Varold explained. "People from Babelia and Kaltarborog who fled the perpetual war along with folks like you, Manuel, forced by circumstances to leave their native era. They created a retreat that they guard even more jealously since it's not yet totally real. They replaced the war of destruction with a war of creation and this, too, is kind of a perpetual war because Manoon will remain forever conditioned by the work of its inhabitants. We are also Conditionals but by common and constant effort we let in a higher degree of reality than those others."

He looked at them both in turn and went on.

"You still don't understand. I should start from the beginning."

He pondered a moment before continuing.

"For you it started the day I asked to see the first rector of Kaltarborog. I knew that the Babelians had decided to send an emissary to Manuel Esteban, the 20th century biochemist. I was sure that the Kaltarians were sending one, too, namely Anton Borg whose mind I got control of for good. In this like in many other matters, we in Manoon uphold the technical progress made in past centuries. You've seen it. Yes, Manuel, Borg was under my orders. Until his betrayal, which I wanted, because at that moment he was of no more use. So, Manuel was enlisted in the Kaltarian ranks and started with a mission to Babelia. He was supposed to meet Gelia, you and not another, for a reason I'll reveal later. When he met you, he looked like Jorik, but he had to finish his sabotage mission he'd been sent on. That's why I stopped him from destroying the power plant in Babelia—if he'd done it, the balance of the war might've tipped over to Kaltarborog's favor and the future of the two cities would've changed, thus putting at risk the precarious existence of Manoon. Meanwhile, I got Borg in the non-time to find out about Manuel's future and what he saw made him remember his envoy. In fact, the future was alarming because of the Kaltarian attack. Anton brought Manuel back, which saved both Manuel and Jorik. There was some truth in what you told Gelia, Manuel, about the influence of temporal frequencies, but you would both be dead if Borg had left you in hibernation. As for your second voyage, it was knocked off course by the Conditionals. They're the ones, as I said, who sent you to the Tertiary and now I can explain why."

He paused.

Then he went on, "Time is not a flux that flows in a line and always in the same direction. It is a star-shaped dimension whose center is the non-time. Everything that happens in every century is, in a way, happening at the same time if we look at it from this special line of sight. A bunch of causes get tangled up at every instant to produce an infinity of possibilities located in as many parallel universes. But these worlds have a degree of reality dependent on the probability of the effects. The Conditionals are beings spawned from these worlds and are trying to bend the curve of causes in their favor so they can attain a higher reality, thus pushing the others into a semblance of existence that verges on nothingness. There are other

Manuels and other Gelias who don't know each other, who surround us at crucial moments and try to push us back into their place."

"Other Varolds, too, I guess," Manuel said.

"No. I'll tell you why. Concerning these beings... I should call them the *Improbables* instead of the Conditionals—they inhabit the cracks that run between parallel worlds and luckily can't act except during a voyage, never in the concrete reality of a defined continuum, a thing that the creators of Manoon can do, which allows us to know the general outline of events and therefore to bend it here and there by replacing one probability for another. Manoon is inhabited by men and women like you who have acted in a specific direction. We know this direction and sometimes we've completely changed it. But even in your case, where I've only followed the strongest probabilities, the events had to be *experienced* by you for you to be able to bring to Manoon an extra quantity of existence."

"They're doing it now," Manuel interjected.

"Not really... which reminds me," (it did not really remind him but Manuel felt like Varold was stalling), "I appreciate your discretion in not telling Borg about our meetings, even if it wasn't necessary."

Varold smiled, uneasily, and added, "Yeah, you were surprised at how I insisted on staying when the king's guards surrounded us, but the mission about Nicolas Flamel was just a pretext. I knew we were going to meet Jorik and Gelia."

"But why?" Gelia shouted. "Why was I dragged into all this? Why me?"

Varold looked at her strangely, "I promised Manuel to reveal the reason why I deviated the course of events in this direction and not another. It's better that I tell both of you. Know that in Manoon, each of us has to secure his or her own existence like securing a foothold on a shaky bridge. Securing mine came down to bringing you two together. I will exist for real if you two really want it."

Night fell on Manoon. Gelia batted here eyelids, dumb-founded. Manuel felt his lips trembling. It was difficult to speak.

"You are…"

"Yes, I am… conditionally. That's why I said you still haven't *experienced* every event."

"But how come you look… let's say the same age as me?"

"I look, that's all. My true age is that of an unfertilized ovum—a negative age. Don't forget that Manoon belongs to a universe that is only probable. It's up to you to give it part of your reality for me."

A shadow of melancholy drifted over his eyes, then he concluded, "If you don't do it, Gelia will soon be yanked from here and sent back to Babelia right before Jorik's departure for his mission. Manuel to the moment of Jorik's psychic invasion of his personality. No one will be able to predict your destiny. As for me, I'll be wiped out for good. I won't even have tried to exist."

He smiled at them and dissipated in the twilight's per-fumed air. For a long time Manuel and Gelia stared at each other without saying a word. A bird sang three notes, then everything fell silent again.

"Come on," Gelia said.

Hand in hand, the two of them went down into Manoon.

Le 32 Juillet

KURT STEINER

★

ANTICIPATION

Editions
"Fleuve Noir"

THE 32ⁿᵈ OF JULY

CHAPTER I

The parachute opened reluctantly. Someone once said that I had nerves of steel… but the strongest steel turns to mush when a parachute hesitates to open.

I kept falling, but more slowly, in complete darkness. I had no idea how I was going to land even though they had informed me that the ground was, in theory, bare. The wind whistled through my brain but I was focusing all my attention on the need to make my body as flexible as possible—ready for the brutal crash coming up.

Something darker than the sky came rushing up toward me. Then the crash. My legs bent and then my thighs and my whole body, like a worn-out spring. I ended up tangled in a web of ropes while the light canopy slowly shrouded me.

I hastily freed myself from the premature winding sheet while checking for injuries. Nothing broken. All was well. But what a crash! Why not make bigger parachutes? There must be some technical reason I don't know about.

Standing on a vast plain, I tried to get my bearings. At best I could say that the horizon stretched along the border of this scrubland whose strong scents almost choked me.

In theory, I should be north of Avignon, if the pilot wasn't off course. I didn't have much to fear on that score since I'd been all over this region in the past with my old friend Dr. Gercourt. What was he doing now, I wonder?

Finally, I managed to get my parachute folded up. In the humid heat on the ground I brushed off my French-tailored clothes, changed my boots for a pair of dress shoes, a little too pointy for my taste. The parachute went in the bag and I started across the thyme and lavender, keeping an eye out for a rare bush or ditch where I might hide the gear. The dark night forced me to use my flashlight. At least if I wasn't near any roads, there was no danger.

I searched the inside pocket of my coat—a wallet full of money and identification papers—and in my pants pocket—the excellent Luger that I wouldn't (hypothetically) have to use.

A mission like any other, basically. But this time the American agent HB 54, whose real name was Kenneth Broad, was called Alain Farrel.

Weird and winding roads—that's what existence doles out to you. Fairly serious studies at Yale University interrupted by the reversal of the family fortune. And no grants to help finish the program... no desire to do it, either, for the same family reasons. A loyal friend with good contacts in the State Department and, from one contact to another, the track is set, oddly enough, for the CIA.

You can find every kind among the secret agents. My extensive knowledge of mathematical physics had naturally got me assigned to certain, particularly important missions. It is generally believed that a spy just needs brawn and quick reflexes because his job is to take pictures of secret plans in hazardous conditions. Nothing is farther from the truth. You can be 70 years old with a white beard (which is not my case) and still render important service to your country—or another—in the field of underground activities.

What brought me to France required a minimum of scientific knowledge. If I didn't have it, I would, of course, be working in the dark, taking the part for the whole and the trivial for the essential. It was about some research being done at the limits of our knowledge of quantum physics, research that was bound to interest any nation that got wind of it. There were certainly not a lot of these nations, but I shouldn't underestimate anything.

A certain Wenceslas Petrowics, a professor at Warsaw University, had emigrated to the West two years ago. The well-informed circles inside the CIA—well-informed but late out of the blocks—wondered why Petrowics had left Warsaw. The physicist didn't seem to be in conflict with the regime and nothing in his personality would lead you to believe that he was going to escape. Some intel, however, had hinted that the affair dated back to his marriage.

Wens (I called him this to keep things simple) had met a German chemist three years ago, a woman who had gone to Warsaw for a conference. The marriage took place three weeks later. Now, the character of Margareta Schiller—Greta—was surely not very pleasing to the top brass in Poland because of a tendency to non-conformism, which made her suspicious.

Whatever the case, the couple had headed out for greener pastures and France welcomed them for a lengthy stopover, though not with open arms: West Germany was not very pleased with Greta either, especially after marrying a Pole, thus making her suspicious in their eyes too. It was a total mess.

But the strangest thing of all was about the origin of the funds that were financing the Wens' research in France—I'd never been able to find out anything about them. For me, the explanation was simple: the funds were American but they had sent them without a quid pro quo—the quo was me. It was up to me to find out the object and the state of the research. I guessed that Wens had refused to communicate his results but would he accept help now in exploiting them? They had supported him, but it's rare to see a government lose interest.

They'd sent me to rummage around his lab. Basically, it was for their own good. If they cut off the funding, another power would step in and do it. Plus, too much pressure on him to send out results might kill the hen laying the golden egg—in the CIA this man had a reputation as a genius and we had to

133

avoid upsetting him, at all costs, before getting (by force if necessary) any unsatisfactory results far below what he could produce in the future. Something was telling me that he'd already been reluctant to reveal anything to his own country and his marriage wasn't the only reason for leaving Poland.

In short, he was a guy to be handled with great care... or more precisely, not to be handled at all, just approached. The ideal would've been to gain his trust and become his assistant. My ID with the name of Alain Farrel said I was an engineering consultant and I was also carrying in my wallet a certified copy of a fake PhD degree from the University of Paris. But was I going to run into a real graduate from there who might, for example, be a French secret agent?

I decided to do some reconnaissance of the Wens house first so I could get some idea of what exactly his research was about. Then it might be easier, after I've met him for real, to pique his interest by pretending to be working along the same lines... for this I'd need a lot of luck in my investigation and a lot of nerve in the subsequent meeting because Wens was no doubt as far beyond me in mathematics as I was of a high school student, if not more. I guess the CIA couldn't find anyone who was truly qualified... and who'd accept.

While thinking back over the facts of the case that got me parachuted into France, I had walked quickly through the balmy night. Streaks of light not far away indicated the presence of cars driving down a road.

A small house in ruins with an old well outside, three quarters caved in, was a lucky find for me. I dropped my parachute in the well and covered the opening with stones. When my task was done, lightning lit up the whole landscape, revealing its mystery for a split second. Immediately afterward a loud crash spread over the sky and earth and died out in the distance. The heat got heavier. Without waiting for the rain, I started off again.

When the storm broke, I was on the road. Through the warm rain that started falling I saw the first houses of a city.

Odds were nine out of ten that it was Avignon. The light rain-coat slung around my shoulders made me hard to see, but I was being careful on the roadside because the drivers couldn't see more than 30 feet through their windshields.

At last, I passed a sign that bore the big letters of the name of the city where I was going. Now I just had to pull up the map I had in my mind to locate the Wens villa. I did it easily and faster than hoped.

It was, indeed, a big white house built on the outskirts of the city, not far from the Rhône whose raging waters mixed their uproar with that of the sky. First, I passed by the front gate that stood before a small, well-kept yard lavished with flowers. The windows of the house were shut tight, letting no light leak out, which didn't mean the owners were asleep. However, it all looked too deserted to try a home visit. It was no great loss of time because I could find a way to meet up with Wens the next day... and I already had in mind a few clues on what to say. I raked my hand through my drenched hair.

A quick glance around assured me that all was clear. As I was climbing over the fence, another lightning bolt flashed through the clouds and a deluge from the heavens was un-leashed. Caught in mid-air by the sudden light I thought that if Wens was guarded in some way, I had zero chance out of a hundred to pull this off. I got under a fig tree and waited for a while, hand on the butt of my luger.

Nothing happened, so I crept up to the house. If there was any secret surveillance, they must've had my description along with orders to let me pass... unless something else? I didn't understand how the French, at least, couldn't know about it. They were right here, for God's sake!

But no. I forgot that the importance of Wens' work had barely leaked out. He kept up appearances here and the neces-sary funds to buy his equipment came as donations. After all, maybe we were the only ones really interested in him...

As I snuck by the long window on the ground floor, I heard a woman's scream, faintly through the thick walls and noise of the storm. Then there was another scream—a man this time.

I stood still for a moment, my heart racing. No, I was the only one in the game. Somebody had beaten me here. Someone who was apparently sabotaging the work. I hurried over to the closed door and right then felt the barrel of a gun in my back.

A voice whispered in my ear, "Alain HB."

It took me no time to realize it was a friend. No one could know the name chosen for me except a friend.

I answered back, "54."

There was a rustling behind me. I turned around. No one in sight! The guy must've raced around the corner of the house and disappeared.

Inside, it seemed, everything was quiet again. An ominous, uncomfortable silence. I pulled out the tiny instrument they'd given me to pick locks. It only took seconds and I was in, the door closed behind me.

Standing in the dimness of the entrance, I thought fast. What enemy could've snuck past the surveillance of this ally who'd just checked my identity?

A door was ajar at the end of the hall with a faint, greenish light leaking out. Gun in hand I approached noiselessly and almost gagged on the stench of ozone.

Three feet away from the door I stopped and listened. Only one sound came from the room: a kind of gentle snoring, cut off briefly by muffled clicks. Nothing human about this sound. Nothing to do with the screams I'd heard, no moaning, no heated argument, not even a whisper.

I stepped forward and keeping my gun raised I snuck a peek through the opening. I didn't see much at first. Just a jumble of machines made of dark plastic, connected by a maze of wires and cables... and at the back of the room that was obviously the physics lab, I could see a green light in the shape of a screen casting its murky glow over the room. I stood frozen to the spot for a few seconds, watching the phenomenon that held some kind of secret fascination. But I soon pulled myself out of this risky reverie to run my eyes over the walls and the web of conductors. Lastly, I scanned the floor and recoiled.

Not far from the glowing phenomenon that kept rippling vertically like a sheet ruffled by the wind, I could see the shape of a human body lying on the floor.

CHAPTER II

I went for broke. Taking out my flashlight and holding it out, I kicked open the door, which banged against a black stand. At the same time, I swept the cone of light around the lab.

"You can come out," I spoke calmly in French. "I'm not the police."

And I jumped back to get out of the way of any bullets that might answer my call. Nothing. No reaction at all. As if I were alone in this damned house.

I swung around and lit up the nooks and crannies down the hallway. They could attack from behind while I was playing the hero in front of the open door of the lab…

Nobody. Not a peep. I turned back to the wide-open door.

And if I were alone, the only intruder? Carefully I felt along the wall for a switch, which I found right away. A white light flooded the lab whose layout took on a little order. The glowing green sheet lost most of its brightness, but didn't disappear. I stepped in.

Where was the woman? I knew I'd heard a woman's scream. There was just the body lying on the floor. I went over without letting down my guard.

At first sight I recognized Wens. They'd shown me a photo of his face and profile: in his fifties (his wife was 26, so it was no wonder he got married three weeks after meeting her), regular looking with a short, gray beard—a typical, old-school scientist.

I got on one knee and felt for a pulse, still holding my automatic. He was alive. But some shock had made him pass out because his heart was beating slowly and he was lying as still as a log.

Something suspicious for no specific reason kept me far away from the undulating green screen. Under the bright ceiling lights it was blurry. And yet, you could see it rippling to some complex rhythm that kept its shape but distorted it into countless, continually shifting paraboloids. The whole thing stayed within a metal frame as tall as a man and of equal width, topped by an eight-inch assembly of cryotrons and spools whose purpose I couldn't figure out. It was around the frame that most of the wires came together from the other machines: dynamos, condensers, transformers, oscillographs with quivering sine waves...

In the middle of the lab a rather loose coil of copper supported a tube that clicked at regular intervals at the same time as it emitted a tiny flash inside a column of light. I thought of the pinch effect, of fusion experiments... This was definitely something else. I glimpsed a glass integrator at the foot of the back wall that was completely occupied by a huge, electronic calculator.

I turned back to Wens. It was crucial that he wake up from what seemed to be a simple lab accident since there were no other intruders but me.

Crucial? In fact, I didn't think he was in danger. Wasn't I finding myself in ideal circumstances to get all the information I could on his work? I was in his lab! On further thought, it did me no good. There was a good chance that the fluorescent patch was the crux of his research, but I understood absolutely nothing about its nature, its purpose or how it got there. What I needed were notes, calculations, his curves.

Wasn't there a desk in the corner of the lab? No. Nothing like it. Just a plastic board lying across two rows of condensers on which four or five sheets lay next to a pen. When I picked them up, my head started spinning. What good was four years of mathematical physics. What I read there was using group theory applied to a series of differential equations with multiple variables. Einstein would've been lost.

I'd figured as much… but I hadn't had such proof of my ignorance before. The only way was what I'd planned to do first—get in close contact with the physicist.

Then something bothered me. Leaving this guy unconscious on the ground to examine his work… oh, of course, you either do your job or you don't, but I'd trained for a different profession and fell into this one almost by mistake. On the other hand, my two previous missions didn't force me to murder anyone. Basically, I was lucky and I was going to let my third mission sacrifice my last remnants of humanity.

I started slapping Wens.

I got no results. The physicist must've suffered a serious shock. I rolled up his sleeves to check for electric burns, even though he didn't look asphyxiated. But I found no trace whatsoever. A different kind of shock, then… but what?

I finally decided to look for some help in the house. Without turning on the lamp in the entrance hall I called out in a normal voice. Again, no response.

A few minutes later, after a quick search of the upper floor, I came back down without seeing a living soul and without finding a single medicine cabinet.

Sitting on the floor of the lab, Wens watched me come in.

It was a great relief for me… but also a desperate surge of energy, a sudden focus on what I was going to tell him. I had to play the savior.

Wens looked at me with wild eyes. Was he crazy? That was the last thing I needed right now!

But when I leaned over him, he choked back a sob and whispered in French, "Help me…"

I got my hands under his arms and lifted him up. He fixed his sleeves, which I had rolled up checking for burns.

"Who are you?" he managed to stammer, looking me up and down distractedly.

"Alain Farrel," I said, "from Paris."

I had no accent. He, on the contrary, drawled out his words.

"Ah… and how did you get in here?"

"Your front door wasn't locked," I said brashly. "I heard two screams while passing by your house. I thought someone might need help."

He nodded, then turned to the green screen and pointing. "Don't get near it," he muttered.

He swung around abruptly and cried out, "Need help?! God, if only you knew!"

He lay his head in his hands, so it was hard to hear what followed:

"But who can help me? Who can help *them*?"

I said nothing. The guy was obviously in great pain and trying to fight against it. And he was undoubtedly suspicious of me and being careful not to say anything about his work.

But his emotions got the better of him. He raised both his arms and made a sweeping gesture as if to empty the lab of everything in it. "To hell with all this!" he shouted. "And me with it!"

He scrutinized me from head to toe as I saw a tear run down his cheek.

"Monsieur…"

He stopped, trying to remember my name.

I repeated, "Farrel. I'd like to help…"

He shook his head, "Nobody can help anymore. Nobody. You don't understand—*they're on the other side*!"

He pointed to the green veil with a kind of fury.

"Listen," I told him, stupidly looking at the space behind the rippling surface, "listen to me—I was really surprised by your set-up here. See, I'm an engineering consultant specialized in electronics. So, if I can help you in any way whatsoever…"

At that moment I was being sincere. I'd half-forgotten why I was there. I felt sorry for him. I stiffened up right away. Nerves of steel… What a joke! I thought I'd spoken too soon and too openly. I watched his face for any sign of doubt.

Nothing. He just shrugged his shoulders.

"Monsieur," he said wearily, "I appreciate it, but alas!" He waved it off and concluded with a snarl, "I can do nothing but go after them now."

Disaster! If anything happened to him, I wouldn't get an iota of information about what he'd accomplished. I couldn't let him out of my sight for a minute.

I spoke as gently as I could, "Come on, maybe all is not lost…"

I hated my hypocrisy. And he ended up seeing that I was on my guard. How could that story of the open door get by without him thinking me a liar?

Then I heard what I'd never expected to hear, but what, in truth, I'd come for.

"Monsieur Farrel," he said, "since you have some notion of physics, you might understand the horrible accident that just happened here…"

My ears opened wide.

"Many people would love to hear what I'm about to tell you," he muttered, "but nothing matters anymore."

He looked me straight in the eyes.

"Isn't that right, *Monsieur Farrel from Paris*?"

He drew out these last words. As I was trying to keep my composure he laughed humorlessly.

"Don't worry. I guessed who I was dealing with from the moment I opened my eyes. But the theft of my discoveries, what they can be used for, my own murder… and the destruction of humanity… none of this means anything to me. Oh, I didn't think like this until the fatal accident."

I shuddered, feeling very uncomfortable. I stuttered, "Your… your wife…"

He couldn't escape me now and my work would be child's play.

"My wife, yes… and my assistant, Iris." He looked at me with bitter irony. "A Swiss assistant, my dear spy. She knows all about my work. It's already the property of her government, which doesn't get involved in any wars."

Everything came crashing down. So that's where the mystery money came from! But as a last resort, wouldn't it be better that if a second country would get the necessary data, it would be mine? There was no doubt that in one way or another Wens' work could be used to build a weapon. Even if the Swiss were no exception, wasn't it better that they were the ones to develop it? I couldn't imagine this peaceful country suddenly infected by the fever of war and carried away by dreams of dominion. I also couldn't imagine them succumbing to blackmail. I wondered if I was starting to feel an *earthly* patriotism on a global scale. But my brain was boiling. What a mistake the CIA had made sending an agent who asked himself such questions!

And about these questions, I was suddenly astonished by the coincidence that brought me here to this precise moment when some tragedy having nothing to do with spy work was unfolding. But maybe my bosses had followed Wens' research closely enough to send me in only when the moment was right. The state of the physicist's work was probably the reason for the accident—a first experience that had catastrophic results...

Wens interrupted my thoughts just when I was starting to think he was being careless in confiding his discoveries even to a neutral country. But I still didn't know if it was really possible to use them for military ends.

"I started with mesons," he spoke as if to himself. "The study of these subatomic particles revealed that *Time had a discontinuous structure*. I discovered chronons or time particles."

I knew that a similar theory had already been proposed, but nobody so far had thought to verify it experimentally. If Wens had gone that far...

"I discovered them first in my calculations. They were *necessary*. And then, a certain experiment proved explicitly that they existed. When I could follow the trajectories I realized that what we take for a uniform, unidirectional flow is really a maelstrom of chronons tightly bound to what comprises the core. Like Space, Time is bound to what we call matter. It's because matter is bound to Space that there's a continuum formed with Time. It's the dance of atomic particles that serves as a bridge between them and gives them meaning."

Was he rambling? Or was he really telling me the results of his research? You'd have to be really obsessed to talk about this while your wife had just... just what? I shuddered again.

"This luminous surface," he said, "is made of a particle screen. Not photons but chronons. If you cross it..." He shrugged, overwhelmed. "If you cross it, *you go across the time that governs us*. You don't travel through it, you leave it."

The idea was completely beyond me. I murmured, "What do you mean?"

The rain outside, the warm rain of July, poured down harder. Through the thick walls I heard a distant clock chime slowly. I automatically counted the twelve chimes.

As if it were a signal, Wens straightened up. "What do I mean?" he repeated loud and clear. "How can we leave the Present without ending up in the Future or the Past?" He stepped forward and shouted, "How am I going to find Greta? Just watch!"

Before I could budge, he lunged at the sinister screen of green light. When he touched it, his entire body lit up briefly, then vanished abruptly.

I stood frozen to the spot for a long moment. The lab suddenly looked to me like a gaping maw that I had stumbled into.

When I could think straight again, I was sure that I'd just witnessed a suicide. I was at a total loss, completely helpless before this dark turn of events.

Then I wondered whether Wens' might not have re-vealed some extraordinary truth to me. The Polish scientist was no impostor. For the CIA to be interested in him they had to have gathered some really exceptional information about him. I thought of what he'd said, "How can we leave the Present without ending up in the Future or the Past?" By dying, of course… but maybe there was another way…

The 12 chimes from the invisible clock were still ringing in my head. July 31 had just ended. And if Wens wasn't dead? If he'd gone across time, if he'd gone with the day out of our continuum completely? If he'd reached *July 32* in a kind of Space fitting that kind of Time?

My head was bursting. No, it made no sense. And yet, if Time was really a whirlwind and not a linear flow, you could, theoretically, go off in any direction.

I felt dizzy. The same craving for excitement that had led me into a job that had nothing to do with what I had planned, the same appetite for travel and adventure was now driving me to seriously consider this mad experiment!

For Wens it was something else. An act of despair, in short, or of hope! Hope of finding the woman he'd lost, even in death? I didn't know how Margareta had disappeared nor the assistant who I didn't even know existed, but I guessed that none of the three had thought of experimenting on the light screen. At least not yet. Maybe Wens had planned to use it for something else entirely and an accident had thrown them through the barrier.

A fatal curiosity was forcing me now to look more avidly at the menacing ripples where Time was bound and whirling its tempest. I knew there was only one way for me to recover from this shock: follow in the footsteps of those I had come to spy on.

I got my bearings again, but I hadn't changed my mind. Still, I wasn't ready to jump blindly into this nonsense. I thought of Gercourt, Dr. Michel Gercourt, a friend I'd met a few years back—a man in the best sense of the word.

It seemed doubtful that Michel would leave his office in Lyon to follow me on this absurd and risky adventure, maybe onto death. Anybody would find it so crazy it'd be a joke. For me there was a slim chance—I knew him well enough. It was not beyond the realm of possibility that he would see the potential... besides, I'd met him by saving his life. A stupid accident on the road and the young doctor was passed out in his car, which was starting to burn. I'd pulled him out after a fierce battle with the stuck door. My hands still bear the traces.

I decided not to waste time. "Waste time!" The expression took on a strange significance in this situation.

There had to be a telephone in the house somewhere. I knew Gercourt's number. I just had to...

Searching room by room I realized that it wouldn't be enough. You'd have to be mad to agree to follow a reckless adventurer on an unknown expedition. Nevertheless, I found a phone and dialed the number.

While waiting to get through, I felt another worry take shape. What if my "friends" had installed a bug? In the unlikely event that Michel would agree, they'd arrest him en route, maybe even snuff him out. And my real name that I'd have to give him? In fact, my name wasn't important. "They" probably didn't know it. To keep Michel safe I had to give him my real name and not the fake one. If need be, he could say he was coming to treat the guy they were sitting on...

"Hello?" a faint voice said.

"Are you still a bachelor? I was wondering..."

I hung up the phone. The conversation hadn't lasted long. Michel sounded like he was in a really bad mood and I barely had time to give him a few simple directions and basic warnings. Since he didn't know about my secret self, he didn't understand why I just showed up in France out of the blue and called him in the middle of the night. Still, I gave him the address, my two names—the true and the false—and the phone number. If others were listening in, they could imagine that Gercourt was part of my network. Otherwise! The important thing, really, was that they let him through to the house.

But then none of this mattered: Gercourt wasn't rushing out here. He told me that I'd gone a little too far and hung up on me.

But if someone went to pay him a visit now and tried to extract information he didn't have? The more I thought about it, the more convinced I was that I'd put him in a real bind.

The harm was done. I didn't understand what drove me to such an absurd and dangerous action. Now I had no choice but to write a detailed letter to Michel (even if he might never read it) in order to fill in the gaps of what I'd told him. I got down to work.

Ten minutes later I put my letter in plain sight near the screen that hadn't stopped working for even a split second. In conclusion I advised him to burn the lab: maybe Wens was bluffing when he said the Swiss government knew all about this work. In any case, there would be no trace and all would be well—I already suspected what kind of weapon could be built with this discovery.

Was I just wasting time? I couldn't help feeling more confident than if I were diving in solo without leaving anything behind me.

When I was standing in front of the window of light, I flinched. My heart was skipping more beats than I could count. It was because I was leaping voluntarily into this madness. No accident was forcing me, no grief was clouding my mind. And I felt I needed to ponder it a little longer.

If I waited for Gercourt? It would take him three or four hours to get to Avignon from Lyon by car. That gave me a little time. And when he did arrive, I could protect him from my dangerous allies who were prowling around the house.

Yes. I had plenty of good reasons. But Gercourt might stay home. And me, I'd leave the house and leave the team of physicists to their secret to report to my employers on the deplorable results of my efforts.

Nothing I could do about it. I was obviously not cut out for this kind of work. And I knew I'd never become a real physicist myself. Before me the green square could be a doorway and finally give my existence some meaning or snuff it out once and for all.

I took a step forward, then two, then three... I felt yanked in all dimensions, emptied of myself, swept up by a maelstrom of powerful forces. I exploded into dark nothingness.

CHAPTER III

A steam bath. And this weight on my lungs... breathing was so hard! Too much water in the air. A temperature fit for equatorial plants.

Unintelligible forms behind by closed eyelids. Multicolored spots battling it out. And in my ears stuffed with wet cotton, a swishing sound, broken at times by lazy downpours.

My eyes opened slowly. The eyes of someone else. Fingers moved. Then came the consciousness of a body lying on spongy ground.

An idea, like an explosion—the green screen!

Only at this moment did I remember everything. But I wasn't sure I was still alive. The landscape my eyes discovered didn't help... on the contrary—never in my life had I seen anything so weird.

I struggled up, supporting myself with both hands on the soft ground. My disoriented eyes gazed upon a yellow sky, like gold, in which a purple sun shined as big as a wagon wheel. A few scattered clouds drifted very low.

I tried to take a deep breath. The warm, humid air irritated my bronchial tubes, which forced a long fit of coughing. I dried my eyes and looked with horror on the rest of the scenery.

I was on a small hill. It looked to me like I'd fallen out of the sky because the fall had left a hollow in the soft ground. Fallen out of the sky? Without killing me? Where in this world was the green portal that had sent me here?

As far as the eye could see was the same gray, porous ground with narrow, dark blue crags sticking up here and there. It took me a long time to realize that there were transparent things crawling slowly or lying still on the ground, throbbing as if animated by some inner pulse. And I don't know what prompted it, but I thought of Wens.

I turned every which way. I saw nothing but what I'd already seen, except for one thing: a narrow passageway was shining like metal, crossing the plain not far from me. But no trace of Wens.

However, I'd taken the same path, so it should be logical that I'd be near him. But there was no one. Nothing but the gloomy landscape, eerily menacing, with its crawling clumps and its metal road.

All of a sudden I became aware of my irrevocable solitude and sank into an awful depression. What stupid move had pushed me into this nightmare universe? I must've been an idiot or lunatic to do such of thing voluntarily!

Ah! I'd lost the cold determination of the fake Alain Farrel. As long as I was working in a familiar universe, I could pretend to scorn danger. That danger was something I could handle. I knew its form and how to protect myself against it. *Here*, no such thing. I was farther from earth than if I'd entered another galaxy. The weight of my enormous solitude crushed me and the idea of a world full of *absolutely unknown* dangers made me skittish as I panned around.

And yet my arrival seemed to have caused no reaction. It seemed obvious to me that these creepy, transparent things had something to do with life as I knew it…

But there was little chance that they were evolved, intelligent creatures capable of…

One of them, in its clumsy squirming, *was heading straight for me.*

I pulled myself together. The thought of communicating with this species of jellyfish made my stomach turn. I stepped forward, finally. My foot sank halfway into the ground from which sprang out a clear liquid, like soil drenched after a good rain. I paid no attention and hurried to put some distance between the crawling thing and myself.

But no, I stood frozen in place: another was coming toward me, then another and another. They were all converging on my spot.

Peering around, I sized up the situation. Maybe these gelatinous organisms were harmless... but if not, I had to get through them. I jumped over the closest lump, maybe two to three feet away, but the spongy ground had hampered my takeoff and I landed too close, barely missing it.

Just as I was getting ready to jump again, a distant object went gleaming by in the yellow sky. I was too involved in my escape to observe the shiny thing closely and a few seconds later it was gone.

Instinctively, I headed for the metal roadway that no jellyfish was crossing. I managed to get there after a few close shaves. Very carefully I stepped on it. I was half expecting something like an electric shock, but I felt nothing. A second later I was standing on the 6-foot-wide strip that stretched from one horizon to the other.

Contrary to my first impression the road did not feel like metal. It was soft and my weight left an impression. On closer examination I could make out a very thin structure that reminded me of a honeycomb. When I looked up, I saw a double row of slimy monsters piled up on both sides of the road. These nameless things felt my presence and an encounter with them would not be harmless; I was sure of it.

On observing them I realized what they reminded me of: amoeba. Huge amoeba. I wasn't too knowledgeable about biology, but I thought that their gray and flabby appearance and especially their way of moving were like the most basic cells with little outcroppings that deformed them and filaments that they used to crawl.

Rudimentary amoeba, three feet long! In a flash I thought of how they would eat: phagocytosis. These extensions of protoplasm, these pseudopods would form a pocket by huddling up behind their encircled prey. The thing or creature being eaten would be covered and digested. I had seen the process under a microscope in my high school lab class.

With a retrospective fear I started marching quickly between the two repulsive piles and was thankful that this road was here to protect me. But after a few steps I shuddered again. What had become of Wens? And the two women?

The purple sun was still doling out the same heat up in the sky that looked like molten gold. Occasionally, a dark green cloud veiled it, but the greenhouse atmosphere never changed. I was running now on the supple strip that made it easy to move and I'd left behind me the monstrous horde that my presence had attracted. Other amoebae were crawling along the track but I must've been too fast a prey to trigger their tropisms.

"God," I thought, "Wens dropped into these disgusting lumps. He might've been eaten before he even woke up... or he tried to escape and they surrounded him..."

Wens had become for me a very dear friend. Why? Because I was hoping to see someone of my own species. Everything living in this transtemporal world seemed monstrously far from human. And I couldn't imagine how I was going to get out of here someday... but what madness had possessed me?

I got back to Wens. Maybe he, too, had reached the protective road? In that case, I would see him again... unless he'd gone in the other direction. As for the two women... I preferred to repress the grim pictures that came to mind.

I slowed down. Panic had pushed me this far, but I was gradually getting my self-control back. I went back to walking, still quickly, toward the horizon that got farther away, and tried to find some similarity between this world and mine.

A mystery was bothering me. I was alive even though, according to Wens' theory, this universe was governed by a different time from mine. Since the chronons were bound to atomic particles, I should've been disintegrated on crossing the barrier...

However, thinking about it, I figured I might be able to solve the puzzle. I was wrong to be positing the traditional notion of "linear" time. For Wens, time was swirling around. My own time particles had not been affected by the passage. In some way I'd just deflected my movement in earthly time and another had grabbed me.

Wens' discovery was beyond genius. It had implications far greater than if he'd just found a way to travel through human time. He gave Time the same kind of surface and depth as Space, multiplying the fourth dimension unto infinity.

In fact, I must've had at least a basic intuition of this since I'd followed Wens on this scheme that had nothing to do with suicide.

I was snapped out this reverie by a certain change in the landscape I was passing through. I hadn't noticed it at first, but now I was seeing that the hordes of amoebae had diversified a little. On the spongy ground at present I saw wide flaps crawling around, obviously made up of big, flat cells. I stopped, awestruck. There was no doubt about it. Cellular colonies covered the ground in some places, rippling gently in the purple light. They turned bronze when the clouds veiled the solar disk.

My heavy breathing had finally steadied itself to a less painful rhythm and I could spend a little while watching this spectacle. As I progressed, was I going to witness all the stages of animal evolution from undifferentiated cells all the way to… to what? To what crowning achievement could this vast, senseless proliferation lead? To what beings is this dully shimmering road taking me? The ones who built it?

Wondering about the food that the creeping life inferred, I remembered the liquid that the ground soaked up. Maybe that was enough to sustain it. In that case, my fears were unfounded.

Maybe… but in the same case, what had become of Wens? I started off again, a little groggy and stumbling a little too.

I saw the break, the interruption in the distance. Torn between two opposing impulses I slowed down. Behind me the road led to the other horizon with seemingly no breaks—it would protect me unto infinity. Before me the land rose and the supple path disappeared at the top of the hill (where I might find a landscape less monotonous and more human). Unfortunately, the road cut off halfway between me and the summit. It would be a problem if I had to face the same difficulties as before when I was out in the open.

I stopped and shielding my eyes with my hand I turned in a circle. I saw nothing but what I'd already seen. It was even impossible for me to spot where I'd woken up. Down there, the road almost reached the long, green strip of a cloud and the glare of the sun on all the little bumps made a blood-red pool beneath the green stain. I was more curious than ever and since my lungs were getting used to the warm, humid, vaguely sulfurous air, the dizziness I was feeling didn't hamper my will. I marched onward.

The closer I got to the danger zone, the smaller I felt, less and less bold. Brushes with danger on the human scale (like I was used to) called for a different kind of courage, a reasonable courage, so to speak, where your chances were equal to the enemy's despite betrayals and ambushes. Nothing of the sort here. I needed that spontaneous, reckless abandon, the blind zeal of a gambler. And I felt more alone than in an empty plaza of an evacuated city, more naked in my ridiculous, tailored earth clothes than if I were wearing a loincloth. Those jade clouds, the huge, pink sun in a lemon sky were rejecting me like the strangest of strangers. We had nothing in common and I was the intruder here.

At first the road swelled up in the middle, bulbous, shrinking on the sides. The bumps had melted into a shapeless mass where I thought I saw some kind of corrosive secretion.

While I was examining it apprehensively, the silence of the expanse was filled with the quiet slithering and flapping sounds of squeezed sponges. Looking up I saw that the ground a few feet away from me was being slowly covered with the same repulsive forms as I'd just escaped. A living traffic jam was forming in the empty space where the road ended, blocking my progress beyond the edge where I stood stationary like on the top of dam.

Anger bubbled up in me, which I nurtured silently. This was where I could hope to muster enough courage to accept a battle with this universe—drawing on all my aggressive impulses. At the same time and right at the edge of consciousness, I was thinking that the most powerful weapon of man was that very barbarity in which still crawled, those warrior instincts so hard to uproot.

And then, what stage of evolution could these lifeforms be at? Had they pass the amoebae of Earth in their hideously exaggerated size? I hadn't killed anything yet in the cruel world where I came from... but destroying these slimy lumps seemed less questionable than killing a human enemy... an eventuality that I had accepted.

Even still, I had to be able to do it. I slowly pulled out my automatic and aimed it at the closest creepy crawler.

Before pulling the trigger, I calmed my fury for a moment in order to evaluate the possible consequences of my actions. Above all, I couldn't forget that in this unknown world the vague similarity of appearances to my own did not necessarily correspond to likeness in nature. These giant amoebae, huge fragments of organized tissue, might be something else all together here than what I imagined. If there were, however, a strange population endowed with intelligence, the dangers I'd already faced would be nothing compared with the reactions to a real act of hostility. I would then become a kind of weird prey, dangerous and rare. My life wouldn't be worth a plug nickel.

I balked again... then my finger made the decision. A sudden flick of the index, an explosion muffled by the silencer still screwed onto the barrel... I squinted to see through the blue smoke that swirled before me...

CHAPTER IV

When the smoke dissipated, the sudden stillness of the things that were just throbbing at his feet startled him. The bullet had certainly only hit one of the protoplasmic lumps and I figured it would simply make a hole that would fill in right away.

In fact, starting from the middle—the impact—a kind of crystallization had instantly spread out. Now I was seeing a bunch of little triangles shimmering under the outer membranes, all pointing in the same direction—at me. I thought fast about the change in structure that certain shock waves can cause inside matter, but I didn't linger on it. I had to take advantage of the gunshot's strange reaction, which left me an open field to the other side of the road. A quick glance around told me I had no time to lose: coming from every direction heading to the point of attack were all shapes and sizes of those cells. On the side of the hill a more complex formation was taking shape. A strip of fibrous tissue was folding itself up into a kind of sack. The nameless thing was 20 to 25 feet long and squirming forward spasmodically. My throat tightened as I put a foot on the closest amoeba.

I sank knee-high into a fragile, crunchy matter like hailstones. The move shattered the fine crystals into tiny fragments that went flying off and showering back down like rain, covering the ground and the other cells with a glittering dust of green, gold and blood.

Surrounded by this multi-colored cloud, thicker with every step, I dashed across the danger zone. Through the iridescent dust I could see the heavy forms dragging themselves along, foot by foot, on their pale pseudopods. I breathed through my nose because I was afraid the crystalline dust might hurt my lungs until I got free of the cloud and with a sigh of relief stepped onto the other road. A few feet more and I could look behind me.

I'd done a lot of damage. The mass of crushed cells was being covered by a swarm of living cells whose contact liquified the crystal dust, dissipated it, absorbing into the membranes. The loathsome, crawling sack was doing systematic cleaning, but it didn't seem to be aware of my proximity. I just tried to shrug off my fear and disgust and I put the gun I was still holding back in my pocket.

What was the meaning of this instantaneous remodeling that caused crystallizations on contact? Oh, you could find similar effects in my universe, even in living tissue that is submitted to extreme cold. But what role did the bullet play? A kind of shock had effects on a molecular level? Or was it the presence of metal in the bullet? The important thing was that I glimpsed a future of constant battles in which I'd have to save my ammunition. But this too I put off thinking about until later. For, I'd been climbing up the hill and what I saw on the other side petrified me.

Picture the steep and lofty slopes of a huge crater whose floor is lower than the plain. And on this floor was the most astounding building you could imagine.

It reminded me of ruins but ruins that were carefully and expertly arranged, joined by shapeless architectural forms that pieced them together like an armature. It was like a roughly circular city more than half a mile in diameter, built by an alien first as ruins, then half-buried under a shapeless massive frame that was covered by black vegetation.

I stood there for a long time, fascinated by the weirdness of the ruins where the shimmering path led. The road ended again a short distance from what could be called a rampart—a pearly pink cliff with a jagged summit pierced in places by gaping holes where no light entered.

In the distance, on the other side of the "city", the circular edge of the crater was molten gray in the yellow sky with occasional glints of purple from some tiny metallic fragment.

The saffron sky loomed over all this silence with the green streaks of frozen clouds and made me deeply depressed. Once again, how could I have been so crazy as to jump into this nightmare that I couldn't escape?

A wind came and brushed my neck and with it the everlasting sounds of suction and crawling reached my ears. When I looked, I saw both sides of the road besieged by two compact columns of flabby things slowly heading my way, creeping over the outer slope of the crater. I was caught in the crossfire: 50 yards away the broken road was swarming with amoeba and down there at the bottom of the huge vat, the "city" awaited me in silence! It showed me its skeletal minarets and bloated gardens... behind those shadowy eyes that pierced the walls. For a moment I was afraid I'd lost my mind and I felt weak and trembling.

However, I managed to get hold of myself. Turning back was the least practical decision. On the other hand, the city seemed to offer more possibilities than the monotonous, perilous plain. I chose the city.

The gravity here seemed a little lighter than in my world, so the descent into the crater was relatively easy. I got pretty quickly to where the road disappeared for good without running into another plasmodium. My presence in this no man's land (I almost smiled at this expression more fitting than ever) seemed to raise no reaction. Was slimy fauna confined outside the excavation for particular reasons? Was it some kind of cattle? I wouldn't like being the cowboy of such a herd...

"Get angry, feed your anger," I told myself, "but don't forget to have a little laugh when you can. Two good methods of survival."

As I was stepping off the road onto the soft ground, my whole body went stiff. A loud scream had surged out of the city and flooded the space, echoing off the slopes, almost making the clouds retreat. A scream of 50 sirens with such human tones that my stomach leaped into my throat.

Instinctively I jumped back onto the road and stood still, sweating bullets, my hands plastered to my ears.

For a long time after the scream had died out, I heard the shrill echo in my brain. I was like an insect you blow away and I couldn't bring myself to move forward again. I was obeying the reflex of not moving that such insects have in the face of danger.

And yet, my thoughts were grinding away, grating and scraping but finding a little oil. It was, indeed, a city. An alarm must've been tripped when I left the road. Many cities on Earth were basically set up the same. But what really froze my blood was the hideously human sound of that mechanical cry. The cry of a mad giant.

I was pondering the petty adventure that had landed me in this warped universe and felt an ironic pity for those squabbles of ants that I'd been involved in. They faded away into the depths of a different time period that my own molecules had abandoned—my species vanished before my eyes like smoke in the wind. The smoke of humans whose memory left me painfully lonesome.

"Enough!" I said aloud. "Stop your whining!"

I straightened up and slowly took out my gun. Steadily but with my nerves on edge from the hellish howl that screamed out again, I stepped off the road.

It was a matter of habit. Once I got used to the noise, it was bearable. But it provoked another worry: such a hellish noise couldn't be for nothing. There had to be a reason and I was expecting at any moment to see something appear on the top of the rampart or in the surrounding plains… something that I instinctively imagined would be human-shaped.

Everything remained deserted and I stopped a few feet from the so-called rampart even though nothing blocked me. I looked up and examined it—not only the fact that it was jagged but it rose up in places more than 150 feet high while in other places it was barely 65. It was a very smooth wall on which the sun left traces of orange lines, especially near the sporadic dark openings. These openings looked menacing, like gaping mouths. Thinking of this comparison I realized that the screams seemed to be coming straight out of them as if they were the visible end of some huge, interior maze of organ pipes. I got closer. The screaming stopped. For a few seconds more I heard the distant echoes, then the landscape fell silent again.

Any second now something was going to jump out. I was sure and after everything I'd experienced, I had to really struggle not to turn tail and run. I found myself pointing my gun at one of the openings...

But nothing happened. The plain stayed empty and silent. Still on alert I started off along the wall. If there were living beings in this city, even a little more evolved than the shapeless lumps I'd seen so far, maybe I'd be lucky enough to communicate with them and get some information about Wens. I didn't even think about how—common sense advised against it.

The same idea passed through my mind again: whoever was living behind this wall must've built the road, which meant they had rather advanced technology speaking in relatively human terms... and at the same time I had to admit that war, in these terms, was a pretty common excuse for an encounter.

"Bah!" I mumbled, "Don't give up hope."

I was talking to myself more and more often. The deep sense of loneliness? My thoughts were jumping all over the place. Why didn't the road lead directly to a gate or doorway or something like that?

While I was looking at the ground in search of some tracks, I saw a ribbon... of white fabric with a pearly button on one end and a buttonhole on the other.

160

CHAPTER V

I bent over and picked it up. I didn't need to scrutinize it to see that it was a belt… from a lab coat… a woman's because of the light and thin nylon. My heartbeat suddenly changed rhythm.

One of the two women had been here. Dead or alive, alone or captured by one the creatures of this world, one of those I was hoping to meet if I couldn't find Wens. Hadn't he been here first at the ramparts and found the belt and picked it up? Who did it belong to? Margareta or the assistant?

The thought of the two women being dragged along this incomprehensible structure filled me with anger and pity. I realized then that I still had human feelings in me and I was glad. But I didn't come here to admire my indignation. I ran along the wall searching for an opening that I could reach. When I couldn't find one, I stopped and examined the wall again. I slapped it with my hand, scratched it with my fingernail and stood puzzled for a moment. I recognized the feeling, the tactile sensation when you take…

I stepped back, shook my head in disbelief, stared at the wall and its gaping cavities, its jagged crests…

The contact—*it felt like bone*. The entire wall was a giant, bony assemblage.

This observation provoked a bunch of crazy, troubling images in my mind. The universe where I'd been stranded had far too many points in common with mine, but these points of comparison were all mixed up.

And with this thought came the realization that the world I came from was not necessarily the best organized in and of itself. I was using false logic by giving it pride of place. And if I did so, it was from anthropomorphism—my native land seemed well made because I was used to it. This other universe was obviously not surprising to the inhabitants here, no more than I'd be surprised by mine.

Basically, what struck me most was the number of similar elements in the two worlds, more than what I imagined as an arbitrary, absurd arrangement. But whatever the direction of Time or the curve of Space, the arrangement of objects and the form of beings obviously correspond to some general scheme of things, valid in all worlds.

I quieted these random musings when I saw that they were doing nothing but sapping my energy. One observation remained true: the rampart resembled bone. The memory of the huge cells that I'd met only reinforced the probability. For, bone is a compound substance where you can find living cells stuck in organic-mineral matter that they secrete. The coherence of this world was being affirmed rather than denied.

As I stepped close to the wall again, something soft hit me on the shoulders from behind.

When I cried out, the city answered with its howling, which cut off abruptly. I forced myself to turn around clumsily while raising my hand armed with the gun when a kind of pulsating strap stuck to my hip. All I could do was fall against the wall. I think my disgust was stronger than the paralyzing fear that seized me at the moment.

But after I started thrashing about a bit and I happened to look up, my eyes almost popped out of my head when I saw what was coming along the wall.

I was obviously something akin to what had attacked me and I felt even more horror and disgust. More cells—in the shape of long spindles with both ends tipped with what looked like whips. The spindle bodies were more than three feet long and less than a foot at the widest point. The whips were just as long and they were all crawling along the wall with squishy sounds, repulsive to the ear.

I spotted at least ten of these reptilian things before three of them dropped on me with their whole body. Then I was bound by the rubbery straps and lifted off the ground. The

162

species of giant protozoa was dragging me slowly up the wall. Then I fainted twice and when I finally regained full consciousness, I was hanging 100 feet up, so completely at the mercy of the disgusting things that I didn't struggle against them. Being in such a vulnerable position, it'd be more dangerous for me to snap one of the straps that bound me than to let them carry me off to an unknown destination.

A few feet above me yawned one of the dark holes I'd seen from the foot of the wall. I knew that if I wasn't dropped, I was soon going to find out what was hiding behind the bony ramparts. Maybe now I could free my hand and use my gun. Could I go on unimpeded to accomplish my mission?

Squeezed between my chest and bent arm the white nylon belt was swaying with my involuntary movements.

The saffron sky overhead was darkening. The green clouds were covering the blood-red sun and a bitter cold wind stinking of sulfur started whistling into the dark opening I was next to. With twenty other lashes helping, I was tossed in and rolled over rough ground.

The rain came down outside, dripping onto edge of the hole. It sizzled and steam rose up in the shadows of the cave-like space in the side of the wall.

As my bindings were quickly released, the whips slid over my body and disappeared. Looking into the back of the dark tunnel I watched them withdraw, then the cells vanished. Still shook up by the sudden attack followed by my aerial kidnapping, I figured the retreat was due to the rain whose drops were blowing into the cave… corrosive, boiling drops if the steam from their contact meant anything.

Then I noticed that I was just out of range, despite the wind. The bi-pole cells had dragged me far enough inside the hole. Were they following orders? Had they been commanded to let me go free in order to move freely inside the citadel?

A chaotic uproar proved me wrong. In the back of the tunnel I saw new attackers and I crawled toward the light to escape them, staying out of the rain, however. And yet, as they got closer I wondered if was going to have to fall out of the opening and crash onto the ground far below.

From the look of them they were more single-celled organisms, but these looked more repugnant than any I'd fought against so far. They were roughly spherical and covered with long cilia that made them look like huge, squishy sea urchins. They moved slowly, wriggling all their cilia like unformed insects with countless antenna.

While I was hesitating to jump, they reached me, surrounded me, pushed me with their cilia and forced me back into the darkness. Every touch of their cilia caused a little burn, even through my clothes. Since my life didn't seem to be in danger, I decided against using my gun and I started walking, but I kept looking back at the light.

The ground sloped down pretty sharply. I'd examined the openings from the outside and had concluded rather hastily that they were a kind of window and that you wouldn't follow a path longer than the thickness of the wall before ending up in courtyards, gardens or directly inside houses built against the wall inside the city.

In fact, they were the mouths of dark tunnels that were unexpectedly long and not only reached the ground but went deeper. This city had nothing in common with the idea I'd come up with. Nevertheless, I pursued my blind way, spurred on, if ever I balked, by repeated burns.

The deeper I went down the damned passage, the harder it was for me to convince myself that I would ever get out. The blistering nudges did nothing to encourage hope.

Soon, however, a dim, reddish glow revealed the shape of the hairy spheres around me. A few feet more and I came out into a huge oval room whose walls emitted a bright red phosphorescence. The group of living spheres scattered all over the place before I had the chance to see where they went. I turned around and saw no trace of the tunnel I'd come out of. A triple curtain was sealing it off and within seconds it blended in completely with the wall.

I went to the wall and stretched out a trembling hand. No doubt about it, the curtain sealing off the tunnel was *living tissue*... I recognized the big polygonal cells and my fingers felt a warm, elastic surface with almost imperceptible movements.

Shut off, I turned around and looked at the ground, the walls... Nowhere did the room look like anything but tissue. I had to admit it and the idea made my head spin—the city... was not a city but a living being. I had stumbled into the guts of an astounding animal that screamed when something approached it and compensated for its natural immobility by dispatching different kinds of cells. The walls were the skeleton or carapace. Their bony structure had indeed worried me, but I didn't have the courage at the time to follow through to the necessary conclusion.

With a lump in my throat I turned around every which way. What was this "Leviathan bound" going to do with me?

From the time I'd entered the huge cavity, the light from the walls had clearly gotten brighter, as if my presence had tripped some kind of mechanism in the heart of the living city to produce more light... something like the freeing of electrical discharges after a modification of membrane potentials? Would these electrical changes produce particular enzymes like the luciferase in glow-worms on my home planet?

But whatever process the thing was following, it couldn't be without a definite purpose. For light like this to develop inside a biological cavity it was probably a stage, a cause and effect in some kind of chain reaction. I was afraid of being the object of both, the starting and finishing point. I became terribly anxious thinking about the secretion of gastric juices to process food. What effect on my body was this light going to have? It seemed particularly full of the longest wavelengths... infrared and ultraviolet, meaning the most harmful.

The more I thought about it the more convinced I was that the radiation was part of some kind of digestion. If it was, my trip was over and I wouldn't have the pleasure of meeting the other travelers.

I revolted against this absurdity and stormed back to the wall I'd entered through. Using my feet and knees and shoulders I tried to tear through the curtain. The big polygonal cells were soft but rubbery and they resisted.

All around me the light got brighter. I had to get out right away if I didn't want to get burned by the damaging waves. I decided to use the last resort: I pulled out my gun and fired at the wall.

Despite the silencer the shot made an infernal racket in the living cave. When the smoke cleared, I felt victorious on seeing the same results on the surface of the wall as I'd got outside on the broken road. I stepped up and pulverized the layer of cells into crystalline dust.

But behind the layer a bony, pale ivory plate had formed. I stared stupidly at the tiny hole the bullet had made in it.

There was no way for me to destroy this new obstacle. It must've been very thick and all my strength was useless against it. I had to face the inside of my prison and watch out for the first signs of radiation damage on my skin and limbs.

Without paying too much attention, I saw some weird forms slowly emerge in the blood-red glow as it got stronger. Their stillness surprised me. I moved away from the wall and walked over the spongy "floor".

I remembered that although ultraviolet light doesn't burn instantly, I should have immediately felt the heat from the infrared. But I still felt nothing. I had hope: just like a normal stomach protects its lining against the ravaging power of its juices, so the cells carpeting the inner surface of the cavity shouldn't suffer damage from the radiation. Maybe my body was protected in the same way? Or else the radiation had nothing in common with the rays I was familiar with.

This particular worry took a backseat for the time being. I was focusing on the scattered forms I saw more distinctly. I went closer until I was standing in front of a metallic shape whose sharp angles caught the purple light. I walked around the huge thing and became sure that it was from some kind man-made machine. A mechanism made by intelligent beings, a complex instrument that had been liquified into shapelessness and thus impossible to identify.

Right or wrong, I felt less in danger, which cleared my mind enough to examine the curious sight around me. I left the metallic remains and went over to a faintly shiny patch a few feet away. I leaned over and easily recognized the honeycomb structure I'd seen in the road outside. The patch, moreover, was patterned enough to match it to the road. It was a strip with two parallel edges and toothed ends. I'd bet 10-to-1 that this was an actual piece of the road.

This made me think: did the road lead into the bowels of the city and had it somehow crumbled? Or had the moving cells dragged the piece in here? I suddenly felt hostility toward the city, an obviously inexplicable hostility.

But another shape caught my eye, an oblong thing sitting in an alcove in the wall. An unaccountable feeling of disgust first held me back, but when I overcame it and got closer I saw that it was eerily similar to a human form. I remembered Iris and Margareta. I stepped up to it fearing I'd guessed right...

I recoiled. It was not a human being. At least not completely... for two reasons. First of all, the general shape was human but it had undergone modifications—nothing to do with putrefaction—that made me think otherwise. Secondly, what was still identifiable was an arm ending in a hand... *a hand with six fingers, specifically two thumbs.*

The sight fascinated me for a long while. It was a hand and not an animal paw. But I'd never seen anything as weird as those four fingers of equal length framed by two symmetrically opposable thumbs.

The rest of the body had undergone a simplification that could've made it anything. Despite all my efforts, I couldn't come up with even a wild guess at the kind of being whose remains I was staring at. But there was no doubt that such a

167

distinct hand couldn't belong to the branched cylinder that barely had a head.

I finally left the corpse in its tomb since I could learn nothing more from it. After such an experience I had to check my body again for effects of the radiation that probably killed the two-thumbed creature. But despite being a stranger to this universe, I seemed to be safe.

I was like a sleep-walker now, roaming around in the blazing glow through the wreckage scattered on the floor... a floor paved with pentagonal cells whose membranes were so resilient that it felt like walking on flagstones. Other machines were sitting in the middle of the stomach-cave and some of them still looked very complex. I also found other fragments of the road and two more corpses. One of them was pretty much just a lump but the other still had a recognizable head... a head like a man with huge eyes and a very pronounced skull. I was struck by the resemblance and took a little comfort: if there were humanoid corpses here, then there should be living beings on the outside. Even though I was learning about it in these macabre conditions, the presence here of a race so close to mine lightened a little the burden oppressing my mind.

But hadn't this race fallen prey to the monstrous city? I saw horrific images of peaceful villages being invaded by giant cells and depopulated in seconds. I saw captives being carried away into this deadly cave where I was imprisoned, slowly killed by radiation and absorbed into the living thing. These images shook me out of my apathy and I suddenly forgot all about the contents of the cave so I could concentrate on my escape.

Nowhere had I seen a trace of the two women. But finding the belt made me think that they'd been captured like me. Which meant that they'd been here shortly before me. So, there was an exit they'd used—or else they'd forced their way out.

Walking along the walls I was hoping that my reasoning wasn't false and that the two women had really been captured,

168

otherwise nothing justified my hope for an exit. I suspected that the cellular wall was completely reinforced by a bony skeleton resistant to bullets. If this skeleton had any chink in it, I had to find it. But how could I know where it was hidden behind the layer of cells?

Just when I was asking myself this, I jumped back to avoid a hole that yawned open before me. Since I was examining both the floor and the walls, I could swear that it hadn't been there before. It seemed to have been dug out in seconds and yet the inside of it and the edges looked exactly the same as the floor whose mosaic was unchanged.

In truth, the hole was vertical at first but quickly opened up onto the bowels (this word came by itself into my mind but it was no less displeasing), a narrow, elliptical passageway that led to who knew what other strange viscera.

I had no choice. I slipped inside.

Here again the walls were luminescent, but dimmer and a greenish yellow hue. Maybe this new light had a precise function… maybe it was just the normal action of the cells… metabolic waste.

The atmosphere, too, had changed. The faint odor of sulfur, which had given me coughing fits, faded away as the oxygen level increased—the air seemed more invigorating. I was taking full breaths and feeling so euphoric that I wondered, deep down inside, if it wasn't due to some narcotic gas instead of oxygen.

Whatever it was, I pictured the future with unbound confidence. The rescue of the women seemed practically accomplished. I'd find Wens and the four of us would head happily back home. How? I didn't let the useless thought stop me. All that counted was success and it was virtually a done deal. In this weird state of bliss, I hurried down the tunnel, scrambling down the steep slope.

There was a bend and I came out suddenly into a space that threw me so off-balance that my excitement just evaporated. I was in another room, as far as I could tell, a room completely divided up by transparent formations pierced with holes, hollow columns, tufted stalactites and stalagmites sharp as needles. I squinted in the green half-light and felt my pulse racing. From the back of this maze I heard a weak moan.

CHAPTER VI

I summoned up again the optimism and need for action that had just been spurring me on. I was right, I was prevailing. The two women had survived like me and I was going to get them out of this. I would shout out my triumph and strut around gleefully. This air of unknown composition was influencing my brain and making me crazy. I noticed it vaguely just then, but I could do nothing to control myself.

Why was one of the prisoners moaning? She must be hurt, otherwise she wouldn't be acting so pitifully. I marched into the open space and went through the first opening into another. As I went around a column I passed through another opening and like that I followed the green glow emanating from the transparent walls, guiding me to the moans that got louder and softer.

The farther I went in the absurd place, which reminded me of attractions at some county fairs, my enthusiasm and confidence faded away. In short time I was reasonable again, only to feel scared. Had I just had a fit of madness? I had a clear image of chemicals suspended in the air and I figured that the openings in the obstacles acted as a kind of filter on which the suspected substance got stuck or destroyed or diluted—useful here but harmful out there. This carnival setup must act like a purifying organ, a kind of kidney. And I knew why the two women weren't feeling the bliss I'd just experienced.

I was about to shout out to tell them that I was coming, to give them courage and get a response to guide me to them, but something ridiculous stopped me... Was I going to call out, "Madame Petrowics?" That sounded so ludicrous in this situation that I couldn't bring myself to say it. And my inbred manners kept me from yelling out "Margareta". I shrugged, annoyed, and found a simple, embarrassingly stupid solution to the problem

I shouted, "Iris! Where are you?"

There was a brief silence, then almost a shriek of joy. "Here! Over here! God bless!"

I was obviously expecting a "Here", which didn't help me at all. But the sound of the voice was enough. A flood of words, with plenty of German, was coming through the staggered openings. The voice sounded young and fresh despite the occasional sobs amidst the laughs. Iris—whom I was itching to finally see—sounded on the verge of a nervous breakdown. I wasn't surprised. Her mind might very well not stand the strain of such an adventure. Hastening to reach her I slammed into a column that warped and then went still again. For a second I was afraid I'd see it transform into an army of giant protozoa. But the city didn't seem to have such an advanced level of metamorphosis so I could breathe easily.

"Are you alone?" I yelled as I wound my way through the crooked gaps.

"No," the still distant voice answered. "I'm with your…" She stopped short, then with surprise, "But you're not the professor."

"No, but he's also in this… infernal land."

Silence, then, "It's Mrs. Wens… who's with me. She's fainted."

Mrs. Wens! How weird. I guess she couldn't think of the right term in French. She must be Swiss German, her accent proved it.

"I was surprised that you called for me first…"

Vanity will out, even in this cadaverous light.

One more partition and then I saw them.

I saw only two white shapes, one standing over another that was lying motionless. I didn't see the shapes clearly because one last partition pierced with many holes was separating me from them. I was in front of it in a heartbeat. A hand reached out and grabbed mine frantically while the laughter and tears intensified. Through one hole I saw Iris' face. Even in the unfavorable green light I could see that she was not un-attractive—with her you don't think about beauty but about seduction. As for Greta, I couldn't see her face.

"I'm Kenneth Broad and I'm American," I introduced myself formally.

At that moment I thought it really clever to act like we were in a salon. But I didn't see the use in giving a fake name. The mission that had brought me this far meant nothing any-more.

Iris quieted down but laughed again. I'd never seen any-one look happier.

"Me, I'm Iris Hagenshtall, Swiss," she responded. She pointed to the shape on the ground, "Margareta Petrowics. She's alive but... completely passed out from the start," she added gravely.

The start, meaning since she crossed the chronon barrier. A blackout lasting so long was cause for worry. Long? How long? How could we tell?

"We're prisoners," Iris said. "Be careful, these things build themselves faster than you can imagine."

I glanced behind me. She was right. Buds were sprouting around me in a half-circle about six feet in diameter. For the first time I noticed how small was the space where Iris was standing. Margareta's body measured the limits. Plus, no opening was big enough to even put your head through. The city had put them in a cage and looked like it was doing the same to me. We were indigestible foreign bodies, so it was turning us into cysts.

"I see. But I'm not waiting for..."

I cut myself off, grabbed the edge of my big peephole and started rattling the wall. It shook but didn't break.

"Oh, it's very solid," Iris remarked. "It's like bone."

"No," I shook harder, "just... cartilage... and full of cells... you can see them through... the hard substance."

"Maybe," Iris admitted, "but what does it matter?"

I stopped wasting my energy. "We'll see." I pulled out my gun. "Stand as far back as you can from this wall."

I was putting all hope in the weapon. Though deadly for cells a bullet was useless against bone. But this intermediary tissue? Maybe it could destroy it...

"Watch out," I repeated as I stepped back and took aim so that I would avoid hitting the very ones I was trying to liberate.

The cartilage buds were growing so fast around me that I was already walled in up to my thighs. Iris moved Greta's body out of the line of fire.

"I was carrying her but I passed out myself. When I woke up we were in this prison..."

She huddled up against the opposite wall right before I fired.

It was the third shot since I'd got there. So, I had 21 left (five in the gun plus two extra clips) and I suddenly felt the terrible need to be sparing.

The effect was different from what I'd seen so far. The cartilage acted like glass. The bullet pierced it and cracks fanned out from the hole. I banged it with the butt of the gun and it shattered. Iris shouted with joy as I climbed through the jagged slit.

Iris threw herself into my arms like I was the great love of her life. And she almost trampled Margareta while doing so.

I said, "We'll have plenty of time to gush later. Let's get your friend out of this prison cell and far away before it builds another one around us. I don't have enough bullets to destroy the whole damn jungle here."

"It's lucky you were armed," Iris replied. "Are you from Chicago?" she added with a sidelong glance.

"No, my job requires... required...it doesn't matter. Let's get out of here."

I lifted Margareta and threw her over my shoulder, cursing the reputation that Hollywood's made of Americans. Iris followed me and we went through the new wall that was almost as tall as us. Beyond that, I dove into the cartilage jungle but went around the other side of the broken prison cell, not the way I'd come, in order to avoid the cave.

Margareta's position made blood flow into her head and she moaned. I lay her on the ground in an empty space and sped up her recovery by slapping her. Iris knelt beside her and called her name. I made a quick comparison of the two faces, the different hair, and I opted for Iris, the blonde with prominent cheekbones and a pointed chin instead of Greta, the brunette with even, regular features. Besides, I was bringing Greta back to her husband…

But Iris who had welcomed me as her savior…

Greta also spoke French but with a stronger accent than Iris. I tried using English but they both maimed it so badly that conversation became torture. Because I had to answer their deluge of questions. I cut them off when Margareta was on her feet and reminded them that we had to get out of there. They were so frightened by the place that they'd given up hope of finding an exit.

The maze of glowing walls was endless. I was afraid we were going around in circles until we came into a new empty space that narrowed into a corridor. I decided to take it, wherever it might lead, and they followed behind me docilely. Before heading down it, I glanced at my wrist. My watch had stopped. But was a watch any use in measuring the hours of July 32 and the impossible days after such a date? Why not, after all? My heart and other organs were still working… In any case, many hours must've passed since I awoke in this universe, hours corresponding to my physical Time, real hours.

Iris and Greta went with me down the tunnel while talking excitedly—the fear of another encounter with other dangerous cells was temporarily fading away.

I, however, was wary of a different peril: even though the light in the corridor was dimmer than in the maze, I could

175

make out the muscular elements shaped like elongated fibers. There was surely another layer behind what I was seeing, a circular layer able to *contract* the duct and shrink its diameter until we could no longer go forward or back. At worst, I saw us half-suffocated, forcing our way through the muscular actions like pieces of swallowed bread. Such a fate belittled the idea I had of man and woman.

But nothing happened. I'd obviously deluded myself with the crude analogy. But thinking of the pieces of bread, I was surprised that I wasn't feeling the least bit hungry or thirsty. I mentioned this to my companions and they, too, were amazed.

"It's very possible," Margareta said, "that the air is charged with molecules that are absorbed directly…"

Thinking about it I had to admit that it was possible. The air came from the outside, but it obviously went through the cave where I'd been brought in. That cave where bodies and other things slowly evaporated in the strange radiation. We might've been washed in a nutritive spray with molecules so diffused that they passed directly into the blood through the walls of the pulmonary alveoli.

"Living on thin air, as they say, in every sense of term," I ended up saying.

They both laughed politely, but nervously.

Of course, the first thing Margareta had questioned me about was Wens. On learning how he had deliberately jumped through the chronon field to follow them, she couldn't hold back the tears. Tears full of joy and a great deal of anxiety. Wens had really put a spell on her. She thought of nothing but him.

As for Iris, she seemed very impressed by my own departure. I was starting to think she wasn't completely neutral to me. It must be said that I did come in like the Messiah.

An accident had cast them both out of our world. Greta had carelessly got too close to the generator screen and had been sucked in, so to speak. She'd tried to jump back and had inadvertently touched Iris' arm. The assistant had been swept away by the same uncontrollable force. I figured Wens' fainting when I got there had come from some desperate attempt of his, which hadn't affected the energy feed.

Iris had woken up far from the road and was terrified and disgusted by the giant protozoa surrounding her. But the huge cells had not threatened her life. They just kept her from moving until a big swathe of tissue wrapped her up for delivery—along with Margareta—into the walls of the city. Greta had never woken up and Iris envied her ignorance of the hideous voyage.

It was only when they were in the glowing cave that Iris had dragged her into the cartilage filters that had caged them like invasive foreign bodies. They'd been there a long time, according to Iris, until the sound of my voice came "like an angel into hell". She had no idea who she was talking to, otherwise she'd have changed her tune…

The tunnel had many forks and by instinct we kept taking the biggest one.

Iris understood the reason for this, "It's like we're in some huge vascular system and we're heading for the heart."

This was a revelation to me. The city was just a gigantic animal in the shape of a habitation. What weird mimicry had guided its development? These branching tunnels were, in effect, its blood stream that transported oxygen and nutrition in the form of gas instead of liquid. The hypothesis seemed so likely to me now that I took it for granted. And with this in mind, the progressively wider tunnels meant that we were going to run into some enormous muscular pump. We could definitely feel a constant air current flowing the same direction as us and something had to be causing it. It couldn't have been a difference in temperature with the outside—it was just as warm inside. I just wondered what dangerous organ we were going to face before finally getting to the surface, in one way or another, of this monstrous body.

As we entered a tunnel that was almost 15 feet in diameter, Margareta shushed us.

"Listen," she whispered. "Hear it?"

We stopped. From the dark depths came a muffled but constant noise like a waterfall. I was suddenly scared that I'd misinterpreted the role of these tunnels. What if they were periodically flooded with liquid? We'd be drowned without any means of escape.

But the sound didn't get louder. It got closer only when we started forward again. Then the "ground" rose up, getting so steep so that we had to hold onto each other to keep from tumbling backward.

The new cavity we reached was much smaller than the big cave, but there was something so marvelous that we were speechless. A fluorescent liquid curtain was falling from the ceiling and rushing into a trench separating the room into two parts. The cells covering the walls glowed the same color as the rest of the circulatory system but this light reflected off the liquid curtain with a purple or reddish light like in the big cave, though much brighter. I saw gas bubbles being generated in droves by the liquid and wondered what it was for.

Then Iris shouted, "Look! The heart!"

At the same time I understood that this weird organ was, indeed, the heart. How? It was simple: the circulation of gas could be produced by a muscular pump if it was based on the principle of a water or mercury pump. A jet of liquid constantly generating gas molecules, which causes a suction effect in the living ducts, maintaining a continual depression in the cave, filled by the draft from outside. The big cave, therefore, was communicating with the atmosphere through the openings I'd spotted.

The cycle was obviously closed beyond the waterfall around capillaries that got tighter and tighter, some of which must have been encircling the cave with a nutritive network to be constantly feeding the ever-moving air…

"Basically," I said, "we explored the digestive system, the renal system and the cardiovascular system. Do you think there's a central nervous system? Nerves and sensory units?"

"Without a doubt," Margareta said uneasily.

She wrapped her lab coat more tightly around herself, which in this light looked prettier than a brocade dress, and explained:

"The free cells, which I haven't seen yet, are a little like independent locomotor units and maybe, in some way, the sensory units. I don't really see how a sensitive and motor nervous system is connected to free cells... but the absence of nerves doesn't necessarily mean there's no brain."

That was my opinion and Iris', too. But this discussion wasn't getting us any closer to an exit. The longer we remained prisoners of the Leviathan, the less likely we were to get free. Margareta stood still and silent, staring at the waterfall, almost hypnotized.

"This fluorescent cascade looks like the chronotron screen," she spoke as if to herself. "What happened to Wenceslas?"

I saw iridescent tears well up in her eyes and I couldn't let her give up hope, even if just in the interest of the group.

"If he was captured like us," I reminded her, "then we'd be here together at the same time. So, he must've landed somewhere else, out of reach of the city. I'll go even further: Iris obviously saw the humanoid remains in the big cave..."

"I did," she admitted. "But I can't say I got up close to them."

"Well, why couldn't Wens have got in contact with these other forms of life while we've been flirting with disaster?"

"Who says those humanoids are peaceful?" Greta asked.

I could find no satisfactory response.

We were at a dead-end. As expected from how the weird heart worked, the only way out was either to retrace our steps or to follow the liquid. I went over and bravely put my hand into the luminous waterfall. My bravery was due mainly to the presence of the two women behind me. The liquid felt like blood: warm and a little thick and sticky. All in all, unpleasant. But not harmful. I inspected the crack it poured into. It was wide enough for a person, but I could see nothing else underneath the frothy turbulence. And yet, given how much stream there was, there must've been a passage if the cascade served any real purpose because the air had to be constantly circulating to other parts for the organ to react to anything.

"I'm going," I swung around to Iris and Greta who were watching me silently.

"Oh, no!" Iris cried out. "Don't leave us!"

I shook my head, "Listen, I'll give it to you straight. If nobody tries to get through, we have no choice but to stay here or go back… to the stomach-cave that has no exit. We have to keep moving toward…"

"And if you drown in the… the drool," Iris interrupted, "what will become of us?"

"Nothing better, nothing worse," I said.

She fidgeted, then approached me, sounding a little embarrassed, "I… I don't want you to risk your life…" And suddenly finding an explanation for her troubled thoughts, "You saved ours!"

"Precisely. In this situation I can't save us in one fell swoop. By helping you out already, I've taken on the responsibility of getting you out of here for good. Otherwise, I'll just give up."

She said nothing, so Greta spoke up, "Maybe we could find another way? Is it not possible to go directly through the walls of this chamber by using your weapon like you did before?"

"I don't think so," I answered. "I believe all this tissue around us is only covering patches of bone that bullets won't destroy. And I prefer not to waste my ammunition trying to find a weak spot."

They kept silent. I used the moment of confusion to slip over the edge of the crack, making sure to get a big lungful of air. I heard a double scream, which reached me over the roar of liquid in my ears, and I was swept away by the current.

It was brief. I was quickly lying on a spongy, porous floor that drank in the liquid as it fell. Apparently, it rose back up through the thick tissue by some rhythmic muscular contraction that I couldn't see or feel… or else it was permanently secreted into a sac located high enough up to give it the necessary kinetic energy and the porous tissue accordingly. These hypotheses flashed through my mind in seconds while I got to my feet.

Right away I was afraid the women wouldn't know what to do after my disappearance. I tried yelling over the sound of the waterfall:

"Iris! Margareta! Come down here! It's okay!"

They must've really hated being left alone because they obeyed in no time flat. Iris came first, coughing and spitting with disgust, followed by Margareta whose hair was lumped together like she'd taken a bath in oil.

I couldn't help laughing after the fall. Our clothes made us look like canned sardines.

"Luckily," Iris said, "we heard you. What would we have done if we hadn't?"

Greta looked around. We were in an oval cavity that opened onto a new tunnel.

Iris had taken off her lab coat and was wringing it out, screwing up her face. She was using it now like a bath towel, sponging off her face and hair, her arms and legs. A real towel would not have been much use and the wet nylon was even less so. Next she took off her stockings, with a little false modesty, and kicked off her high-heeled shoes. Greta did the same, sighing, but kept her white coat. I had a hard time not giggling.

But I kept my voice serious and said, "Now let's get moving."

After a few feet I had to comfort Greta who had just stopped and was crying quietly. I knew that as long as she hadn't found Wens, nothing would be OK and my consoling words were futile against her understandable distress. Iris needed all her willpower to back me up. She had clearly lost hope and her voice lacked conviction. However, somehow, personally, an unwarranted confidence buoyed me up and refused to accept the worst. We weren't hurt even though we'd landed here in a pretty sticky spot. Why would Wens be worse off? That's what I tried to explain and finish with the need, the obligation for us to escape the living prison. This tunnel had to lead somewhere…

The size of the artery was shrinking. If the *thing* we were trapped in had any relation to our own vascular system, we would soon reach the capillaries that we'd have to crawl through. I wasn't afraid of them getting too narrow for us because of the size of the cells, but what would happen if we hit a dead-end… or almost?

I was assailed by these crazy thoughts. I went so far as to think that we could block a passage and create a solid embolism in this gaseous circulation, thus causing a kind of heart attack that could neutralize part of the area that we could then finish off mechanically and open a passage through the tissue into the open air.

But that could take a long time and the area affected might be surrounded by healthy tissue. A new phenomenon made me forget these irrelevant plans: we were skirting around a huge sac that we could see inside like looking through a glass picture frame. We stopped, stupefied.

Inside the sac shone the same greenish yellow light but much brighter than everywhere else. The light bathed a swarm of free cells some of which detached from the top now and again. They were spawned from the top after growing big enough that some long filaments were visible in their lump of cytoplasm, filaments that were probably chromosomes on the same scale as…

We couldn't see the lower half of the sac, stuffed as it was with the cellular swarm in which we noticed all kinds of tissue threads, but the bottom must've opened like a giant funnel to drain the things onto the plain surrounding the crater...

"We've got to go through that," Greta shuddered.

"Hmm," I was hypnotized by the living mass. "We won't get through, even if all those jellyfish are harmless..." I shut my mouth and remembered the hairy, burning spheres. "Besides, there are some that are dangerous."

The idea of this path to salvation being blocked by thousands of monsters was discouraging. Giving up on attacking the reproductive reservoir, we were careful not to damage the transparent wall lest the things escape. I turned to the closest fork in the way and the two women followed me with relief.

The farther I went, the slower I walked.

"It feels like some power is repelling us," Iris spat out, answering my thoughts.

"Repulsion," Greta snarled.

The force worked in two ways: on the mind and on the muscles. I felt like I was walking through thicker and thicker air, which demanded more and more effort on my part. At the same time, I was fighting against the irresistible desire to give up, to stop and turn back. My companions felt exactly the same.

Straight in front of us the tunnel opened onto a hazy area emitting a *gray* light. Despite the invisible barrier hobbling us, I mustered all my strength. Maybe the exit was in there, protected by this prohibiting power.

It took enormous effort for me to go just a few feet. Greta and Iris dropped to the ground next to each other and struggled not to leave me alone. I was finally overpowered and fell against the curved wall, resisting the silent command to turn back.

The tunnel opened onto a space I could not tell how vast because of the intricate, interlocking web of cells stretching in every direction. Just seeing this dreadful mesh made my head hurt.

"…Head hurt…" I thought. "Head… brain… this is *the brain*. It's protected by a barrier of frequencies. Electromagnetic waves that are bio-physical, the same that control the free cells. It's the frequency emission from the brain that replaces the nervous system… no need to press on. Nothing to do but go back…"

But behind the dull pain that was pulsing in my temples, I felt like I was seeped in a kind of huge, organic consciousness. I felt, kinesthetically, the reality and the presence of the big stomach-cave, its life and the turmoil of its slightest biochemical reactions, the flux of its destructive light. Simultaneously, I felt the constant deposit of toxic molecules on the cartilage filter, the huge osmotic pressure in the secreting cells of the liquid shaft that circulated the nutritive air… and many other processes partaking of the unconscious life, frantic and silent, all jumbled together in the great central consciousness that had nailed me in place and whose flux was carrying along my own thoughts.

I also knew how to get out…

Impregnated with this knowledge, I surrendered to the repelling force and staggered back to the women. I didn't know to what extent the metabolism of the city's nervous system might be hijacking the energy reactions of my brain… the contents of the stomach-cave didn't seem to be replenished very often.

"I know the way," I stammered.

The women reacted weakly and struggled to get up as quickly as possible.

"I'm terribly tired," Iris explained.

I helped her with my hand around her waist, which felt nice, but only managed to exhaust more of my own energy.

"I get it," Greta muttered. "Maybe you've felt this… huge presence…"

"I have!" Iris said. "You were closer to the end of the vessel…"

"I was a few feet from the first layer of neurons," I said.

Iris turned to look at me, "The brain!"

I saw her little cat face framed by blond hair still soaked with the fluorescent liquid. She was such a strange beauty that I wondered for an instant if I was with the real Iris or some diabolical emissary of the city, fabricated just to entrap me. The idea was ridiculous and I had no trouble casting it off.

Then began the monotonous march through the tunnels. We didn't speak but kept focused on the hope of escaping this eternal twilight, these dry arteries, the silence that loomed more eerily since we felt the presence of life all around us. We stopped many times, not out of physical fatigue but because of a mental lethargy from the grim series of endless branches, the sickening curve of the maze-like tunnels or from the hypnotic path that never went straight. It was like we were in an interminable dream where time had lost all meaning, where there was no landmark to mark the distance or duration of the journey. Our organisms fed on substances that were totally absorbed—I was sure of it—so we acted like engines with an unlimited supply of gas. We must've been sweating out the waste from the combustion. Time passed, infinite, and we kept up the same rhythm without even thinking of measuring it.

Later, I would imagine we ventured on this blind and almost unconscious voyage without anything to do with it…

I walked confidently. The certitude of being on the right path never once abandoned me. The spatial sense of the invisible was once and for all settled in me like a sediment and I was convinced that I could rely on it henceforth—at least as long as I stayed within the limits of the city.

There were an infinite number of branches where I always chose the way without hesitating. One of them, however, was hard going because it was so steep. I started dreaming of ropes. Helping each other we managed to get over it. A few feet on and the tunnel widened like a musket barrel. We were in a huge cavity whose walls were made of long fibers.

"This is all muscle," Greta observed.

Iris suddenly pointed at the ceiling and cried out, "Look!"

We obeyed and my heart jumped in my chest: a crack of purple light stood out against the hazy yellow fluorescent. A narrow passage that let in the rays of the red sun—at last an exit.

CHAPTER VII

I had some idea where our path would lead us to get out. But what I didn't know was what the place meant, its role in the gigantic organism we were trying to escape from. Greta and Iris were even more in the dark than I was since they could never have entertained the idea.

I was examining the inside of the huge, pear-shaped cavern looking for little cracks or bony spikes we could use to climb when Greta stepped away and called out to us.

"Come here."

I went over, followed by Iris.

"What do you think this is?" Greta asked in s strange voice, pointing to an object embedded between two fibers.

I almost jumped back, "Don't you see?"

It took a few seconds for Iris to recognize it. She screwed up her face and said, "I've seen that before, I can't remember where…"

"In the big cave," I clarified. "Greta won't remember because you told me she was passed out."

Iris let out a little scream, then her voice choked out, "I kept my distance, but not enough to…"

She didn't finish. The object was a hand. A hand with six fingers, four of equal length between two symmetrical, opposable thumbs.

The silence was palpable. A humanoid had escaped the radiation cave and managed to reach this place, a stone's throw from freedom. I pictured his long and lonely trek through the maze of vessels, all his energy focused, like ours, on escape, denying death. Maybe he'd been accidently guided, like us, by the big brain lurking down in the patchy tissue. He'd probably seen the light of his sun, more beautiful for being unreachable.

Only his hand stuck out from the wall. He must've gotten into the lethal cavern, armed himself with a piece of metal torn off those deadly machines and run off haphazardly, dogged by terror. When he got here, desperate to haul himself up to the crack, he tore into the muscle fibers, tried to break through the wall, but the layer of tissue was too thick for his crude tool. It scabbed over, healed itself the farther in he got and he died of suffocation before he even got completely inside the thick muscles. His hand remained, calling out for help.

Iris had certainly pictured pretty much the same thing because I had to hold her up.

I described to Margareta what she'd missed in the big cave.

"I was hoping," she said, "that it was an animal paw, a bird claw that maybe flew through the crack up there and couldn't get out..." She broke off and glanced around, concluding, "A bad omen."

"What's that supposed to mean?" I was outraged. "You, a doctor, talking about omens!"

She didn't react and I judged it wise not to press her. Discouragement was gripping me again. It sapped my energy, even the need to speak. Once again we three, desperately fragile and completely powerless, surrendered to a dismal silence that none of us had the courage to break.

Finally, after an obvious effort, Iris spoke up, "We have to get out of here. For the first time we're lucky enough to be in a place leading directly outside. It's too stupid to stay locked up in here just staring at the exit."

Too stupid! I was thinking... nothing's too stupid. Absurdity knows no bounds. This wouldn't be the first time someone was killed on the morning of the peace treaty. But I kept this dark vision of things to myself. Since Greta had decided not to open her mouth, I forced myself to talk, almost cheerfully.

"Of course… This creature is not too resourceful. I'm sure that within half an hour we'll find a way that it hasn't imagined."

The idea of counting Time crossed my mind again. What did half an hour mean?

Iris seemed to read my mind because she repeated, "half an hour… 72 multiplied by 30… 2,160 heartbeats…"

Basically, that was the truth of it. We needed—as I'd vaguely felt—to focus on the physiological aspects. However, almost without thinking, I started winding up my watch. What would happen if the hands ticked off minutes containing barely five or six beats or, on the contrary, five or six thousand? But no, such an eventuality meant nothing: my watch and I were stuck in the same system of referents. Nevertheless, in spite of everything, there was a weird little twinge in my chest.

All went well. Time didn't cheat on Duration. Just as Wens had proposed, time and space were only functions of matter, meaning of energy. And since life is a circuit of energy, we had nothing to fear from the hazards strewn around this alien universe—at least up to the moment of our death and right now the problem would become meaningless. I'd barely concluded this comforting speculation when the rubbery floor started rippling under our feet while a low moan came out of the ceiling.

Iris and Greta started screaming in fear, but the movement stopped and the sound faded away. Finding our balance again, we stood frozen, glaring through the green shadows and the silence, glancing up at the high ceiling where the thin line we called Freedom was still shining.

A smile crossed my lips, "Do you know where we are?"

Almost before I finished, Iris jumped and cried out, "I've heard that! It's higher and louder here—the city's scream… we've entered the organ that makes it. a natural siren… alive."

"A larynx-lung," I commented. "That bright crack up there is edged with two membranes. Look at it. They're like brackets. They're giant vocal cords. The air is compressed here by the contraction of the muscular walls. And it produces a cry that I, too, have heard before. For it to sound so much like a human voice is probably because the larynx up there is crowned with cartilage formations like our nostrils. It's all so baffling. Not just that we're standing inside an anthropomorphic monster in spite of the inherent differences, but that it's here in a universe that's totally unhuman…"

"No," Greta broke in. "Not totally. Think about… that hand… those creatures you saw. If they look like us on the outside, why would their insides be so different? And why would this city be completely foreign if it belongs to the same universe?"

I had to accept her logic. In fact, I preferred it this way: we'd escape more easily from something that resembled us than from a being that was hopelessly alien.

Iris came up to me, grabbed my arm and suggested, "Can we make it scream?"

What had made me smile a few minutes before was precisely this idea. I replied, "I wonder if this sac would empty out all the air it contains. And if the walls would contract enough to push us up to the membranes…"

"We can always try," Greta said.

"There's something else. The contraction might very well crush us."

"Phooey," Iris snorted. "Should we just stay here forever?"

"My thought exactly," I agreed. "We just have to figure out how to make it scream. Every time I shot my gun, I heard nothing."

"Maybe," Iris said, "but that crack is open to the outside. That's probably why it's connected directly to the brain, more sensitive to an attack than the formations deep down inside where there's usually only harmless prey."

"Good," I approved by pulling out my gun.

I aimed carefully at one of the membranes.

The explosion was horrendous and I thought my eardrums had burst. But I didn't have time to check because I felt myself being lifted up into the air by a wild whirlwind of gas like a dead leaf in the wind. Upside down, limbs flailing, I was thrown to the ceiling and plastered against the very membrane I'd fired at while my ears were seared by the mad howl that I thought would shatter them for good this time. In a flash I saw a white shape slipping through the crack I could almost touch. Then another body smashed into my hip and made me groan in pain.

In my clumsy scrambling I tried to overcome the pressure that was crushing me against the muscles that had turned as hard as steel.

All of a sudden, swept up by a gust, I, too, rolled out between the membranes and was tossed like a ball against an obstacle that bounced me over to another, then another... where I passed out.

A sound droned somewhere. Like something rubbing together near my ear or an engine idling in the distance. Two possible interpretations of the same auditory sensation.

I opened my eyes and propped myself up on one elbow. But no, the second one made no sense since I was in a foreign universe, a universe without engines, without cars, without men.

My mind cleared in waves and reconstructed a consciousness that the pain in my muscles and bones had already started waking up. Beyond the transparent walls piled up like useless windows, night had come. A magnificent night where the green clouds were forming isles of phosphorus.

All the events that had happened before I passed out surged into my memory, as real as if I'd relived them, and the first name that came to mind was Iris. I struggled to my feet, broken everywhere. At first I thought my leg was fractured. Luckily, I could stand up, which was a great relief—how would I survive in this madness with a broken leg? I would've been like an old horse on the side of the road, waiting for a compassionate hand to put me out of my misery. And there would be no compassionate hand here.

I was a few feet from the rough orifice that looked out onto the exterior. The first images I'd recorded on regaining consciousness I'd seen through the transparent formations around me, closing off the maze with a ceiling that looked like a cartilage filter. I remembered the brutal shocks I'd suffered when the jet of compressed air shot me against the walls and almost at the same time what we'd said (who had said it?) about the nostrils and the human sound of the screaming...

But I wasn't interested in these details. What mattered now was finding Iris. Iris together with Margareta. I turned around and was shocked: in the back of the compartment, close by, lay a white shape. Certainly the same as I'd glimpsed before being thrown between the membranes. And my blood froze because I knew that *Iris had dropped her lab coat* after getting past the waterfall...

I had to help Greta, but I think I would've almost willingly left her there because I felt so disappointed that it was her. And this disappointment was so close to actual sorrow that I had to question my feelings. Had Iris captivated me so much? If so, I was in a real scrape, what with that weird mental disease called love... And yet, I had to admit it—there was physical evidence that didn't lie.

I went around an overhang that I almost ran into because it was hard to walk around in the semi-darkness with all those transparent walls. In fact, I was hoping that Iris had been tossed farther away, out of sight, or that she had got out through an exit I hadn't noticed yet. Was there an exit? With this transparent stuff, visible only by its internal ribbing, that varied the refraction index, with this stuff you couldn't bet on anything...

Greta woke up quickly and her first words were once again about Wens. Promptly, however, she was talking about her assistant, surprised that she wasn't there. I tried to reassure her along with myself:

"Oh, she's not far, I'm sure. We got caught in a real wind tunnel. I don't see how she could've stayed behind."

Greta stood up. Her left wrist hurt but otherwise she was fine. We went in search of Iris.

The windstorm had dropped us in a firm hollow, relatively small because we just had to get around three short walls before finding one of the jagged openings onto the outside, which I had seen on awakening.

Nowhere, alas, was any trace of Iris. I was only searching for her for peace of mind because the transparency of the walls allowed us to see wherever she might be. But I didn't want to take a chance and Greta felt the same. During the search we stopped for a few minutes by the double membrane whose edges were barely a foot and half apart. Truthfully, we were both lucky to be out of that ghastly sac. We cupped out hands around our mouths and yelled out Iris' name into the chasm where she'd probably stayed, but no answer came back to console us. I remembered the awful contraction of the muscles and I became terrified: maybe Iris had been crushed when the cavity closed up completely.

I had to shake off these dark thoughts and keep searching. Undoubtedly, she'd got outside before us, right?

We left the deserted place and slithered through one of the exits. We landed on rough ground in the middle of a jungle where shapeless ruins overrun with vegetation stood out against the phosphorous clouds.

Seen from the outside, the place we'd escaped from looked like a truncated pyramid, a small, almost crystalline building where we could see two overlapping images among the ribs and honeycombs. It was like a prism for the clouds and a mirrored horizon for the rest. The whole thing reminded me of a huge diamond hollowed out by dwarves for a hive to fit their size.

Greta was also staring at it and neither of us dared to speak. I knew that she was thinking of Wens. Had she guessed that I couldn't stop thinking of Iris?

"Is it always night here?" she asked.

"No," I said. "When I entered the city the sun was shining. A red sun in a yellow sky."

I'd barely finished the phrase when I noticed that the sky was purple, almost black, and studded with twinkling points of every color. This universe had stars, no doubt as far from each other as the ones in my universe. But no rocket ship would bring me through them back to my native solar system. I was farther from it than if 1,000 galaxies separated me. Somewhere else, in a different duration, another star field was flying around the vast whirlwind of Time. Eternity, too, was represented by an infinite circle "whose center was everywhere and circumference nowhere." We traveled a stranger path than that of Space.

"Do you think she got out before us?" Greta wondered.

A warm wind had kicked up while I was contemplating the heavens. My hair blew across my forehead, which made me think of Iris'. "I hope so."

I looked around. How could I let myself get lost in a reverie of the night—as phenomenal as it was—when Iris needed my help? I saw Greta's figure walking along a wall that stood a little distance away. In the phosphorous glow her white coat looked a little like ectoplasm.

"Search over there and I'll go around the pyramid," I shouted.

I took one step forward and froze. I'd just realized I'd lost my gun.

It was very serious. I suddenly felt like a child lost in a forest, a completely helpless child facing unknown dangers prowling all around him. I'd already seen how effective the shots had been and now I thought bitterly about trying to save ammunition. What ridiculous caution!

One of two things: either it was in the cavity or it was outside. If it was back where Iris was still stuck, she had a way to get out. And that was preferable.

Feeling a little better, I went back to the pyramid and walked around it. Instinctively I looked at the ground hoping to find my weapon and realized that the ground I was walking on was a little like thick skin. No surprise but it was creepy to recognize that once again I was an ant on an elephant's back. And no trace of Iris. It was unlikely that she would've gone off alone to explore this chaos without looking for us first. Plus, we were easy to spot with the see-through pyramid and the blast couldn't have shot her too far...

No, the gust of air hadn't lifted her out. She was still prisoner in the sac. I looked up at the pyramid, sure that my gun was still inside, and called out her name again. The same gloomy silence answered. Crestfallen, I went back to Greta who was still next to the wall. The closer I got the more familiar the wall seemed to me. And then I shuddered—it was not a wall but a huge *fingernail*, maybe 15-20 feet high, free-standing, alone, vertical, pointing up at the stars.

Greta turned her terrified face toward me and almost whispered, "I... I can't go any farther. Do you see this claw?"

She wasn't exaggerating. I saw the rest of the passage in a new light: spindly trees whose tops were tangled in an indescribable confusion were nothing else but *branching hair*. I had no idea what the little hills were but I had no desire to find out. To my left a rolling esplanade shined with an oily glimmer. It was a *tooth*. A tooth that must've measured 65 square feet. I felt like I was losing my mind.

And yet, what was so surprising in this new biological chaos? Didn't we pass through much more distinct, more complex organs whose dimensions were the same size? But I sympathized with Greta's jitters. In these exterior formations the resemblance was much closer to human anatomy. A resemblance that bordered on a nightmare, hard to take after the trials and tribulations we'd just been through. And the greenish glow from the clouds spread such a funereal atmosphere over everything that I felt like we were in a mass grave for giants.

"Come on," I made my voice stern, "there's nothing dangerous here. We'll have to…"

A muffled explosion interrupted me and the city's scream rose in the night.

I ran back to the pyramid but I was halted by the jet of air shooting out of it. I was blown back against a block like a leaf onto a rockface. The scream died down quickly, taking on a weird, distant, muted tone. I started forward again, fighting against the wind, but Greta reached the pyramid before me.

In the middle of it white tissue was already sealing over the crack and its membranes. A web of filaments was weaving together like a cocoon.

"Quickly!" I shouted, "Iris is there. The city's making a bony plate and she'll never be able to get out."

I tore into the filaments with desperate fury but it was getting thicker every second and I couldn't stop it with my bare hands. But this fossilization, this scarification was not just on the surface. It was filling in the space directly under the membranes. My efforts were in vain. Presently the matter being secreted was too hard and too compact for my fingers.

Another detonation exploded under our feet and a bullet flew out of the ossifying tissue, whistling by my head.

That was it. I fell back, hopeless, while Greta cried out Iris' name. No answer came back.

CHAPTER VIII

I lay prostrate for a long time, my mind drained, my will sapped, all initiative lost. I barely noticed Greta leaving and the light of dawn slowly illuminating the pyramid.

It was daytime when Margareta came to shake me out of my lethargy… if you could really call this crimson light day-time.

"I went pretty far," she said. "The… things are less scary than at night."

She avoided mentioning Iris. I was grateful for that even though I refused to give up all hope. I forced myself to answer with a monosyllable.

"I reached the edge," she added.

I had to say something, so I sighed, "What edge?"

"An edge. We're on a kind of uneven plateau covered in spots by that vegetation we saw. It's cut off by a sheer drop of almost 100 feet. I followed the edge and it rises up twice as high in some places and half the height in others. You can see the slopes and a line of hills.

"I know," I muttered.

All of a sudden I became aware of the stifling heat in the big crystal. I was sweating. For the first time I was hungry and thirsty—the air was no longer nutritive.

"I'm going back the way I came," I decided. "I'll find Iris and help her get out through another opening."

"I'm coming with you," Greta declared. "I don't intend to abandon her either. Besides, it's the best way to find food."

I couldn't deny the contradiction in our decision: going back into the city to help Iris get out (if she was still alive) knowing that the only way to survive was not to escape. But there was no other solution for the moment. What was most important was to be together again. Afterward we'd find a satisfactory arrangement.

While I was gathering all my forces to get to my feet, Margareta remarked that the color of the light was changing quickly—from purple to a kind of golden bronze that turned into a dark and moldy verdigris. I thought of an eclipse, but immediately rejected the idea because I'd noticed that this world had no moon.

It was impossible to see through the walls of the pyramid anything but a greenish curtain at the zenith. We left and one curious sight struck us.

Above our heads was spread a huge, dark green cloud whose nearness revealed a structure that was continually in motion, like the swirling vapors from smokestacks that blacken our Earth cities. Curls and currents constantly springing forth, indicating the presence of a chaotic wind, a silent cyclone limited to this portion of the sky over the city.

"That's weird," Margareta observed. "That cloud took shape really fast and right over our heads. There's not another anywhere in the sky."

"Sure there is," I responded. "Over there, that small one, but it's not the same color at all."

As I was finishing my sentence, blinding white lightning flashed through the bizarre cloud. Silent, perfectly straight lightning like a sword blade. I thought of the Angel of Judgment. Uncontrollable associations followed this thought: damnation, hell, fire and brimstone…

Greta started yelling in pain. I did the same a second later. Big drops of rain were pelting our hands and face. The rain was boiling hot or corrosive. We ran back to our shelter and stayed near the opening, panting and petrified. The ground in front of us was fuming.

I'd seen this phenomenon before when the cell strips tossed me through the bony wall. But I didn't have the chance then to really watch it. Now, under shelter and out of reach of giant protozoa, I could observe the ravages made by the corrosive shower.

Every spot touched by a drop fizzled and bubbled, then gave off a puff of smoke followed by bunch of steam. And the organic matter on the ground was corroded, hollowed out in seconds. The rain was so dense that few places escaped its scorching. I wiped my face with my right hand, then felt my left wrist, which had been hit by the first drops. It still stung but there was no blister. Being more vulnerable to this sinister rain than to the destructive radiation in the big cavern, we'd reacted quickly enough to the chemical catastrophe. The city's tissue was faring much worse than us.

Margareta looked up and said, "As long as our shelter holds up."

The substance of the pyramid had lost its transparency. The outside had already darkened, like glass in contact with hydrofluoric acid, but much faster. We heard the screaming from the outside.

The giant voice of the city scared me more than ever. It proved that the cavity where our poor Iris was still imprisoned was not the only organ of its kind that the city could use. But did the second "larynx-lung" exist before or was it newly formed after the first was blocked up? In such a case I feared the blockage would be followed by a total cave in of the cavity because it'd be immediately atrophied and so lose all its func-tionality. And thus Iris had to go back through the tunnels if they weren't already being cut off by the ultrafast secretion of bony plates like I'd seen happen twice already.

Gradually, the light lost its funereal hue and was back to its bloody tint. Neither of them was comforting but the second meant that the cloud was scattering.

Indeed, the rain was letting up too. It ended up stopping all together and we risked venturing out into the desolate land with ditches and bumps everywhere and dark patches cut out of the hairy forest. What Greta had called a "claw" was re-duced to a kind of spike in the aftermath of the selective de-struction of certain vertical zones.

We walked among the wounds towards the top of the rampart whose jagged edges we'd seen 100 yards away. The clear sky spurred us on and we reached the edge without need-ing to protect ourselves from any new dangers. But when our viewing angle was wide enough to give us an overview of the crater, we were petrified.

The slopes were covered with gleaming figures that were rushing down to the city. They moved silently and orderly and new phalanxes kept showing up on the ridges.

"Men!" I cried out in a fit of excitement. I was about to start jumping up, waving and shouting when Greta recalled me to my senses.

"They aren't men," she spoke calmly. "That *can't be a human army*... if it's an army."

I shut up. She was right, obviously. We were undoubtedly looking at the race whose specimen we'd seen inside the city. But these were very much alive and besieging us. So, there was a war between them and the city and we dropped in during full battle mode. Once again we were caught between a rock and a hard spot.

"Why would they be hostile to us?" I wondered aloud. "They're fighting against something that has nothing in common with them, whereas we look like them..."

"Humph!" Greta snorted. "Don't bet on it."

But I couldn't shake the joy I'd felt at seeing, for the first time in this monstrous land, living beings that I could recognize some affinity with the human race.

Nevertheless, I remained a little suspicious, which kept me from exposing myself stupidly. We were hidden well enough to see everything without being seen ourselves and the sight was worth it.

It certainly was an army. Every soldier came with a glittering breastplate over a tight-fitting outfit of undefinable color. We could see their rounded helmets with an extension on both sides of the face to protect their cheeks. They bore individual weapons that were completely unfamiliar to us.

When the first ranks were at the foot of the ramparts, we lost sight of them, but we heard hissing and a fog rose up to us—a yellowish fog that reeked of chlorine. They were attacking the city with gas jets that were obviously noxious to the walls.

We were about to retreat from the irritating clouds of gas when Greta yelled. She stood out in the open and pointed at the armed mob scrambling down the slopes. I saw, at the same time as her, the black and white figure she spotted. It was Wens.

Over the hissing of the gas compressors we started screaming together and thousands of helmeted heads turned toward us. A moment of hesitation. The attack let up. The hissing stopped. Nothing could be heard but the distant jets attacking other parts of the wall.

In the distance, Wens' voice was faint and unintelligible. I saw him running towards us, parting the cohorts. When he was close enough for us to understand what he was saying, we heard the name Greta, over and over again. There were sobs in his voice.

100 feet away from each other, we had a short, rambling conversation befuddled with joy. In our despair of not being able to reach each other, I got an idea.

"The trees," I said to Greta. "The hair is growing all the way to the edge of the wall. What if we use it to reach the ground? Some of it's no thicker than your wrist at the base. It could make excellent rope…"

She didn't hear the rest. She'd run off without responding. I followed her and we dove into one of the weird groves that stretched to the edge of the rampart. Choosing carefully, we settled on a kind of vine whose bulb was rooted very deeply in the ground but that didn't break when we yanked hard. Soon we had a firmly anchored rope whose length should have reached the foot of the wall.

They were watching us from below and when I tossed the line over the bony crests it caused an uproar. I dared to go first, hanging on the best I could to the smooth cord, then I slid down with my feet against the wall. I got to the ground without any trouble. Wens was waiting there, laughing and waving his arms wildly. We gave each other a quick greeting and Wens turned to watch nervously as Greta descended rather clumsily. However, there was no accident and we were finally reunited. Wens and Greta fell into each other's arms in front of the staring humanoids who had stopped their attack. They didn't show much emotion, just seemed to be waiting for Wens to notice their presence. In the distance could be heard hissing mixed with faint explosions and drawn-out wailing.

It was necessary to back away. Clouds of gas were being wafted by the wind directly into us and our lungs were putting up a fight. On the other hand, the soldiers around us were breathing freely.

When we had reached a spot where the air was more breathable and Wens and Greta were a little calmer from their reunion, Wens asked us what had happened to Iris. He was already worried about her absence but a quick explanation was enough to reassure him. Now we just had to know if she had a chance of survival and her fate, in my eyes, became a priority that had been pushed aside to save Greta.

I related our adventure in short order and confessed my fears. Our conversation was a chaos of questions and hypotheses rolling off the lips of each of us. Iris, however, was at the top of the list.

"For the month or more that we've been separated..." Wens said.

"A month?" I cut in.

"Well, a month on this planet, counting 30 revolutions around the sun..."

I was dumbfounded, "A month! We were imprisoned in the belly of the city for a month?"

"At least. I was able to learn some of the language of the Atols and I've already been on two futile raids with them."

I shook my head, "Listen, Wens, any conflict we had before landing here is in the past. We're humans in a strange world and nothing can come between us from now on. I think I can trust you completely just like you can trust me."

He shook my hand vigorously and in his Slavic accent, protracting the vowels and softening the Rs, he said, "You helped save Margareta. We're united like the fingers on a

202

hand. That's why we have to get Iris out that prison no matter what."

"I believe," I admitted, "that I'm even more attached to her than you."

He smiled and slapped me on the shoulder, "You see, we'll figure it out. She'll know how to hold on until we do."

At that moment, an Atol wearing an orange chest plate came up to Wens and said something in a strangely squeaky voice with snatches of abruptly metallic sounds. Wens answered him slowly and the Atol went away.

I was mystified, "How can you get your throat to make such sounds? I thought they only came out of cricket wings…"

"I worked at it, worked hard," he said modestly. "You know how gifted Slavs are at languages. A kind of intuition helps us reconnoiter the terrain while the map is on another level… as Korzybski would say. But I'll tell you everything when we're in a better situation. The Atols are a very evolved people."

It was hot. Wens took out of his pant pocket a dusty handkerchief and wiped his forehead. The Atols all around us had resumed their offensive. Over at the foot of the rampart the gas jets were cutting into the bony material, creating breaches that we could see were growing wider. The openings halfway up had sealed off long ago. The city was retreating into its carapace like a turtle in its shell.

"They won't get anywhere," I observed gravely.

Wens frowned, "They're trying a new tactic, but I, too, fear it won't have much of an effect."

"And those explosions?" Greta asked.

"I taught them how to make explosives," Wens sounded a little tense. "Yes, I know, I broke my rules, but what choice did I have? I'm their ally and it's a chance of unhoped for survival for all of us. Besides, this species of biological monster has nothing human about it… I mean except for its origin."

"Its origin?"

"Oh, yes," Wens said, "you have so much to learn. So, this huge living thing is the result of a physiology experiment gone out of control."

"The result of a…"

I was astonished and Greta's eyes were popping out of here head.

"Yes. What they're fighting is a kind of teratoma that grew around a lab and whose basic elements are nothing but the biological cells and organs of the biologists doing their research… the whole thing 100,000 times bigger."

This revelation left me speechless. So, all this was just the result of a laboratory accident… a little like our presence here. In short, an accident threw us into another accident on another world. The coincidence was daunting.

I contemplated the gigantic mistake that had evolved by itself, as far as it could, and I remembered the wreckage of machines in the big cave. Everything made sense.

"We know its insides," Greta said, trembling a little, probably from the thought of wandering around in the monster's organs.

"That will be very useful to us and the Atols," Wens replied. "They can't get rid of it and the Krall is threatening them with more and more aggressive cells every day."

"The Krall?"

"Yes. That's what they call it. It means something like 'the transplant' with an idea of mutation. Their biologists had built a very well-equipped lab and they were smart enough to build it far from their city like they do with all their labs. A road leads to the bottom of the crater. They were working on the stimulation of the processes of cell division and growth under the influence of certain kinds of radiation. One night all the buildings were covered with a bone-like formation issuing from the trays of serum where the giant osteoblasts were kept. The technicians were caught inside and apparently not killed but integrated into the uncontrolled proliferation that had started spontaneously. Their bodies were used as building blocks and the thing grew and grew, deformed, multiplied…"

"We saw... the Krall's brain," I muttered. "So, they're the neurons of those biologists who were the first elements..."

"Undoubtedly. That's what we have to get to and destroy. The growth of these misshapen bodies and the freeing of cells controlled from a distance is getting more and more adept. The day this thing becomes truly intelligent will be the day it takes over the planet."

"The Krall is *already* intelligent," Greta said with a shudder. "Its brain is buried deep inside the bulk of body and probably in the ground where the anatomical formations dug in like roots. You can't get to the brain because of the paralyzing frequencies. Just getting close nearly killed us. Monsieur Broad almost communicated with it..."

"Better to say I was probed to the depths of my being. That awful thing must've learned everything I know about earthly bodies. If it knows how to make use of this knowledge, we're in for a very tough time. And how are we going to help Iris under such conditions?"

I pushed this thought as far away as I could but it kept coming back and stinging me like a red-hot needle. I who had smiled the first time I saw her, hearing those cries of joy, holding her close to my chest when she hugged me! I had smiled at the idea that she treated me like I was the great love of her life... I wasn't smiling now. I was driven to despair on discovering that I needed her like I needed food or air.

"Don't lose hope," Wens said firmly. "We'll do whatever we must for her."

He looked so confident and so cheerful that I wondered what could possibly be putting him in such a good mood. Was it only the joy at being back with Margareta or was it seeing my interest in Iris was deflating his fear of seeing Greta interested in me? There were plenty of reasons for Wens to worry about me at my age... but no, he couldn't doubt Greta's feelings for him—they were obvious in all the affection she showed for him. Besides, I had displayed nothing but impartial courtesy toward her. The last thing we needed was a rivalry of this kind to make our exile unbearable...

We heard a raucous commotion in the distance and saw some Atols retreating. They had managed to break through the bony wall and the underlying tissue all the way to the vascular system that I knew quite well, whose branches could be seen through the breach. But the inter-tissue space was teeming with spherical cells and the flagella that were clumping together around the soldiers. Their weapons were flashing through the clouds of yellow gas and blowing up the cells.

The retreat was blocked by the officers in orange breastplates and transformed into a stampede into the depths of the Krall. Just then the gray ground, in different spots, started sprouting free cells that spread confusion through the ranks and split off the supporting forces. Withing minutes the wall began its scarring, which an explosive charge rapidly attached could not slow down. From then on, the flagella infiltrated the army on all sides and chaos reached its peak.

An officer ran up to us, shouting something at Wens.

Wens turned to us, "Quickly, let's get up to the crest. They're going to use the corrosive rain they used before the attack as an artillery preparation. They're not too vulnerable with their helmets and armor, but we'll be fried from head to toe."

We scrambled up the side of the crater while a group set up on the edge was aiming a massive instrument with four identical tubes at the sky. Presently, the tubes shot jets of green smoke that fanned out over the fighters.

The smoke took on shape, rolled and reeled, unfurled like sheets, just like I'd seen before the other attack. Along the crests other similar weapons were adding their own vapors until a white flash shot out horizontally from one crest to another. The searing rain started pouring down and we saw nothing but a maelstrom of green clouds, columns of rain and yellow gas mixed with the fumes rising from the ground. It lasted several minutes during which the multi-colored mist kept lighting up, here and there, with every explosion from the handheld weapons.

When it was all over and the air was finally swept clean by the wind, I saw the reorganized Atol army holding their ground all the way up to the rampart. The protozoa were just bubbling jelly strewn all over the place.

"That went well," Wens sighed, "but we didn't get a step closer."

At the thought of Iris still imprisoned in the impenetrable citadel I got a big lump in my throat. I was angry at myself. As Wens had suggested, not being able to take it was one thing, acting was something else altogether.

"Don't they have some kind of drilling machine?" I asked.

"Yes," Wens replied. "But how can they use it? Even with the breaches caused by the explosives, they can't open them up before the scarring endangers any soldier caught inside the tissue. The big problem is we're not faced with a fortress of steel or cement but a thing that rebuilds itself wherever we get through."

"We've got to inject toxic gas into its circulatory system. Oh no! Not with Iris!"

"You see…"

"Anyway, the filter would stabilize it…"

"We have scant knowledge of the physiology and anatomy of the Krall," Wens noted. "You'll be a big help."

"Yes," I sneered. "Do you think a commando unit could get in and out? I'll gladly lead the team."

"We'll have to consider that if we don't find another solution."

The Atols were retreating. Slowly, the army was leaving the field and climbing the slopes. One group was dragging along a huge fragment of secreted tissue in the shape of a funnel, which they had taken great pains to capture.

"Why capture that?" I asked foolishly.

"Come on, Ken," Wens spoke paternally, "haven't you heard of observation, experimentation and other ways of getting information about your enemy's forces?"

I actually turned red and said curtly, "Listen, Wens, do me the pleasure of not making any more references to my past life."

He laughed, "Don't get angry! I know very well that if you'd been truly devoted to your job, you wouldn't be here scolding me for reminding you…"

"Okay, okay," I forced a smile. "Let's drop it."

Greta had listened to us with curiosity, but she withheld any comment.

When the columns were formed, they started marching down the road I'd taken and headed off to the horizon like a legion of ants. Wens introduced me and Greta to a group of senior officers whose black armor didn't reflect a single glimmer. The physicist had taught them the meaning of a handshake, so I cordially grasped the first one's hand.

I was startled. I had totally forgotten about their anatomy and when I felt my fingers gripping two thumbs, I almost jumped back, which would've been taken badly, as Wens later informed me. I glanced into those almond-shaped slits of eyes that reminded me of cats and I figured there were pointy ears under the helmet. A fit of dizziness made me break off.

"Well!" Wens smiled. "The Frenchman had the same reaction as you."

I turned my eyes on him and almost shouted, "The Frenchman? What Frenchman?"

"Oh, it's unforgivable, I know, but we had so much to talk about. Your friend the doctor…"

"Gercourt!" I yelled. "He's here?"

"Well, yes. He arrived just after you. Look, there he is over there on the ridge."

I left Wens standing there and ran over, waving my arms like a madman.

CHAPTER IX

The army was moving on foot only because Rapal, the Atol capitol, was so close. For the siege weapons, however, for the big cloud-makers, there were vehicles. Perched on one of them, in the middle of a group of sullen officers, I continued the heated discussion I was having with Mike.

The damned fellow had reacted to the phone call a lot more enthusiastically than his voice had led me to believe. He told me my call had yanked him out of the doldrums that he'd been wallowing in for a month or so. A love story... Warned by my cryptic message, smelling something fishy and then remembering the distinguished duty I was performing in my job, his mind was made up. He grabbed the essentials: toothbrush, antibiotics, an excellent Mauser with 100 rounds of ammunition and a Leica. And he was on the road before daybreak.

When he got to Wens' villa early in the morning, he ran into no guards and could enter the house easily, which he couldn't understand. So, he had followed my instructions and tossed the match as he crossed through the chronotron.

"And the injured?" I asked.

"I left them in the capable hands of an assistant."

Seeing this old pal of mine right in front of me cheered me up. I saw the same guy with short, black hair, tall, still wearing gold-rimmed glasses and acting in this parallel world with the same self-composure as in his office. His dark gray suit didn't have a wrinkle.

Wens and Greta interrupted our chummy conversation. Greta wanted to get a biologist's opinion on the Krall. As she was talking, I was distracted by the vehicle in front of us on the shiny road. It had no wheels and glided on a thin cushion of compressed air created by holes on the bottom—or so Wens had told me when I climbed on the one carrying me. This levitation surprised me not so much by its strangeness and perfection but for what it reminded me of: I was well aware that a company back home was doing research in this same method at this very moment.

Bringing my mind back to the conversation at hand, I heard Mike saying, "I have nothing more to say... but I'm doing research with some Atol biologists on the captured cells. I think Ken was right to contact me before chasing after you. It's very likely that I'll be getting results soon with the help of Wens on the physics and math. We've done a lot of work this past month..."

A month! I remember when we were wandering in the vascular maze, we'd lost all sense of Time. We'd marched through the semi-darkness with no notion of night and day, just the constant passing of this new duration. I remembered winding my watch, calculating Time by our bodily functions. I'd concluded that Time hadn't changed but I'd made an odd mistake: what was different here was not the physical Time but the psychological time. It differed from Earth, but it didn't pass at the same speed inside the Krall as outside since Mike felt his month of research was a really long period...

"I think," Gercourt added, "I can even do the conclusive experiment today."

He turned to me, "Which doesn't mean I can help you right now in rescuing the girl stuck in the Krall's guts. But very soon if all goes well."

Then a bitter grin crossed his face. "I especially want to help you out since I've just been through a rough period myself and I understand perfectly well what you're feeling."

He stopped talking and stood still, looking off into the flat distance. A strong wind kicked up by the tubes expelling air out of the vehicle in front blew through his short hair.

In the meantime, Wens was talking with an Atol officer. He spoke slowly but the officer seemed to be following his thought perfectly and forcing himself to answer just as slowly. Mike was curious about their conversation and struggling to listen in for a moment.

In the end, he told me, "I can barely understand... This Wens is something else. It took him less than a week to put meanings to the sounds and then his vocabulary skyrocketed. The Atols can only babble a few words of Polish that he taught them. For me, whether it's Polish or Atol doesn't really matter... I think they're talking about the big tissue fragment they captured."

"Exactly," Wens shot out in French. Then he went back to his discussion. Wens could think in several languages and follow more than one conversation at the same time. I'd never met a man whose mind was so clear. Greta watched him with veneration and I was starting to understand why.

But the road now had risen up to a land of red lichen and we suddenly saw a wondrous sight. A city, a real city made of slender buildings, laid out on the edge of a huge bay. An ocean stretched out to the horizon, with only a few gentle waves lapping the feet of the farthest buildings. The sea reflected, almost too brightly, the crimson light of the sun so that it looked like an ocean of lava. I saw a port and ships docked in the bay. Ships... I supposed. The craft were like the ones carrying us but must've been much bigger, judging by their size in the distance. It also looked like they were building fortifications all around the city.

"That's Rapal," Mike said.

There weren't suburbs, properly speaking, but a ring of low houses whose façades were hidden behind lichen that seemed to be the only vegetation able to grow here. Again it's stretching the word to speak of lichen: up close you could see some grayish fronds moving gently as well as cat fur underneath...

We entered the outskirts. The road went straight as an arrow and split into multiple branches. Whereas in my home the roads between two cities were wider than the streets inside—except for a few boulevards—here it was the opposite. I mentioned this to Wens who pointed out the heavy traffic of individual vehicles:

"You see, the road itself is almost never used. Even for expeditions against the Krall, only one way, about seven feet wide, is enough for the Atols. So, the life of Rapal is kept entirely within the walls of the city, which they're finishing up now, and since the urban vehicles are all individual, you can imagine the need for spacious streets."

All the vehicles were the same shape, a particularly simple shape: they were disks, about 20 inches in diameter and four inches thick, with an Atol standing up on each one. A vertical shaft on the edge of the platform contained the controls.

"Note," Gercourt said, "how skillfully they handle those things, their Kzecs…"

I did, indeed, admire the extraordinary expertise they displayed. They could fly around at up to 50 miles an hour—as far as I could judge—without ever bumping into each other. They changed lanes defying centrifugal force.

"Is there anti-gravitation?" I asked Wens.

"No. The gadgets are based on the same principle as what we're on. Cushions of compressed air for suspension—did you notice the honeycomb structure of the road to support the cushion?—and the horizontal expulsion of air in any direction for propulsion. They've become so skillful at riding the Kzecs that they can offset the centrifugal force in the turns by reducing the air pressure on the part of the disk inside the curve, which they do solely with their bodies."

I kept a close eye on them or tried to. I felt like I was surrounded by flying bees.

"And what's all the hubbub about?"

"Just like in our world. They all have work to do and even though their time doesn't pass the same way as ours, it's no less precious in their eyes."

We parted the crowd like a boat sailing through a school of fish, but without arousing their interest. Wens and Mike must've been riding around the city all month.

"They don't care much about the color or style of their clothes," I observed. "They all seemed to be dressed the same, in that kind of suit of undefinable color…"

Mike furrowed his brow, "Their clothes…" he repeated hesitantly. "That's what bothers me. Their clothes…"

I furrowed my brow in turn, but in order to analyze the problem, which got me nowhere.

"I'll explain later," Mike said as our vehicle slowed down outside a sparkling building.

This building, which I'd noticed when we came over the hills and I had an aerial view of Rapal, was five storeys high and had a weird shape: a giant cupola at the base and other domes, smaller and smaller, rising up and topped by a sharp, incredibly tall pinnacle holding a dark-colored banner fluttering in the wind. The whole must've been over 650 feet high.

"The Government Palace," Wens remarked. "It's also the arsenal."

The big Kzecs were parked along the glistening courtyard in front of the monumental door of the palace. A cloud passed by and hid the sun. I thought of the rain, the corrosive rain.

"By the way," I told Wens, "I got caught in that sulfuric rain when I entered the Krall. Did you launch an attack a month ago?"

"The Atols found me on the road. It was a commando team. Only a matter of hours and we all would've been together."

All… including Iris…

The officers jumped down. We did the same, Greta behind Wens and me on the heels of Mike. The physicist and Gercourt were clearly accepted by Atol society. They could enter the palace at will.

"Follow us," Wens said, "we're going to ask to see the Premier."

We left the eternal sunset to enter the light of an aquarium. The entrance hall of the palace—majestically huge—had walls hung with… luminous things. Things. I couldn't think of anything to compare the lighting with: spots of light but glowing like lamps. No windows, as I noticed from the outside. I told Wens how astonished I was. He replied briefly:

"Local ionization."

There was a crowd of Atols rushing around every which way. I saw a lot of officers in their black or orange breastplates but without helmets. The sight of all those pointy ears was a little disturbing. Indeed, in their eyes, we were probably the ones who looked like monsters.

Wens introduced me and Greta to person whose clothes were decorated with a green metal disk. His name was Xal. He had a senior post in what corresponded to the Department of Defense, something like the head of the research labs for all offensive weapons. Wens and Mike talked rather lengthily with him while I looked around the office we'd entered... the office or the room serving as such.

We were sitting, almost lying down, on chairs shaped like gutters that conformed to the body. The Atols must've found these seats very comfortable but not me. I was as cozy as in a real gutter but I was no rat. But it would've been rude to refuse a place to rest during our first appointment. At least I could examine the décor from here.

Gray walls tainted green from the light, pleasantly curved, perfect for calming the mind without distracting mental concentration. A little furniture, probably functional—and that alone—but whose use I couldn't even guess. Several sliding doors. And in the watery light, the chirping of conversations. A dreamy atmosphere after the nightmare where Iris was left behind.

"Come on," Mike said. "We're going to see the Premier."

We didn't go far. The Premier held meetings in an octagonal room adjoining Xal's office. A completely bare room with a dome-shaped ceiling with a kind of spotlight in the center, which was turned off.

The room was steeped in an unsettling half-light. I looked for the Premier with the feeling of being caught in an ambush.

"There's no one here but us," Greta sounded just as uneasy as I felt.

Xal had disappeared. The four of us stood still in one of the eight angles and waited so long that I got the desperate desire to run away.

But presently the spotlight lit up and what followed was like a dream. It wasn't just the light that spilled out but the forms. Forms that took shape around us and gradually built the scenery of a luxurious room. It was almost as if it was all real, that the atoms of the white wall coverings and the red and gray striped furniture were forming themselves before our eyes. But something made me think it was nothing but a television show in relief. Greta reached out and tried to touch the edge of a weird tapestry that suddenly appeared on the wall next to her. Her fingers passed right through the sumptuous material.

Did the Premier fear an attack so that he only met people in an artificial environment? I whispered my idea to Mike who explained.

"Rapal is a huge city. It's not totally under control of the Security Services. Moreover, it's not the only city on the planet, of course. The other cities are under the same government, each with its own Premier but the central administration is here in Rapal. The Council of Premiers legislates and decrees as a last resort on problems of planetary interest. It'd all be fine if there weren't opposition factions among the Atols just waiting for some excuse to rise up and revolt. These factions don't really have a specific program opposed to the Council but they're led by individuals who want power and rely on two separate sides: one, the under-evolved people of the slums along with the nomads of the lichen steppes; and secondly, the mid-level bureaucrats who crave the posts of high dignitaries. The Krall affair has naturally become a kind of political abscess and since it's dragged on for more than a year in this world, passions are getting fiercer every day. We came in at a critical point when the Atol civilization is being attacked on two fronts: the Krall is threatening to extend its destruction and get control of the planet, which would mean the death of Atols, their corpses to be used as raw material... but this danger could be preempted by the political breakdown which would cripple any attempt to stop the Krall."

Mike stopped talking—the Premier had just appeared in the middle of the room.

Even though he was surrounded by all the pomp, the Premier of Rapal wore the usual dress of the Atols, lacking any emblem of his rank... not even Xal's green disk.

He was of middle height but his eyes drew your gaze like two lamps. He looked at each of us in turn while Wens talked in the perplexing language and I felt my mind drained like during my mental contact with the Krall's brain.

I couldn't tell how long the meeting lasted. My clarity came back when everything was dissolving around us and we were left alone in the room again. Xal showed up then and led us back to the gates of the palace.

"Wow," I said to Mike, "it seemed like forever to prepare that meeting but I can't remember a thing about it. How crazy!"

"It's because you don't speak Atol. I think Wens got into a lot of important matters."

"Yes," he overheard us. "From now on we just have to give the word to Xal and we'll have the Army Research Services at our command. The decision is crucial at this point in our work."

"Did you ask THE question?" Mike wondered. In French he used the informal "you", which surprised me, but after thinking about it I saw that their exile together had made them friends, which made me happy.

"Yes," Wens replied again. "He said no. I think you're going to get to go as soon as things are cleared up."

Mike shot me a sidelong glance, "We've got to make sure, first of all, that your assistant isn't in any danger from my attempt."

"Of course… I keep hoping that…"

"Come on, you two," Greta spoke up right as I was opening my mouth to do the same. "Can't you tell us what you're talking about?"

Wens smiled, "But of course, of course. Wait a second. We're standing in the middle of the entrance hall and blocking traffic. Let's all go the labs on the seaside where an apartment's been prepared for Ken. We'll discuss the plan together."

"One thing first," I had to close my eyes against the gleaming forecourt, "that question… tell me what it was?"

Mike looked straight into my eyes when they opened again and answered, "Does cancer exist here?"

CHAPTER X

I didn't have time to ask for details. As we stepped onto the esplanade the wind bore the echoes of a distant noise. The constant traffic of Atols had turned denser and faster and I saw several big Kzecs loaded with armed soldiers. In less than a minute the vehicles had raced off towards the outskirts.

"Riot," Mike said. "I didn't think it'd break out so soon. Just in case, grab a weapon, any weapon. We have to get to the labs on foot and just might have to fight our way through. It'd be better if Margareta stayed in the palace... don't you think so, Wens?"

Wens opened his mouth but Greta shouted first, "It doesn't matter what he thinks. I don't think so and I'm coming with you."

There was no need for discussion. Wens ran into the palace and came back with an armful of shiny tubes.

"I ran into Xal," he panted. "He's leaving for Jarol, a port located a day's journey away by Kzec. It's not good. The North and West quarters are in full revolt and thousands of nomads are headed toward Rapal."

"The Atols don't have any airships?" I fired off.

"No," Mike said, "except for the individual platforms, which are not built for long distances. Let's go."

The lab on the seashore was, fortunately, far from the districts in revolt. But we could feel, on the way, that the rebellion was rumbling toward the port. Our appearance and our weapons were able to intimidate the groups we crossed so we reached our goal without a hitch after more than 45 minutes of walking.

The Atol technicians and assistants there told Wens some news that shed immediate light on the current origins of the riot: a remarkable number of polymorphic cells had reached the walls of Rapal. Others had attacked hordes of nomads and driven them to the already half-infested city. The road to Jarol isn't cut off but they were expecting it to happen within the next few hours.

"But," I said, "the road protected me when I first got here. The protozoa aren't at risk of…"

"I know," Wens cut in. "The matter they're made of used to set up a potential barrier, but not anymore. The reports agree that the roads are infested with amoeba like the rest of the territory. The Krall has managed to adapt its free cells on the bioelectric level… and what's worse is that they are obviously remote-controlled by the brain you saw in there whereas before they were just obeying basic instincts."

"These weapons," I lifted the shiny tube I'd been carrying in front of me, are they effective?"

"Not too much," Mike frowned. "They shoot a jet of irritant gas. Be careful not to press the button for the tank…"

I put the weapon on the edge of a yellow stone tub that stood next to the electronic calculator Wens had built in the room of biological physics where we were. At that moment an Atol came running in. He was out of breath and Wens had a hard time understanding what he was saying.

Finally, the physicist turned to us and simply said, "The clothes."

Mike shuddered. I looked at him with nervous curiosity. He had vaguely mentioned the clothes to me before.

"That's what I was afraid of." He turned to me and Greta, "The Atols' clothes are *alive*. They're epithelial tissues different from their bodies but symbiotic. Normally, they adjust their metabolism to their host, giving or taking away heat, absorbing sweat and using it. The settled people trade them to the nomads for lichen that's rich in heavy elements and these symbiotic clothes are of great help to them when crossing the deserts because they can also provide nourishment directly through the skin."

He stopped talking for a moment.

"The Krall is starting to control the symbiotes. In some outlying regions they've half devoured their hosts."

I was learning some new wonder of this land all the time. But this one was a serious threat to our situation.

"Communication has been cut off with Jarol and three fourths of the audio-visual facilities in Rapal are down. Nobody understands why."

In horror I supposed that the Krall was already—as I feared—making use of the knowledge it extracted from my memory.

"We have no time to lose," Wens said. "Where's the transplant experiment at?"

"It's going," Mike replied. Then to us, "Let's start at the beginning. After I got here and as Wens learned the Atol language, I found out that the Krall was able to resist the civilization that had involuntarily given birth to it. No offensive measure was effective, so I turned to methods in sync with their goal—biological methods. And what weapon would be more effective against a living creature like the Krall than cancer?"

He pondered for a few seconds before continuing.

"From me being here Wens found out about your passage through the chronotron. We agreed that you were trapped inside the Krall. It had to be since no Rapal patrol and no party of nomads had run into you—unless you were unlucky enough to drop into the ocean, a thought that we refused to accept. It was then that the idea of grafting cancer cells onto the Krall became part of a double experiment—one part finding the receptivity of cells from an Atol organism (as is the case with the Krall) and the other making sure it was harmless to humans. All this, you can imagine, was secondary to the possibility of creating a tumor on a fragment of an Atol organism, then finding a way to graft it onto the Krall."

I listened in awe. What an idea I had to call Mike! If we pull through this, as well as the Atols, and Iris gets out of the Krall, it'll be thanks to Gercourt.

"I first leaned towards radiation. Wens built everything I needed, but the irradiation of a piece of skin tissue I got produced no results. The physical agent needed to be joined with the right chemical agent, a really potent cancerous body. I extracted it from the ocean waves that wash against the lab. There are trace amounts of a genetic catalyst in the liquid (which is nothing like water) and is the basis for the reproduction of marine animals like our own reproductive functions are dependent on vitamin E…"

"This is all very judicious," Greta said, twisting the word, "but we have to get to the Krall to graft the tumor, supposing it'll work, of course. And right now we can't even leave the lab."

"I know," Mike agreed hesitatingly, "but I think Ken will find a way while Wens and I finish up our work."

"I've already got an idea," I said. "If Wens can get me an Atol who can teach me how to drive one of those Kzecs."

Everyone looked at me.

Mike looked stern, "It's not that easy and besides, I doubt you'll find one here."

"I'll take care of that," Wens spoke up. "It's a solution to gain us some time and maybe allow one man alone to reach the Krall." He paused before adding, "But it's very dangerous, Ken."

On saying this he snuck a glance at Greta. She didn't blink.

I really didn't care what Greta thought. Although, it wouldn't have broken her back to take a little pity on my fate. But no, after all, she was right: Wens was staying safe inside the building.

Satisfied, Wens called over an Atol technician who was passing by and spoke to him. The answer was long.

"There are a few platforms in the central courtyard of the Institute of Physiology," Wens translated. "But most of them were sabotaged last night. The uprising had been planned. We're going to find out if there's at least one in working condition. If so, the Atol will show Ken how to use it."

The technician hurried away.

"We have to be careful of everyone now," Mike said. "Things didn't get this bad overnight. From now on, any Atol from the other camp might slit our throats at any moment."

"You see, I'm not the only one running risks," I said. "Take all necessary precautions. Thanks to Mike we still have a chance to save Iris and maybe pull through this. This is no time for stupid mistakes."

A distant commotion could be heard through the walls. The fighting must've reached the port.

While Wens and Mike gathered around them some trusted collaborators to finish up the ongoing experiment, Greta got busy on organizing the food provisions given by the Atols. I just waited for the technician to come back.

Greta served us a lichen jam that was rather tasty, but had so many tangled fibers that it felt like eating a hairbrush. Then came the "fish", straight out of the ocean and cooked. The fish looked like a fat insect and tasted like orange. The beverage reminded me of beer by its foam but milk by its taste. It was all very confusing.

"Are you sure there's nothing toxic in this wizard's food?" I asked Mike.

"Yes, I'm sure. I analyzed it a long time ago. Wens and I have eaten nothing else and you can see that we're doing just fine."

Which reassured me.

"In truth," I admitted, "I like eating strange food almost as much as I like breathing nourishing air. It's nicer…"

The commotion grew louder through the walls. It turned my thoughts toward more serious matters.

The Atol wasn't coming back. Outside, night was falling. I checked my weapon, half-listening to Wens and Mike talking while leaning over a crystallizer in which a shapeless thing was soaking.

"Yes," Mike was saying, "I know cancer doesn't exist here or at least there's been no case in Rapal. But I wanted to know the Premier's opinion about it. I would've asked sooner if they weren't always moving around."

There was silence. Wens was turning knobs on a metal panel sparkling with transparent tubes.

He observed, "The irradiation is speeding up the proliferation and multiplying the cellular monstrosities... but we can't yet conclude anything about the effect on our own skin fragments."

"So far," Mike remarked, "they're still normal. The serum bath is keeping them alive but the neoplastic transplants aren't 'taking', although they're distorting the histology of the Atol grafts. If we refer to the rapidity of the aberrant mitosis, the prognostic is excellent..."

"Yes, but Iris is in there. We can't run the slightest risk of hurting her."

The name of Iris caught my full attention. Greta left the machine she was working on and joined us.

"The Atol microscopes are giving weird images," she said. "But I can see the cell structure well enough to confirm that the human chromosomes are not affected at all. Considering how fast the Atol tissue invaded, your samples should be in total chaos by now."

There was another profound silence, which I broke this time.

"I know very well that we have to take all necessary precautions to protect Iris from an eventual contamination, but, look, we've never seen cancer transmitted by touch alone, even though it is sometimes transmitted by a virus. Plus, the experiments you've done show good results and we have to remember that time is pressing."

"Hmm," Mike growled. "Indeed, indeed... But the weapon I'm perfecting will only work on the Krall itself. One thing is encouraging: the malign tumors don't end up rotting but in a dry necrosis without infection, with a crystallization of the cytoplasm. That will allow us, if we succeed, to find Iris before she runs out of air."

"I'm ready to try it right now," I offered.

But my offer was a moot point—the technician hadn't come back. When I went to the sliding door of the lab, I found someone outside had blocked it.

In all my life, I'd never been so angry. Here we were, grinding away at planning an attack on the Krall and a stupid political quarrel, the petty ambition of a few Atols was going to ruin the whole thing. That we're fighting for Iris and not for them doesn't mean a thing. They'd profit from the victory as much as us since it's their civilization and the existence of their race that's threatened. I raised my weapon and aimed it at the door.

"No!" Mike yelled. "You'll suffocate us all!"

I got hold of myself. I'd forgotten that I wasn't holding one of those radiation weapons I'd seen flashing at the bottom of the crater but a gas-thrower that could only be fired in the open air. I walked back to them, brooding and frustrated.

A swoosh behind my back. I swung around. The door was open. And the technician rushed by me like a shadow. He stopped in front of Wens and stood tall and proud, giving him a long speech. When he finished, Wens shrugged his shoulders and gave a short answer in reply. The Atol seemed satisfied and left just as swiftly.

We all huddled around Wens. He translated:

"The revolt is winning everywhere. The Premier can't be found and three fourths of the army have joined the rebels. But the leaders are already clashing. The nomads who invaded Rapal are acting vilely and the army is starting to drive them back into the outskirts where they're fighting in the streets. Beyond the walls the Krall cells hold all the land and we can't count on reinforcements from Jarol because it's a bloody mess. They just asked me if you're ready to help the new Premier installed in the palace to destroy the Krall. Of course, I accepted on your behalf…"

"Was all this carnage really worth it just to end up with the same problem to solve?" I was furious.

"Of course it was," Mike said with a half-smile. "For those wanting to command instead of obey, it was worth it…

provided that the Krall doesn't promise them the same fate as the victims of their massacre."

"The Atols," Greta concluded, "really are just like us."

CHAPTER XI

My pilot training started during the night. Nothing in the Atols' behavior showed that their government had changed hands. We remained their allies and they kept acting politely to us. I was trained by Jnor, the technician who had locked us in, and Wens had to leave Mike and Greta in the lab to act as interpreter, which made him nervous and distracted. It'd been a while since I felt Wens' jealousy but his worries didn't surprise me. Greta, however, was far from fickle, Mike had someone else on his mind and none of us had any inclination to replay those precious French melodramas here in Rapal. But Wens was itching to go, so I let him as soon as I could. I would've laughed at all this if my own mind wasn't preoccupied by the fate of Iris.

What was she doing? She was probably still wandering around in the Krall's vessels or maybe she'd reached the brain and was being held prisoner, drained of her thoughts like a fly being devoured by a spider in the middle of its web. I feared the worst. She certainly had emptied my gun and had nothing left to defend herself if, by chance, a giant white blood cell attacked.

I committed myself wholeheartedly to my pilot training.

The machine was similar to those flying platforms being designed by the US Army before I left, but this one was perfected, even if its "battery life" was very limited. The Atols called it a Kzectl, the last letter referring to its vertical dimension. I was starting to learn a few words but most of the time I found them unpronounceable.

Piloting was simply the coordination of three discharge controls. It was this coordination of movements that made it hard to learn fast because the slightest mistake created dangerous wobbling that could easily throw you off.

After a few hours of gliding around at around five feet off the spongy ground, I felt more confident. I shot up over 60 feet in the air and veered into a really nice turn that almost flipped over the platform. I pulled it steady at the last minute and landed gently. The Atol seemed satisfied. Myself, I was happy they didn't decide to give the mission to a native pilot—if anyone was going to help Iris, it was going to be me...

I left Jnor and his Kzectl and observed the lab in the early morning glow. The sun was about to rise over the ocean. A breeze infused with strange odors blew along the seashore under a sky that gradually turned the color of sulfur. As I entered the building, the crimson sun was just peeking out.

In the electrobiological room Wens had left alone Mike with his pet tumor. With Greta's help he was putting up a series of formulas on a board... a white board with black chalk.

"This system is interesting," he showed me the board. "The surface is loaded with static electricity, the opposite charge of the chalk. Then, by pressing this button the board drops in contact with the floor. It discharges and the chalk particles sprinkle down into this tray as a powder."

I gawked. Wens smiled.

"It's coming together. I think that in a few months I'll be able to build a chronotron here. By some unbelievable luck I found a piece of paper in my pocket on which I'd noted down the frequency used, which will keep us from being marooned in another temporal universe other than our own, if we manage to bid farewell to the Atols."

I acknowledged his confidence with joy, but such hope scared me again that Iris might not be going with us back to Earth.

I was leaving Wens and Greta alone to go help Mike when someone entered the lab. I was stunned. Except for a few fleeting glances, I'd never seen an Atol woman. She would've knocked the socks off of any red-blooded man despite her four thumbs and pointy ears... She was wearing a white tunic.

Mike spoke from behind his machines, "Let me introduce you to Jalia, Jnor's sister." For the first time since we'd been reunited, his face was glowing. And I knew that he was not insensitive to the charm of the other race. This gave me great comfort because his melancholy had seemed incurable.

I stammered something. Jalia uttered a kind of weird squeal and shot me a look with those huge eyes that almost made me forget Iris.

"Uh… well," I sounded like an idiot, "so, this is your… biology partner?"

He laughed. "Not exactly. Seems she'd been bugging Jnor for two weeks to give her something to do. Her brother offered her to work under Wens but I'm the one who chose her. What do you think of her?"

I got close and whispered, "Super. She's pretty as hell."

He smiled again. At last, the old Mike.

The transplant was ready. We sealed the fragments into five small, transparent spheres full of serum and wrapped them up for protection. The Kzectl was waiting for me outside.

"Our counter-attack has become critical." Mike told me as he handed over a radiation gun. "The Atols can't wear their symbiotic clothes anymore and have to destroy them. You saw how Jalia was wearing a tunic. Plus, they' seen protozoa with big, wide membranes that they use to get off the ground and drift on the wind. Everything's getting worse."

"I'm ready," I said. I pointed to the Kzectl and added, "I think I'll do just fine with this machine."

"Great. Well, you know what we say in France to wish good luck…"

"Thanks. It's really the words of a general that fits the situation."

I got behind the controls and waved goodbye to Wens and Greta who were coming out of the lab to see me off. The Kzectl rose up slowly and soon Mike, Jalia, Wens and Greta were just four little dots in the immensity of Rapal.

I got my bearings. The city underneath me spread out to the edge of the ocean, flooded by sunlight like a city in flames. Above me was the yellow sky with scattered, coppery clouds. I gazed along the recently built ramparts until I found the glittering ribbon of road leading away from it. Veering gently, I headed for it while continuing to rise up.

This mode of transportation was really pretty spectacular. I felt like a soap bubble floating through the air. But I was still a little uneasy on that five-foot round platform, gripping the vertical command shaft.

When I was high enough, I saw that the road made a long, wide curve through the lichen but I took the short cut. Not far from Rapal a horde of nomads was fighting with a mass of flat cells. I saw weapons flashing and heard Atols screaming. I felt some bitterness at the attitude of Rapal toward the nomads, sentencing them to death, sooner or later, by the Krall. But I hadn't witnessed the violence carried out in the city.

As these thoughts rattled around in my brain, my Kzectl started wobbling badly and something came whistling by my right side. The men I'd just been feeling sorry for were shooting at me. I heard the sound of billions of sparks from the lethal ray flying through the particles in the air, which made it sound like whistling.

I dared to put my Kzectl through a series of complicated evasive maneuvers to get away from the nomads until they stopped firing. They had other fish to fry. I imagined what I must've looked like to someone on the ground and remembered the luminous object I'd glimpsed in the sky when I woke up in this world. Now I understood that it was a reconnaissance Kzectl from some commando unit that was going to launch an attack soon after.

I was nearing the crater and could already see the whole monstrous body of the Krall. All shapes and sizes of cells around the carapace were moving onto the plateau. I descended cautiously.

My heart was pounding. I thought of the Krall's heart, that organ that worked differently from the Atols—I'd learned about it: the Atols' inner anatomy was much like our own— the Krall, however, was just an amalgam with the Atol biologists as a base element. Was there from the start of this gigantic growth an "organizer" comparable to the substance that we isolate from embryos in their initial stages? And did this chemical organizer have the power to create all the parts of an organ adapted to a specific function? If so, a weird mutation had affected the Atol genes being used from the start.

But this was not a burning issue. I saw something rising up toward me like a leaf carried on the wind, something transparent and huge. I got my gun ready after putting the three controls into hover mode.

It was one of those new-fangled protozoa. There was no doubt that besides the wind a frequency emitted by the Krall's brain was driving it towards me. A bright ray took care of it. The membranous cell fell in crystallized shreds. Others were coming at me, so I had to get away. I had no choice but to land.

A dozen yards from the plateau something was moving around in the forest of cable-thick hair. Reacting faster than I could think, I slammed the vertical control and the Kzectl shot up. Even though I almost crashed against the floor of the platform, I could see a big pink funnel racing up and lashes whipped the air just under me. But I was already out of range. The funnel settled back in, as if pulled to the ground by a spring. I thought of the infusoria called vorticellids. I'd narrowly escaped something similar.

With my heart racing I slid the Kzectl sideways and stopped over a free space where nothing could be hiding. As an added precaution I sprayed the ground with the ray gun and saw black, fuming lines trace over the area. I quickly landed in the middle of the space.

The presence of the huge infusoria proved that the Krall had accelerated its proliferation of free cells and had increased the polymorphism at an incredible rate. It was, indeed, time to act. I broke one of the spheres directly on a burn mark whose scar tissue absorbed the contents in less than a minute. I moved on to another and did the same thing. After the last one I ascended over 150 feet and hovered there to watch. At first I had to battle a few protozoa that floated up to me. The last one I destroyed was over 30 feet in diameter with its membranes spread out, fluttering its cilia.

But the Leviathan's metabolism was already being tortured by the grafts. Cells were sagging all over. The brain must've been mustering all its nerve signals to encyst the transplants and so it couldn't control the free cells. I couldn't believe it. It seemed so unlikely that the process could work so rapidly. And yet, remembering the tumors created by Mike, I had to admit that the rhythm of mitosis was pretty much the same, even though the peripheral cells being contaminated were immensely bigger. The graft was working. It was working on every spot I'd stuck one. It was working so fast that blisters and craters were forming before my very eyes. And the more it spread, the harder the tissue became, forming a shiny mass that decomposed in the variegated light—from yellow to dark red.

Then the Krall let loose a scream, piercing, ceaseless, more human than ever, multiplied by the existence of ten other larynxes. I beat a retreat. My Kzectl shot up at an angle, swept up in the commotion like in a hovering tornado.

The Krall howled until twilight. When the horrific cry stopped, it took a long time for all the free cells on the plain and in the crater to turn into glittering dust. In the silence that I felt had to be broken at some point, I descended among the spreading darkness.

The Krall was just a mountain of crystal reflecting the varied colors of the stars. I landed on the top of the bony rampart and pointed my weapon at the plateau. The ray caused a phenomenon more bizarre than anything I'd seen so far in this universe. Starting from the point of contact, with a low rumbling, the cytoplasmic crystals evaporated one after another and their vapors dissipated in the night. The evaporation fanned out all the way to the ends of the destroyed monster. I stood still on the rampart for hours, just watching the extinction.

In the first light of dawn I was standing before the skeleton of the Krall—only the mineral concretions had survived. My weary eyes saw them far in the distance along with the jagged stones and dark ditches of a monstrous castle in ruins. Among the columns and arches of ivory there was a tall peak risen up over the dead gaping mouth of the underground.

As the sun caressed the edges of the crater and glowed over the bony summits, I snapped out of the meditation that the sight of this ruined hell had plunged me in. A voice struck my ears. A distant voice like from the depths of the earth.

Jolted by the cry I jumped on the controls of my machine and started flying over the wreckage of the nightmare. The hissing machine did not drown out the voice so that I was soon setting down on a relatively flat entablature.

"Ken! Ken!" cried the voice.

I found Iris on the edge of the black abyss and I pulled her up on the Kzectl, which wobbled dangerously as it rose up. We hugged so tightly that anyone seeing the machine from the ground would never have guessed that I had a passenger. Under us the astounding ossuary faded away in the morning mist as we rose into the sky of blood and gold.

RESEARCH DEPARTMENT

Mr. Pan stared sternly at Mr. God who looked quite contrite.

"What possessed you to embark on such an absurd experiment?" asked Mr. Pan.

"But sir," replied Mr. God said with some difficulty, "I thought we might find some practical applications..."

"Practical applications! Ha!" retorted Mr. Pan insultingly. "What could we possibly get out of your... what do you call it, again?"

"Universe, sir."

"Universe, yes. Well, the only thing I note is that it takes up a good half of the lab, and you're hindering your colleagues in their research."

"They're only jealous, sir, but if you want my opinion..."

"I don't want anything of the kind," interrupted the head of the research department. "In fact, I don't want to hear anything that remotely resembles advice coming from your discombobulated brain. You are going to do me the pleasure of cleaning up this laboratory asap, and submitting a new proposal for a real project with some real value."

"Yes, sir," said Mr. God meekly.

"I'll talk to you later," said Mr. Pan more pleasantly, "but keep in mind that Albert Satan is still trying to get your job."

"I know, sir. Thank you for having faith in me."

After the Head of Research had left, Mr. God returned to the lab. Everyone had gone out to lunch. It was deserted. Mr. God went to the generators and successively cut gravitation, space, and finally, time. The universe crumbled before his eyes.

He heaved a sigh of regret.

"Mr. Pan wasn't wrong," he muttered to himself, "it was taking up half of the lab…"

He chuckled. "Satan is going to be furious that the boss didn't fire me…"

A slight noise made him turn around. A gorgeous girl had just walked into the lab.

"Ms. Lilith!" exclaimed Mr. God. "Didn't you go out to lunch with the others?"

"We don't have much time," she whispered seductively.

She kissed him. He took her in his arms. She pulled him down under a work bench cluttered with various instruments.

"What about Satan?" asked Mr. God.

"No problem," Lilith replied. "He's fixing the heater."

Too busy kissing, they did not notice a little spark floating out of the lab and through an open window. This spark was a star called the Sun. She was taking with her her nine children who circled around her like little chicks around the mother hen.

While the two lovers were rolling on the floor, the tiny star merged into the Great All.

Luck was on her side: it would not be easy to find a needle in a haystack, or a single star amongst billions, especially when no one would be looking for her...

CPSIA information can be obtained
at www.ICGtesting.com
Printed in the USA
BVHW081051230123
656900BV00002B/64